Back Kingdom Road House

"RARELY DO MEMBERS OF THE SAME FAMILY GROW UP UNDER THE SAME ROOF."

—RICHARD BACH

Powder River Publishing

www.powderriverpublishing.com

THIS BOOK IS DEDICATED TO THE SELKIE HAGS. YOU KNOW WHO YOU ARE, AND WHAT YOU ARE — WRITERS, ALL.

- SHELLIE LEGER

Published by:
Powder River Publishing LLC
147 N. Burritt Ave
Buffalo, Wyoming 82834

Copyright © 2021
ISBN: 978-1-956881-00-4
Printed in the United States of America

Book One
Chapter 1

Uncle Doug's and Westover, Maine

Elspeth and I often talk about the winter our mother lost her mind. Really went mad. Vermont got a nasty late snow. It was mid-April, and dad was driving home from a night shift. The roads were greasy, he was tired, who knows. But he never came back. We heard our mother screaming at 4:00 in the morning and bolted out of our room. The Scream, as we now call it, Elspeth and I, had an unearthly timbre to it, swollen.

I keep thinking that's what it would sound like to rip out someone's spleen with a meat hook. And I think mom did think of dad as an organ. We found her in the wispy pre-dawn light. She lay on the pumpkin-pine boards of the kitchen floor, the place where it sloped toward the back hall. My mother loved that floor. It always shone a deep gold--the color of a summer sky after a storm.

She was wearing blue flowered long underwear, and her purple-black hair was wild— spread out behind her against the orange wood, like her head was oozing India ink. She was just curled there, and two police officers looked on. They took in the scene of the two little girls and tried to ask my mother if there was anyone she could call to take care of us. She couldn't hear them, I don't think.

Elspeth and I have different recollections from this point on. It isn't really that important. The real issue is that life as we knew

raise for Back Kingdom Road House

"At times haunting, and at times, nostalgic, Leger creates a sparkling world, set against ncient pines, that resonates long after the story ends. Through the eyes of Liza, whose endearing ruggle to make sense of her nonsensical world reminds us of what it's like to be human, readers come quickly engaged by Leger's cast of characters: Liza's grieving mother, Violet, her twin ster, Elspeth, her Aunt Serena, and Karl, the eerily familiar stranger that lives across the street. l are deliciously flawed, but refreshingly real. To this, Leger blends longing and passion, sprin- ing in a whiff of cedar every now and then. Back KIngdom Road House is a must read."

ristin Leonard, author of The Ninetieth Day: Poems About Love, Loss, and Leftovers For Break- st and recipient of the 2019 Maine Literary Award (Dramatic Writing)

"BACK KINGDOM ROAD HOUSE-- like a badass lesbian version of HOUSEKEEPING— acks the wild roundabout road that rebellious LIza takes as she leaves behind, then circles back her sister Elspeth and their troubled yet loving mother, all grappling with a 'batshit-crazy' mily legacy amidst the vividly depicted splendor and isolation of rural Maine. In BACK KINGDOM)AD HOUSE, Shellie Leger creates a powerhouse portrait of two fierce generations of sisters. I ve this frank, funky, darkly comic and deeply moving debut novel!"

lizabeth Searle, author of I'll Show You Mine; Tonya & Nancy: the Rock Opera; A Four-Sided Bed

"With a voice that is so incredibly authentic as to make one wonder how autobiographical e novel might be, Leger develops her rich characters in such a way that readers are forced to not ly meet them, but recognize them from our own lives. Every subsequent reading will now be e visiting familiar people. A book definitely worth reading!"

evin St. Jarre, author of Aliens, Drywall, and a Unicycle and The Twin

"Is it a coming of age novel? Yes. Is it iconic Maine then and now? Yes. With a fast paced ot, brilliant character development and settings so vivid, and dialogue so nuanced when you se the book you'll need to shake yourself to get back from Back Kingdom Road House. What's ost impressive is Leger's masterful economy of prose, and skill with tone and style. Read it r the experience, reread it for the same, but also read it simply for Leger's excellence with the aft."

avid Grubb, author/poet, his work appears in Toasted Cheese, The Bookends Review, and The ad Mule School among others.

"Back Kingdom Road House sparkles with darkness and humor and optimism; a cozy com- g of age tale. Leger's voice is wholly her own."

ara Hoffman, author of So Much Pretty

"Back KIngdom Road House is one of those rare novels that gets so close to the human art that you can touch it. From the very start, Leger's novel unfolds with a tone and mood rem- scent of work by Marilynne Robinson, and the narrative never lets up. This is a novel that will y with you well after you've finished."

organ Talty, author of Night of the Living Rez

it blew wide open. The next month or so we were shuffled around a lot, back and forth between my mom's friend Shana who danced half- naked in the kitchen, and our neighbor, an old woman named Carmel whose house always smelled like camphor and mint. And then, we were heading south in our mom's rusted-out Ford Escort. To our Uncle Doug's in Baltimore.

Doug was my mother's older brother. She had a sister as well, just a year older, but this sister was "unstable" according to the family. Even my mother agreed that Serena was a little nuts. But her parents were dead, so if she was going to find her way back into the bosom of her family, in the hopes that Elspeth and I would have "a village" then it was going to have to be with Uncle Doug and Aunt Kitty, and their daughters, Brianna and Courtney.

I thought those were princess names. I loved them so when I first heard them. Not hard-sounding names like Liza and Elspeth, which sounded like you were spitting. When our mother showed us the picture of our two chestnut- haired cousins, ages 9 and 11, we couldn't wait to meet them. It seemed exciting to be heading off to a new place where we'd meet relatives. We had no memory of ever having met our Aunt Serena or Uncle Doug and Aunt Kitty before.

So, Dad died in April, and at the end of June we headed out of Bethel, Vermont without a damned thing. Mom was finally able to deal with us and saved us from her crazy friends. She couldn't afford a moving van though, and said there was nothing of signif-icance that we really needed. The furniture was garbage-picked or had belonged to the landlord. We were allowed   some clothes, a few favorite toys, and mom stashed three photo albums, seven books and a shoe box of keepsakes in a recycled garbage bag in the trunk. It was 88 degrees the day we left and the little Escort had no air-conditioning. It only got hotter as we headed south.

"Girls, are you looking forward to meeting the rest of your family?" Mom was trying to be upbeat. We'd noticed this forced gaiety a lot. We didn't call it that, naturally, but later we agreed that is exactly what it was. And it was brutal. The fragility of it on some childish primitive level made us anxious.

"What are our cousins like?" Elspeth asked.

"You know, I don't really have any idea. I haven't seen them since they were very little girls. But I'm sure they'll love you. How could they not?"

We made it from Vermont to New Jersey with only a few bathroom stops, but by the time we hit horse country it was 100 degrees and Elspeth and I had been quibbling non-stop since we hit New York about who our mysterious cousins would like best. Our mother had boundless energy, and a certain kind of rigid focus. If she were heading to Baltimore than we wouldn't stop until we were in Baltimore. But she did stop that night for us; we got a room at a super 8 off the NJ pike with a huge air-conditioner. We all climbed into the big white queen-sized bed and I still to this day recall the sensuous feeling unleashed by the expanse of crisp cold chlorinated sheets. Elspeth also has a vivid recollection of that moment. But she recalls it more as a moment of joining with our mother.

The next morning, we awoke early to the relentless thrum of the air conditioner God, and headed to the I-Hop across the parking lot for pancakes, and then off again with only a couple more hours to go. I remember a growing excitement in my body, sort of like my blood was contracting and expanding, and Elspeth chattering to our mother about Courtney and Brianna.

"I think they're probably sweet little girls, Elspeth. I don't think you need to worry at all about them."

"But do you think they'll share their toys?"

"I bet Uncle Doug will make sure they do."

"What about Aunt Kitty?"

"Yes. Probably Aunt Kitty too."

I remember as they discussed what sorts of toys our cousins might have, an issue for us since we'd left our meager collection of frayed stuffed animals and chewed up Barbies back in Vermont, I began to think about our father. Interestingly, Elspeth didn't mention him, and when I tried to pull her into a conversation about our father she'd simply say, "Daddy is dead in the ground now, and we can't do anything about that."

It wasn't that I thought we could, but I wanted to talk about him. My mother tolerated those sorts of conversations in small doses before she'd fall apart, and then I'd feel like it was my fault she was sad. I thought maybe my cousins would be interested in that sort of thing. So, while Elspeth thought about sharing toys, I talked about death.

We arrived at Uncle Doug's door step around 11:30 with a belly full of heavy pancakes. I'd never seen a one-story house that big, a sprawling suburban ranch in College Park. Brick, a garage stuffed with two shiny cars. The lawn was huge and a sprinkler twirled around and around. I remember thinking it was strange that no one was even playing in it. A long flagstone path led to wide double doors. A heavy brass knocker in the shape of a seashell hung from one of them. I ran ahead of my mother and Elspeth, lifted the heavy seashell and let it fall with a loud clank against the gleaming black door.

I heard scrambling on the other side and the high-pitched bark of a small dog. We'd never had dogs, just cats. Somehow my mother hadn't told us about our cousins owning a dog and I actually jumped up and down.

"Elspeth! I hear a dog!"

"A dog?" Elspeth ran to the door, dropped her acid- green pleather purse (mine was tangerine) and left it there as she hurtled toward the sound of the barking dog.

"Mommy," she said, "They've got a dog?"

"I guess so, sweetie," our mother answered.

The door swung open. A tall slender blonde woman with a deep tan smiled at us. She wore a dress in the middle of a Saturday afternoon. I'd never met anyone who did that. (I'd seen my mother in a dress once, at my father's funeral.) She had lots of gold chains around one bony wrist and her fingernails and toenails were painted a brownish-red. She spoke in a crackly voice.

"Well, hello my dears! Which one are you?"

"Liza," I answered and gazed at the little fluffy yapping thing at her ankles.

"Okay, so you're Elspeth," she said to El and then returned her attention to me.

"And Liza, you're so big for your age! You favor your daddy."

Aunt Kitty hugged my mother. My mom was much softer and fuller and so very olive compared to her sister-in-law. I had pushed my way past them all and was bending down to investigate the dog, whose name it turned out was Spud. Spud the Shitzu.

"Violet, it's so nice to see you finally, and your beautiful twins. And Elspeth, you look just like your mother."

I noticed that my mom smiled at Aunt Kitty, but not the usual full-faced smile I knew.

We'd all made it into what Aunt Kitty called the foyer, a cool dark place that smelled clean and lemony. Big potted trees were placed around the edges of the white walls. I'd never been in a house like this before. I sat on the floor staring at Spud and yearning to squeeze him when I heard a booming male voice from another room.

"Is that my nutty sister?"

A man who looked a lot like my mother with dark springy hair and the same eyes rounded the corner of the hallway and loped toward us. He smiled. His eyebrows formed peaks. My mother got rigid when Uncle Doug hugged her. And she didn't hug him back.

"Where's Brianna and Courtney?"

"Oh! Aren't you a sweetie!" Aunt Kitty said.

"At the pool," Uncle Doug said.

"What pool?" I asked.

Aunt Kitty took this one. "Our neighbors have a pool, sweetie. The Johnson's next door."

"We don't have ours in yet. Next summer," Uncle Doug said.

"Well," said Aunt Kitty, "it's just that we only moved in a few months ago, and there were so many things that needed to be done that we figured it just made more sense to wait on the pool."

We all lapsed into silence for a while and finally El spoke up. "I need to use the ladies' room please."

Uncle Doug laughed. A sound like glass breaking.

"I don't know about a ladies' room, but you can use the john."

We'd never heard that expression.

"Oh Doug. Really." Aunt Kitty grabbed Elspeth's hand and led her out of the cool lemony foyer past the potted plants, the clackety-clack of her heels echoing off the white walls.

"Well," said Uncle Doug to my mother and me, "let's get those bags in here."

The three of us headed down the walk to the circular drive

where our beat-up car sat, looking very much like it belonged in the Sesame Street what's- wrong- with- this- picture vignette.

"Cripes! This is what you drive?"

"Yes," was all my mother said.

She opened the small hatchback where she'd jammed the entirety of our possessions: four medium- sized suitcases and the garbage bag and shoe-box that defined our lives.

"This is what you have to show for thirty years?"

"Yes." Again, the monosyllabic answer we came to expect over the next four months. We began longing for the forced gaiety. We walked back to the house in silence until uncle Doug said, "I bet you girls are hotter than hell! Tell you what, put on your swimming suits and I'll bring you both over to the Johnson's so you can join the fun. How about that?"

That was the best thing I'd heard maybe ever. I bolted toward the house to change and loved suburbia. I didn't know that was its name. I just loved it, for being filled with big lemony cool dark houses with no stairs, and small squeezable fluffy animals, and elegant ladies draped in gold, and aqua marine swimming pools that smelled like clean clothes.

I met my sister and Aunt in the kitchen drinking lemonade from tall fancy glasses that matched and burst out with the news.

"El! Uncle Doug is taking us to the Johnson's to swim. Soon as mommy gets open our stuff we can put on our suits and go!"

"Swim in a pool?"

We'd never swum in a pool. Only in rivers and lakes and once at the ocean.

"Yup!"

"That's exciting." Aunt Kitty smiled at us with her dazzling white teeth.

It was then that I knew I really liked her.

I joined them in a glass of lemonade with a big gooey cherry on the top which my Aunt pulled from a little jar in her bright red fridge, and couldn't wipe the smile off my face.

When our mother and Uncle Doug returned carrying our things Elspeth and I ran for our matching back-packs and stumbled over each other to change in the rose-colored bathroom. It was lost on us that our practical one-piece plain suits were shabby and shiny with wear. The elastic thread at the legs and arms was stretched out, and in some places, exposed and dangling down our skinny limbs. Mine was a solid navy blue, and Elspeths's a solid forest green.

We scrambled out of the bathroom ready to go. Our mother kissed us on the cheeks and Aunt Kitty supplied us with the biggest towels we'd ever seen. Soft and plush. In fact, it seemed like mine was furry and it almost repulsed me. Uncle Doug grabbed our hands and pulled us along behind him as he strode over to the Johnson's. We had a hard time keeping up. At the pool, a large sunken turquoise crater shaped like a squiggly circle, we met our cousins and the three Johnson children.

Our cousins were tall and slim with dainty hands and feet. Both wore their thick chestnut colored hair in top-knots on their oval shaped heads and sported pink and yellow neon bikinis. The Johnson children ranged from the ages of 6 to 12. The girls, Amber and Ally, were 6 and 7, and the oldest, Kyle, became my first crush. While the girls were pale and slight, with flat faces and dull grey eyes, Kyle was ropey and his eyes matched the pool. His hair was yellow and he wore puka shells around his brown-sugar neck.

Uncle Doug placed his hands on the smalls of our backs and pressed us toward the senior Johnsons. They lounged on chaises with drinks festooned with pastel paper umbrellas. Mrs. Johnson had the same flat dull look as her daughters, but Mr. Johnson crackled and seemed boyish for a grown-up. He was the first to bolt out of his chair and greet us.

"Hello, girls! Welcome to Maryland. What a long drive you ladies had, huh?"

"It was a long drive," I said, and he laughed.

He called the kids out of the pool and made them stand there dripping while he introduced us. And then he pushed us all in. The other children seemed to love it. Elspeth and I were not used to this type of aggression. Our father would never have done anything like that. Uncle Doug laughed and said good-bye and we were now part of the Johnson clan. Our cousins ignored us, mostly. We played Marco Polo by ourselves in the shallow end of the pool.

Eventually looking for a way to get our cousins' attention, I dog-paddled over to them and said, "Our father died in April. His car went off the road on ice and into a river. We don't know if he fell asleep or if the road was just too icy. But he died."

Courtney just stared at me, expressionless. Brianna was quiet for a moment and then said, "I know," and swam away.

"I'm real sorry to hear that," Kyle said and swam toward us. "You guys want a freeze pop?"

"Yeah! Do you have a blue one?" Elspeth loved the blue ones, but they reminded me of the toilet water at restaurants.

"Sure. What about you Liza?"

"Do you have lime?"

"We do. We aim to please here in Maryland. Come on into the cabanas."

He hoisted himself out of the pool with one arm. I wasn't sure what the cabanas were, but I followed him to a row of three small cabins painted in a series of pastel colors. He held the door open for me. I stepped inside the little house. It reminded me of a Barbie beach house I'd always wanted.

It was cool inside and furnished with pale blue wicker. The tiny fridge/freezer was filled with frosty drinks and ice-cream treats. This cabana became my new favorite place and I often spent my afternoons in there playing Life or Battleship with Kyle. I will never know if he was being kind or if he really enjoyed the company of an eight- year old girl. Perhaps both. Those summer months were thick and slow. We mostly spent them with the Johnsons. Our mother was job-hunting. She left early and returned at the end of the day, sullen and obsequious. We adored her fawning, but the brittleness of it, much like the forced gaiety before it, jangled our nerves, or at least mine. I expect she felt some guilt over abandoning us all day to Aunt Kitty and her neighbors, but we loved it.

Aunt Kitty made our sandwiches into little diamonds, and always stuck sugary fruit in our cold drinks. She painted our toes and fingers. She let us use her bubble bath. When Courtney and

Brianna were snotty to us, and they were frequently, she repri-
manded them. I am sometimes curious that perhaps she liked us
better than her own spawn. Saw something familiar in us.

Uncle Doug usually came booming through the door from work
(he sold restaurant equipment) around 6:15. The feeling in the
house changed then. Usually by that time Courtney, Brianna,
Elspeth and I were sprawled out on the cool hardwood floor in the
den after a long day in the sun at the Johnson's, sipping our tall
drinks and watching Nickelodeon. By evening we'd usually found
some peace with each other after a day of snide remarks. But
when Uncle Doug clattered through the foyer, his largeness filling
the rooms with sound, we'd all tense up. You could see it in the
posture of a naked foot, or the crook of a brown neck. We were on
alert, like dogs in an electrical storm.

Summer was coming to a close. It was the end of August. Less
than a week from Labor Day. Mom had turned down a few job
offers. She didn't want to be a cashier, nor did she want to be an
aid at a nursing home. Aunt Kitty supported her decisions completely. We'd overheard the grown-ups talking about our mother's
"situation" and were aware that while Aunt Kitty understood our
mother's hesitation to take these jobs, Uncle Doug did not. That
evening, our Aunt Serena was joining us for dinner. We hadn't
seen her in the two months or so that we'd been in College Park.
Uncle Doug clomped into the den. He appeared disheveled.

"T.V. off ladies. Go get ready for dinner."

"We're right in the middle of a show," Brianna said.

"Not any more you're not. Now you're right at the end of a
show. Move it." He snapped off the television.

I always jumped to it when Uncle Doug commanded us. Elspeth
and I were afraid of him. Our own father had been so gentle. He
spoke softly, like music you strain to hear from a distance. I'm
sure he must have been abrupt when he was tired, when we were
boisterous and unruly; but I don't remember any of that. I didn't
have many models for men.

"He's such a butt-head," Courtney said out of earshot of Uncle
Doug.

But we all walked quickly to our rooms. El and I peeled off our damp suits and donned the usual shorts and t-shirts.

"Could you maybe wear something else?" Brianna said and stopped in our half-opened doorway.

"What's wrong with what we're wearing?" Elspeth asked.

"You wear the same thing day after day," Courtney added.

"I like it," I said. It felt good to stand up to her, but it was hard and made my stomach cramp.

But I did like my outfit. Short overalls were in vogue back then and I wore mine with a pale blue t-shirt. Stretched out and soft that said Vermont is for lovers. The truth is we didn't have much else. Aunt Kitty had offered to take us shopping, and we'd wanted to go, but our mother refused.

"Whatever," Brainna said.

"Yeah, whatever," Courtney added. And they headed for the kitchen.

"What do you think Aunt Serena will be like?" Elspeth asked.

"I don't know, and I don't care," I answered, which wasn't really true. I was curious to meet the aunt everyone said was nuts.

We took our time. I lay down on my bed with a book and Elspeth stared in the mirror. We usually liked hanging out with Aunt Kitty, watching her glide around on her shiny kitchen floor, expertly moving from one surface to another, creating whimsical sandwiches and otherworldly drinks. But not when Uncle Doug was there. Even Aunt Kitty lost her graceful flow when he glowered over us all.

"Girls?" It was our mother calling down the hallway. "Come and join us, please. Aunt Serena will be here any minute."

But she wasn't. She wasn't there any hour. And Aunt Kitty's bacon-wrapped scallops, sticky melted brie, baby red potato salad and almond-crusted green beans all sat there, as did her slow-roasted lemon chicken.

"This is what we can expect from someone who lives her life the way Serena does," Uncle Doug said.

At this point, we all had the good sense to eat. I was disappointed not to be meeting the illustrious Serena, rumored to be beautiful, bad and buggy. Elspeth and I shot glances at one another as we ate the boatloads of food that got piled on our plates all at once, since the cocktail hour had long passed waiting for

Serena. It was hard to know where to start. The fat little scallops wrapped in bacon that looked like severed finger-tips? The crisp green beans that were slathered in olive oil and doused with almond slivers? The tiny red potatoes marinated in vinaigrette with green mustard?

Uncle Doug ranted on throughout dinner. Things I remember he said: Aunt Serena was loony-tunes. The elevator didn't go all the way to the top. She wasn't wrapped too tight. She'd probably met a guy on the way over and gone to his place for a roll in the hay. She'd smoked too much wacky weed and fallen asleep. She'd forgotten, because she had so few brain cells left. Her horoscope counseled against going out today. And probably more that I likely forgot.

Aunt Kitty was constantly shushing him but he only got louder at those times. My mother said nothing. I don't remember our cousins adding their two cents to the conversation either. It was pretty much Uncle Doug holding court. The way he seemed most comfortable. We'd all managed to weather his onslaught of discontent when Aunt Kitty left the table to extract a marble cheesecake from the fridge. It was truly spectacular. Elspeth and I had never had cheesecake. I'd pictured a cake made out of slices of provolone cheese since that is the cheese we knew best. I wasn't looking forward to it.

Just as Aunt Kitty was cutting it for all of us, we heard Spud barking at the front door, followed by the tinkling voice of a woman.

"Spudley! You bad bad little man-dog, you. Come here and give me a big wet kiss. Come on now. You know you want to!"

I knew who this was. I looked over at my mother whose face was recognizable as the face I used to know. Her eyes were half-closed, her smile was huge, and a full-throated laugh erupted around us all. She almost tipped over the table getting up.

"Serena! Serena!" She bolted toward the foyer. I chased her, and Elspeth chased me. We were our own little family again.

My mother's arms enveloped her sister. She sobbed. I hadn't seen her sob since Dad died. Serena pressed her head into my mother's breasts. A large jeweled bag lay at her feet. Tiny bells adorned her sandals. I wanted a pair just like them, desperately.

She was bony, unlike my voluptuous mother. But the same blueish hair fell in thick waves down the middle of her back. She wore a purple velvet jumper, and I peered over my mother to see her face. Her features were delicate. Everything seemed too small, with the exception of her huge dark blue eyes. She smelled like cedar.

Elspeth and I stood there for several minutes. Uncle Doug, Aunt Kitty, and our cousins didn't join us in the foyer. Finally, my mother released Aunt Serena.

"Oh my God. You're the most beautiful thing."

"You too," Aunt Serena said.

They laughed and fell into each other's arms again. I was longing to be in those elegant be-jangled arms. And that is when she turned to us.

"You're the twins."

She fell to her knees and gazed at us in awe, like we hurtled from space with an important message for the world. She reached out and stroked both of our backs and stared alternately into our eyes.

"What beautiful, beautiful creatures. What kind and good souls. Old souls, especially you," she said to me. And she pulled us into her warm velvet clad body. I inhaled the cedar from her skin, and leaned into her for more. Of everything.

Uncle Doug appeared in the foyer.

"You're an hour- and- a- half- late."

"Really?" She gazed up at him still stroking us from her spot on the floor.

"Yes, really. Don't you keep track of the days and times?"

"I know it's dark out right now."

My mother let out a loud snort-laugh.

"You're as bad as she is," our uncle said, and stomped off to the kitchen.

"Are you hungry?" My mom took her hand.

"Starving, as usual," Aunt Serena answered, and they linked arms and whispered in one another's ears as they headed to the kitchen where Aunt Kitty was packing up the remains of dinner. I longed to hear those fluttering words, and Elspeth and I trailed behind them. Aunt Serena was a character from central casting in those days. A cross between Stevie Nicks and Elvira. A Wiccan in purple, but we didn't know anyone like her, so we couldn't stuff her in that box and ridicule its finite edges. To us, she was irresistible.

Aunt Kitty heated up a heaping plate of our tepid leftovers and made a space for her at the bar.

"So," Uncle Doug said, leaning against the fridge, arms crossed against his barrel chest "you just saunter in here at any old time, and you don't give a rat's ass, is that it? Because you know people like Kitty will say it's okay that you don't respect us enough to be on time."

Beads of sweat popped up on his forehead, despite the central air that always made the house a little too cold.

"People like Kitty? What does that mean, exactly," Serena asked.

"Spineless people. People who don't dare say what needs to be said."

Our mother started to say something, but then turned away instead. Aunt Kitty was wiping counters and packing food into Tupperware, acting oblivious to all the things being said about her in her red kitchen. Our cousins left the room, as though on cue. They disappeared into their bedroom at the end of the hall; the one they shared to make room for us.

"So, you have to say all these things for her, is that it," Aunt Serena asked.

"Yes. That's exactly it. So, what was it this time? Did your coven have virgins to sacrifice?"

"No. We had children to boil." Aunt Serena looked at us and winked and smiled.

"I would expect you to say something like that in front of little girls."

Aunt Serena placed her arms around both of our shoulders. I caught a whiff of the cedar again. A smell I loved from my Vermont home.

"They aren't afraid of me, Doug. I suspect they're more afraid of you."

Uncle Doug lunged toward her. She didn't flinch. He stopped a few inches from her face, too angry to speak, it seemed.

"Why do you hate me so much," Aunt Serena asked.

But Uncle Doug didn't answer. He just left the room, knocking a vase off the counter as he went.

"Bastard," Aunt Serena said under her breath, and bent to pick up the shattered crystal.

That night she remained at the kitchen bar with our mother and Aunt Kitty for hours, entertaining them with risqué stories about her lovers. We listened from our safe hide-a-way in the linen closet. Elspeth and I were sleuths extraordinaire. Aunt Kitty giggled and squealed at our aunt's antics. Another point in her favor, as far as we were concerned. But we learned more than the number of her lovers (26).

We learned that Aunt Serena's "alternative lifestyle" (as Aunt Kitty referred to it) was not what made my mother, Aunt and Uncle say she was nuts. They said this because she'd landed in institutions more than once (4 times since 1976). We fought to stay awake in the stuffy linen closet. The louvered doors let in some air and light, but not much. We were exhausted from a day at the pool, but they were still talking.

"So, how've you been doing lately," Kitty asked.

"You mean have I suffered from prolonged periods of sadness? Am I finally taking my medicine? Or needed to 'rest' at the loony bin again?"

"I'm sorry," Kitty said.

"Was that really necessary Serena?" My mother's voice was low. We knew that voice—it was the one she used when she was "disappointed" as she referred to her anger.

"No no," Aunt Kitty said. "That was way too forward of me."

"It's okay, Kitty," Aunt Serena said. Through the louvres I saw her reach out for Kitty's hand. The women sat in silence until Aunt Serena changed the subject.

"Violet," she said to our mother, "what are your plans?"

Our mother laughed again—the second time that night. "Plans? What are those?"

"We're Chabot women, are we not? We always have a plan."

Aunt Kitty crossed to the fridge and took out a bottle of white wine. She filled three tinkley glasses. I never saw my mother drink, but she grasped her dainty glass and pulled it to her mouth.

Aunt Serena turned it down, and Aunt Kitty said, "Lovely. More
for me." They all giggled. At some point I nodded off, but Elspeth
shook me awake.

"Liza! They've got a plan!"

And they did. Our mother and Aunt Serena mapped out a bold
move. I cracked the louvered doors of the hallway linen closet
enough to keep the three women in my sight. This was big.

"I know of a B and B in a little town in Maine," Aunt Serena
said.

My mother straightened in her chair. Aunt Kitty looked from
my mother to Aunt Serena, poured herself another glass of wine
and settled back.

"Where exactly," my mother said.

"Westover. It's a town of a few thousand nestled in the White
Mountains. It's not unlike Bethel, Vermont." Aunt Serena knew
my mother had loved Vermont. "Some friends of mine own it and
they're taking off to South America."

Elspeth grabbed my hand and squeezed. It's true we loved
the swimming pool, the fancy food, and Spud. But in the quiet at
bed-time we'd talked of wanting our mother back, and our old life,
even without our father, because what choice did we have?

"How long," Aunt Kitty asked, and left the table for another
bottle of wine. "Not that I want to get rid of you, Violet. In fact, I
wish you could stay forever."

"I know most of the business is from October to April. It's in
the middle of ski-country. Hikers doing the Appalachian stay there
too. They can't pay much, but the place would be rent-free. I was
thinking of doing it, but I hate to go alone."

None of them said anything for a few minutes. Aunt Serena
drummed her fingers on the glass table top. My mother twirled
her wedding ring and examined her nails, and I couldn't see Aunt
Kitty. She'd gotten up again to fill her glass.

"What's it called," my mother said.

"Back Kingdom Road House."

"It would certainly buy us some time," my mother said. "Let
me sleep on this."

"You're kidding, right Violet? What's to sleep on?"

"I'm not you Serena."

"Well, thank God for that," Aunt Kitty said. And all three of our beloved women hooted. We crawled out of the closet and down the hall to bed. Once safely in our room we hugged each other and muffled our joyous shrieks in one another's necks. A week later we had a date to leave for Maine with Aunt Serena: September 26th, and we felt as though we were bound for the moon. We loaded up our little Ford early on a Tuesday morning. Aunt Kitty walked us to the car. She pulled us into her arms and quickly released us. She smelled of grapefruit and vodka. I'd opened the big bottle in the freezer a few times. I had not drunk from it, but I was curious about the smell.

"Take this," she said, and handed our mother a cooler. "I put some cheesecake in there, and egg salad sandwiches. And lemonade."

"Thank you, Kitty. For everything." Our mom hugged her. The cousins never appeared.

We headed toward DC, where Aunt Serena rented a basement apartment in a small two- family house in Columbia Heights. She'd sublet it, cat and all, and was ready to "get the hell out of Dodge" as she was fond of saying. She'd given her two weeks' notice at a screen-printing shop, cleared out her bank account, thrown her stuff in an oversized batik bag, and was sitting out on her front steps when we rolled down 23rd Street. And we literally sang our way to Maine, with two pit stops, one somewhere in New York and the other just north of Boston. Our mother and Aunt Serena created the most intricate harmonies I'd ever heard. I hadn't realized my mother could sing. They had a fondness for old spirituals. Elspeth and I were entranced.

Chapter 2

We arrived at the B and B in the early hours of the next day. It was balmy, much warmer than we'd expected. Almost as warm as Baltimore, but still, a freshness wrapped itself around us that we hadn't known that summer. We'd slept in the car while mom and Aunt Serena shared the driving, but a deep fatigue made me wobble when I slogged out of the backseat, and an inky starless black gathered around me. The opacity of it was frightening, but the sounds of small creatures carrying on their nocturnal rituals harkened me back to Vermont.

Elspeth had fallen asleep in the back seat. Aunt Serena scooped her up and carried her into the sprawling farmhouse that would be ours for longer than we could possibly have guessed. We all headed, in a sort of daze, up a narrow staircase at the back of a large open common area to a series of smallish single rooms on the second floor. Aunt Serena placed Elspeth on the top of a double bed, and instructed me to join her. She pulled a lumpy, musty-smelling quilt over us. I'm sure I fell asleep immediately. She and our mother kissed us goodnight, and headed for the room across the hall.

It was noon when I woke up to find myself in a strange bed, alone. It took a few seconds to figure out where I was. The heat of the sun through the window pressed heavily against me. I liked

the color of the walls, though, and the furniture. The walls were
a celery shade of green, and the furniture a random assortment of
vintage stuff but somehow elegant. The double bed was high off
the ground. It occupied most of the rectangular room.

I smelled bacon and coffee. This had to be the work of my
aunt, because my mother didn't like either of those things. But I
loved bacon, and was lured by that smell. I found the narrow back
staircase and entered a huge kitchen with an apple green picnic
table, two shabby plaid couches, a big television and VCR and
shelves filled with books, movies, and board games. My mother,
aunt and twin sister orbited around each other humming snippets
of songs from our long ride.

"Good morning, sunshine," my mother sang to me, and dragged
her fingers across my head, and retrieved orange juice from the
fridge.

"How'd you sleep, pet?" Aunt Serena asked.

"Fine, I guess."

"You guess? You either did or didn't. Which is it?" My mother
regaled precision.

"Fine," I said, and sat at the picnic table, gazing out a window
at the town fire station and general store.

Elspeth joined me at the table and we chatted about going outside and exploring the woods. Our mother reminded us that we
had a trip to the local elementary school. I was looking forward to
the routine of school and fourth grade, and besides, it had a beautiful name: The Star School. The school was in the next town
over, and it would take about a half hour each way by the school
bus to attend. But we were not strangers to long commutes on
school buses.

After breakfast our mother herded us off to take showers. With
multiple bathrooms to choose from, at least until guests arrived,
we didn't have to fight about who went first. At three o'clock,
we were registering for school. There was a total of 47 students
in the entire K-8 group. Smaller even than we'd been used to in
Vermont. On our way back, Elspeth and I asked our mother about
school shopping. We didn't get an answer.

When we returned to the Road House, which I'd begun calling

it, we found Aunt Serena sitting on the deep wrap-around porch with a tall, stoop-shouldered man.

"Hey, all, this is Karl Pulsifer. He lives across the street over the general store."

Karl stood up as we walked on to the porch. I was struck by how much he looked like our father. Well over six feet, whitish-blond hair, a florid complexion and the palest blue eyes. Even the slight stoop was our father's, probably from having to duck all the time. I noticed our mother stop dead in her tracks for the briefest moment. It was barely perceptible, just a hesitation in the next footfall.

"This is my sister Violet and her twins, Elspeth and Liza," Aunt Serena said.

"Pleased to meet you." Karl extended his hand to my mother, who shook it quickly while looking down at the floor, and then mumbled something and excused herself. He then shook both of our hands, and we followed our mother into the road house, leaving Aunt Serena and Karl to talk on the porch.

Elspeth looked at me, her lips parted, about to say something. Of course, I knew. But she decided against it. We watched our mother as she poured herself a glass of water.

"Well, girls, I'm still a little tired from all the driving yesterday. I think I'll take a little nap. Go have fun! Explore the neighborhood, but be careful." And she drifted up the stairs, where it seemed pieces of her started falling off.

Aunt Serena came bounding through the door. Trailing her cedar smell behind her.

"He seems like a nice man, doesn't he?" She looked from one to the other of us, waiting for a response.

"Girls, what's the matter?"

Elspeth took this one. "He looks just like daddy."

Aunt Serena collapsed onto the picnic bench.

"Oh my God. Oh my God. I hadn't seen Tomas in years, you know, really, like years and years. You guys weren't even two. He had a beard, and his hair was long, and I don't know, I just didn't think of that. I can see what you mean. I'm sorry, girls, I am. It must have been like seeing a ghost. Poor Violet."

"She went to one of the rooms to nap," Elspeth said.

"Okay. I'll let her sleep."

Aunt Serena suggested we decide on what rooms would be ours. She and our mother wanted their own rooms, but we certainly would not be afforded that luxury, although we'd secretly hoped. In the far back corner of the third floor was a slightly larger room with a window looking out over the woods. The third-floor bath was directly across from it. We both agreed that was the best choice. Aunt Serena staked out a small corner room in the front of the second floor. She liked looking over the little main street with the firehouse and general store. She also liked the pale lavender walls. She called them opal. My mom would have to choose when she woke up. I wanted her on the third floor with us.

Dinner time rolled around, and Aunt Serena loaded us in the car to find the supermarket. We were hungry. Aunt Serena went upstairs to wake up our mother, but she was in such a deep sleep, she left her. We found the car keys in her purse, and headed to the closest town, about 12 miles away, and loaded up on food. We bought a lot of things that we shouldn't have. As we piled in junk, Aunt Serena just smiled. And we all made dinner. It turned out that Aunt Serena had a lot of flair in the kitchen. The meals were peculiar, but exotic and tasty. On this night, we had pecan meatballs in a sauce made of pureed red bell peppers and garlic. And absolutely nothing else.

Our mother did not wake up for dinner, or at all that evening. In fact, it was Aunt Serena who rose in the morning to see us off on the school bus, with our new supermarket school supplies. When we returned at 3:45, bursting with tales of our first day of school, Aunt Serena was on the porch again with Karl. When the school bus rolled to a stop across the street, in front of the fire station, we bolted across the main road to find our mother. Aunt Serena stood up and headed toward us. She looked more serious than we'd known her. More like a grown-up with something on her mind. Karl also rose, and bid us a good evening and in his slow and deliberate way crossed the narrow road to his apartment over the general store.

"Hey, you two, have a seat for a minute before you go and find mommy."

"What's wrong with her," Elspeth asked. She didn't sit. Nor did I.

"Your mom has just started to see how really very very sad she is about your daddy. Sometimes, in certain people, it takes a while for bad things to really sort of sink in, you know? And that's how it's been for your mom. So, she's going to need to take a long rest, so she can just be in the middle of her sadness for a while."

"Why would she want to be in the middle of her sadness," Elspeth asked.

"That's how it will finally go away, at least some," Aunt Serena answered.

"How long of a rest?" I wanted to know. It didn't sound good.

"It's hard to say. Everyone is different. She may need to rest for a few weeks, or a few months. But I'm betting at least a few weeks. So, here is what I need from you ladies. Are you listening?"

"Yes," we both answered.

"We have a lot of guests registered starting this weekend. Almost every room in the place will be filled up, and a lot of the guests expect to have breakfast, and their rooms need to be tidied up and stuff. When they leave, their rooms need to be all done over again with new sheets, and things like that. Your mom and I were supposed to be doing this together, but she's not going to be able to help. And the whole place needs to be clean. The kitchen, the bathrooms, and even this big room. I'm really going to need some help from you guys. Are you up for it?"

"No," Elspeth answered, and walked away. Serena let her go.

"I'll help," I said.

"Thank you, sweetie." She reached over and pulled me into her cedar smell and hugged me for a long time.

Within the next week, we visited with our mother for an hour or so after school each day. She mostly stared off into space, and seemed to only hear half of what we said. She occasionally managed a strained smile. Aunt Serena encouraged us to keep up the visits. "It really good to keep her engaged," she'd said.

I grew to hate this afternoon ritual. Elspeth less so. She

seemed content to sit at the foot of the bed in her own world. I couldn't stand it and made-up excuses to leave the room.

Karl was making a daily appearance and did some odd jobs around the place, readying it for Friday evening when 7 guests were scheduled to arrive. We went to school, did our homework and played in the woods. This was the best part of our day, when we could slosh through muddy creek beds, and build dams from twigs. What I mostly loved was finding anything that crept or crawled. Small salamanders, centipedes, milk snakes.

Elspeth adored all things winged, but I was earthbound. I had designed an elaborate ecosystem in a series of connected Tupperware containers. I connected the various containers by creating holes in them with an icepick and attaching them with toilet paper rolls. It was this consuming endeavor that made the absence of my mother tolerable. It was the reward after the visits to her room each before dinner where my mother lay zombie-like, greasy-haired and sallow in her musty bed. Elspeth would get bored with our forest adventures and retreat to our room with her books about magical flying dragons. So, I had plenty of opportunity alone in the woods to ponder the nature of sadness. What it was, how long one could "be in the middle of it" as Aunt Serena liked to say, and what forces were at work to make it disappear, and if it would disappear at all.

I wondered if I were sad. I wondered if Elspeth were sad. Aunt Serena, who spoke of her life of intermittent and intense sadness, did not seem so. I understood people could become sad when bad things happened to them, like the death of our father. I turned to my twin to discuss these things, but to no avail.

"Elspeth, are you sad?"

She sat drawing at the picnic table, one of her winged dragon creatures with the head of a dog, a rooster, and a dolphin. Aunt Serena loved these drawings, raved about them, and they papered the kitchen cabinets.

"No." Her tiny little tight body pressed down on her pastels.

"How do you know?"

"I'd be crying if I were sad."

"Are you ever sad?"

"No."

Sadness seemed to run in the Chabot women's blood, at least from what we'd heard, but it had skipped over Elspeth. But on that early fall evening, I needed more information on sadness, so I turned to Aunt Serena who was washing the dinner dishes. She'd been distracted lately. It'd been two weeks or so since our mother took to her bed, and we'd had a full house of "guests," and there was no real end in sight. Aunt Serena was working her butt off.

"Aunt Serena?"

"Yuh?"

"How long should a person be in the middle of sadness?"

"For however long it takes. Everyone is different."

"What makes a person get there?"

"That depends on the person too. Sometimes it's because something bad happens, like in the case of your mom, and sometimes people just come that way."

"Like you?"

"Yes. Like me."

"But you're not sad right now?"

"No. Not really. I'm sad for your mom, and you girls, for not having your daddy around anymore, but that's a different kind of sadness."

"How does a person not be sad anymore?"

"Some people go to the doctor and get medicine for it, but if it's a sadness like your mom, grief-sadness, then the best thing to do is surround yourself with people who love you and ride it out. And that is just what we're doing here."

Aunt Serena put away the last few dishes and came to me in the living room. We never really had any privacy, because guests could be walking through at any time, or even sitting on one of the couches reading or watching a movie. But she knelt down on the floor in front of me, took my hands and looked directly in my eyes.

"What is your sadness like?"

"Well, nothing seems too much fun anymore, except maybe my ecosystem, and sometimes not even that very much."

"Uh- huh. So, if you enjoy that even a little you should do it as much as possible. And when the sad feelings take over, come and find me and talk about them. Describe them. Tell me what color they are, how big they are, what shape they are, give them

names, even talk to them! This way you can control them a little
better. And you should cry whenever you want to. And wherever you want to. That's key. Believe it or not, even your Grandmother Glenna was sad."

"That's yours's and mom's mom, right?"

"That's right," Aunt Serena said, and sat on the couch with me.
I'd met my Grandmother once, but I didn't remember her.

"How did she die?"

"She was sick for a long time--mine and Mom's whole life."

We sat together in silence until Aunt Serena took my hand
and led me to my room. I lay in bed that night and although curious about the exact cause of my Grandmother's death, decided
I wouldn't ask. I realized a few years later that this was the moment when Aunt Serena welcomed me into the club of Chabot
women, the wracked with anguish. I was one of them. Elspeth
was not.

Karl and our aunt began to keep company. Elspeth figured it
out before I did.

"Karl likes Aunt Serena."

"Like a girlfriend?"

"Yes! Like a girlfriend, stupid."

"Does she like him too?"

"I think so. She gets really happy acting when he's around."

One day in mid-November, shortly after this conversation with
Elspeth, I learned that this was true. Our mom was still pretty
much in her bed, but had begun to venture out, though not into
the common areas. She didn't want to run into guests, but she
would occasionally come by our room at night, and we'd seen her
in Aunt Serena's room. She still had a far awayness about her.
She'd ask us about school, but would wander off in the middle of
answering her.

But on one particular night I wasn't able to sleep. My stomach
was bothering me and I was hoping Aunt Serena would give me
one of her herbal concoctions, which strangely enough always
helped. I'd started having lots of bellyaches as Aunt Serena called
them. I was approaching her room when I heard our mother's
voice. I stopped in the hallway and waited for a break in the conversation before I asked my aunt for help.

I could hear everything, and had a feeling I shouldn't be listening. But it had been a long time since I'd heard my mother talk that much. I'm not sure what I hoped to hear. Maybe that she was suddenly all better and that she planned to get up tomorrow and see us off to school or that she loved us more than anything in the world; in fact, more than the memory of our dead father that seemed to keep her in a separate world from ours. But the conversation was about Karl.

"So, you're seeing him?" Our mother's frail voice.

"Yes."

"You're sleeping with that man? My husband's ghost?"

"Violet. I'm sleeping with Karl Pulsifer. The history chair at West Paris Academy. Not Tomas de Kooning, the social worker."

"It's not rational, I understand that. But Serena, he is so much like Tomas. I see him sometimes out the window. Even the way he walks. I hear you two on the porch. The sound of his voice. It's like I'm being tormented. I can't stand it, Serena."

Her voice was flat and calm.

"What do you want me to do, V?"

"Do you have to see him?"

"I want to see him."

"It feels like you've stolen my husband."

"Yes, but you know that I haven't. If you could get to know Karl, you'd see all the ways he's not at all like Tomas."

"I can't get to know Karl."

Her voice was gaining strength. It had some color in it; she almost sounded angry.

"You don't want to get to know him, and I understand that. Although he makes me happy, and I'd like for you to be okay with that."

"What the fuck are you talking about?" She was almost loud. "What the fuck are you thinking? You want me to be okay with your happiness? I can't fucking be okay with anyone's happiness, Serena. To do that you have to be alive."

"You are alive, Violet."

"No. I'm not. My body is functioning. That's all."

"Someday, you will get out of this bed. I know that, because that's how it works."

"That's how it worked for you. You got out of bed. But you never had any reason to go to bed in the first place."

"I didn't have to have a husband die, that's true, to feel like I was covered with leeches and having my life slowly sucked out of me an ounce at a time, for searching for any little glimmer of hope, anything, to make me feel like putting one foot in front of the other wasn't the stupidest thing I could do. So, you can think I never had a reason, like you, to die. I can't stop you from thinking that. But here's the bad news, V, you are not dying."

The room was quiet for a few seconds. But then I heard something hit the wall and shatter.

"But that is what I want Serena! I should be able to have what I want; don't you think? And that is what I want, so why can't I? Make me one of your witch potions. Go get some night shade out of these god-forsaken woods and boil me up a magic death drink, please?"

The door was slightly ajar, and a thin sliver of warm yellow light fell across the hallway. I moved to that place and looked at my mother in Aunt Serena's arms, her body shaking so violently that the spasms were pushing Aunt Serena into the headboard of the bed. Aunt Serena never let go of our mother, and finally lay next to her and wrapped her in her arms like a child.

The next morning at breakfast Aunt Serena looked washed out. She barely managed to produce toast. We had a pretty full house, although the leaf peepers were long gone and November had landed grey and dank. Many of the local slopes were making snow; we didn't have any of the real stuff yet. She kissed us goodbye as we prepared for the bus and said, "I think your mom is going to be making her presence felt, and it could be a little rough for a while, but it's the beginning of the end of her sadness, I bet."

I wondered if that meant she was no longer in the middle, or maybe at the end of the middle, but in any case, it seemed like she'd done that middle thing and I floated out of the house to the bus. My aunt's prediction that she would make her presence known was dead on, and sometimes it felt monstrous.

Thanksgiving had been a slow time in terms of guests. We only filled two rooms and they were hardly ever around. Aunt Serena decided to make us all a nice Thanksgiving. Karl was invited. I knew that Aunt Serena was still visiting my mom's room nightly, and I resisted the temptation to eavesdrop, but I could hear the muffled sounds of loud conversations, or at least our mother was loud. I didn't know if they'd come to a meeting of the minds about Karl, but sort of hoped they would. I didn't really like him that much, but I did want my mom and aunt to get along.

Thanksgiving Day rose up drizzly and warm. Elspeth and I slept in. Dinner was scheduled for two. I tended to my ecosystem, re-read my favorite Roald Dahl story about a boy and a turtle, and chatted with Elspeth. She had been drawing her three headed flying dragons in earnest these days. Aunt Serena couldn't keep her in paper, so Karl had been bringing home huge sheets of brown butcher paper from the school where he taught. Elspeth would unfurl the paper and stretch the sheets across the floor of our room, pushing both twin beds against the wall. I was often trapped on my bed as she swirled her electric shades of oil crayons across the room. We'd run out of wall space for them, so she'd roll them up and stick them in our small closet. I had to start putting my clothes over my single chair.

Aunt Serena called us down to help around noon. The kitchen was too warm but smelled rich and earthy, like she'd put lumps of peat in the stuffing, and I actually worried that she may have.

"It smells like you're cooking a forest," I said.

"Cooking a forest! How fabulous. Cooking a forest, you should be a writer someday."

"Is mommy joining us? She's supposed to, right?"

"That's the plan, honey bunny. Where's El?"

"Making dragons."

"Jesus! More dragons?"

"Yup."

"Look, let's chat a bit about your mother. She hasn't been off the second floor since the beginning of October. So even though she thinks she's up for this, she could change her mind at the last minute, and that'll just have to be okay. She may join us and leave in the middle. Or she may join us and behave strangely, and that's probably the hardest to deal with. Do you understand? This is a holiday she and your dad really liked."

"Yes," I said.

Elspeth came down the stairs wearing a long jade green satin dress and a velvet turban. Aunt Serena had given us some old clothes to play with, and Elspeth often wore them seriously. She wasn't even five feet tall and the effect of the long dress bunched around her waist with a dog leash she found in the basement was macabre.

"I disagree," my sister said.

"Disagree with what, El," Aunt Serena asked.

"I disagree it's okay for mommy to change her mind or act bad at dinner."

"Well, what would you do?" My aunt put her hands on Elspeth's shoulders and looked directly into her eyes.

"I would tell her to get over it."

"Get over it?"

"Yes. That's what my school teacher says, she says 'get over it'."

"Do you? I mean, do you get over it?"

"Yes. I think it's a good way to give people advice."

Elspeth shrugged away from Aunt Serena's hands.

"So, you think your mom can get over your dad's death?"

"Yes. I think she needs to get over it."

"Well, that's one opinion. Do me a favor, though? Don't tell her to get over it today. If you plan to tell her that why don't you wait for just a while."

Aunt Serena put us to work. I was following her recipe for cranberry sauce from scratch, which called for grated orange rinds. I kept grating my knuckles and bleeding into the mix. Elspeth was digging out the innards of a pumpkin for homemade pumpkin pie. Aunt Serena had some sort of Wiccan music playing—a lot of high female voices singing nonsense words, but it was eerily beautiful and created a mood of peace. Even Elspeth seemed content and chattered about a boy at school named Thor. A child we recognized as being somehow like us. Not a local but the displaced child of back-to-the-landers. He didn't fit in either. The three of us often took our lunch together although I don't really recall what we talked about. I do remember that Elspeth liked him. She wanted a boyfriend.

The rain fell in gun-metal sheets against the picture windows and the sound it made on the wooden porch created a hollow space that I imagined was just the right size for my body. At 1:30, with a half hour to go, our mother appeared in the living room. She hadn't been downstairs since Oct, 2nd. Elspeth and I kept track of the days on an old hardware store calendar from 1974. We ran to her and threw our arms around her waist. She half-heartedly hugged us back. Although she had the same faraway look she was dressed for the occasion and seemed almost like someone we knew.

My mother didn't wear flowing robes of deep jewel colors like her sister. My mother's idea of dressing up was to wear clean jeans and a black leotard top. One that generally displayed her spectacular bosom, and she'd apparently decided that this was such an occasion. She also wore her favorite cowboy boots, a gift from our dad, and her hair looked like spun glass. I realize now what strength it must have taken to go to such lengths. I gazed at her in awe. Probably missing how much was riding on this event for her. Aunt Serena, however, seemed to freeze in place, a large wooden spoon in her hand, aloft in mid-air. She knew.

"You look beautiful, Violet. How do you feel?"

"Like shit."

"Well, it's courageous of you to join us all."

Our aunt returned to stirring up the innards of her pumpkin with some cardamom. Our mother slumped onto the picnic bench, as Elspeth and I set the table with an array of mis-matched plates, glasses and silverware. The table looked like a quilt. It was circus-like, the palette of yellows, greens, and reds. I loved it. At exactly two, Karl rang the bell. Our mother startled when it rang. It was an elaborate old doorbell that played eight notes—a spooky little melody. No one moved toward the big oak door. I finally did.

"Hi," I said.

"Hello, Liza," Karl answered in his low, tremulous voice, almost like he was apologizing for speaking at all.

Aunt Serena walked steadily toward him, her usual bounce

gone, probably for my mother's sake. A chaste hug and she ushered him to the picnic table with its curiously festive flair.

When my Aunt Serena said diner was at two, it was at two.
Unlike her, because in most other respects time was a fluid thing,
but where food was involved, she was a slave to the clock. She
didn't do cocktail hours like our Aunt Kitty. No wine and cheese,
crackers and shrimp—if you were invited to eat at two, you sat
down to the full course at two. And so, we did.

My mother smiled up at Karl, managed to stand, and reached
out for his arm. She led him to the table. I am sure she saw a
ghost.

"Here you go, Karl, you can sit next to me, so we can finally get
to know each other a little bit."

It was that forced gaiety. So strained that I could feel my own
muscles go taut just watching her. Aunt Serena pulled out a chair
across from him; I flanked my Aunt and Elspeth flanked our mother.

"This looks beautiful, Serena," Karl said. "Did you ladies help?"
He looked at us.

"Yes," I said. "I helped with the cranberry sauce and El helped
with the pumpkin pie. Aunt Serena made all the rest of the stuff."

"I didn't make anything." My mother produced a shrill quick
laugh, and turned to Karl.

"What can I serve you first," she asked.

Even at the age of 8, I understood flirtation. My mother had
turned her body squarely to Karl's, and her breasts were almost
pressed against his chest.

"A little bit of everything, please."

"A little bit of everything you shall have."

I glanced at Elspeth who was watching our Aunt Serena. Her
face looked like her skin had gotten too small for her skull. Her
long black hair was pulled away from her neck, exposing patches
of bright red skin. Aunt Serena would often get blotchy when she
was upset. Karl was doggedly focusing on Aunt Serena.

"Serena, I'm amazed that you found the time to create this
lovely meal."

"Yes, she is amazing, isn't she? She runs the inn, takes care of
my girls, and me, and finds time for a lover."

"Violet, please think of the twins," Aunt Serena said.

The table fell silent at this point. We all managed to eat, pass things, doing our best to get to the other end of this meal. I thought we'd made it. Karl said all the polite things expected to the chef, chatted about the rain and the strangeness of the unseasonable warmth and lack of snow. And then it happened. Our mother turned to Karl and offered him dessert.

"Karl, would you like me to cut you a slice of Serena's amazing pie?"

"Yes, thank you Violet."

Our mother disappeared into the kitchen and returned carrying the pie, topless. Karl had his back to our mother. I saw her first, and then Elspeth. I'm not sure what Aunt Serena was doing. My mother leaned into Karl's back and passed the plate over his shoulder to the table.

"Here you go," she whispered into his hair, and brushed her lips across the back of his neck.

"Violet!" Aunt Serena jumped up. "My God, Violet, what are you doing?"

I'm not clear on the sequence of events from this point, but I know that Elspeth ran from the room. I stayed, maybe out of fascination. Watching my mother serve us up her madness on a platter.

"I'm stealing Karl." She put her arms around his neck and pulled him into her.

"Violet, I don't think you know what you're doing."

Aunt Serena's voice was soft and steady. Karl was gently unwrapping my mother's hands from his neck.

"Why don't you want me?" She was yelling now.

As he backed away, she slapped him, and this act seemed to trip a lever. Because then she was raving and pummeling him. My aunt grabbed a throw from the couch and put it over her shoulders, but still I couldn't take my eyes from her breasts, exposed despite my aunt's attempt to cover her.

Karl held her away, by the wrists, as gently as he could. Serena was standing by her side and whispering something into her ear. I watched my mother's body slump to the floor, her hair spilled out on the pumpkin pine floors, so much like before.

"The girls should not be here!" Aunt Serena's face was mottled blue and red. "Karl! Please take them upstairs."

She knelt on the floor by my mother's side, the fringe of her long purple velvet shawl splayed across my mother's breasts.

I didn't want to leave, but Elspeth grabbed my hand with great authority and began to tug me toward the stairs. Karl seemed to snap to attention and took up the rear. Our little parade made it to the third floor. It's hard to tell who was really leading who. Karl seemed relieved that his assignment was to manage us. When we got to our bedroom, he rested his arms across the backs of our shoulders and gently guided us in, smiling.

"I think we can dispense with teeth brushing and other nightly rituals," he said, indicating our beds with the thrust of his chin. "It's been a long day, ladies. Why don't you both just climb in bed."

I had to strain to hear him.

"Well, we need to get our jammies on," Elspeth said. She pulled them out from under her pillow.

"Of course, of course!" He seemed too cheerful. "I'll give you some privacy. Is there anything you need before bed?"

He stood in the middle of our bare room, slightly stooped like a white birch.

"A story," Elspeth said.

I was embarrassed for her. We were too old for stories and I thought she shouldn't admit to anyone that she liked being read to.

"Oh, how wonderful," he said.

He clasped his hands together like he meant it, and he probably did. Reading to us was something he could do. "Which one," he asked.

He crossed to the shelves made from planks and cinder blocks and grabbed Nancy Drew.

"This one is okay with you both?" He waved it around like a flag.

"That's my positively favorite one," Elspeth said. "But you have to leave the room to let us change, and you can knock on the door in about 6 or 5 minutes and one of us will let you in."

She took charge as usual.

"Is there a secret knock," Karl asked.

"Yes," my sister replied. "It's two long and one short." She demonstrated on the top of her dresser.

"Okay, I think I've got it." He left us to change, and I watched Elspeth toss her clothes on our floor and pull her nightgown over her head with great speed and purpose. And we'd never had a secret knock.

"I am utterly thrilled that Karl will read to us," she said. "I think I like him more and more each day."

I was not utterly thrilled. I was confused by his presence in our make-shift lives and worried about his bizarre likeness to our father. I was terrified, in fact, that he might never go away and that I would be expected to accept him as Aunt Serena's boyfriend, and watch our mother twist and turn whenever he was around. I just wanted him to disappear.

"Liza, put your jammies on."

"Don't boss me around. I don't want to and I don't want to listen to this stupid book." I got under the covers fully clothed, and turned to the wall. Karl's secret knock allowed him access to the only sanctuary I had. I hated him and I hated Nancy Drew, and mostly I hated Elspeth.

"Liza, will it keep you awake if I read?"

I didn't answer him.

"Liza?"

"Don't worry about her," Elspeth said. "She's just a cranky pot."

I fell asleep listening to Karl's slow deep voice.

Chapter 3

The day after my mother exposed her breasts to Karl, things only got weirder. First, that Friday morning ascended barely into the twenties, after a week of muggy weather. Usually when I woke up, the temperature of the house was bearable. Aunt Serena would get the wood stove going in the kitchen, and the heat would find its way to the upper floors. But not that Friday. I lay in bed, tugging the thin blankets up as far as I could around my ears, wishing I was getting on a warm school bus.

"Liza!" My sister bolted to the window. "Look outside! Quick. Right now!"

I wondered how she could stand there barefoot in her flimsy strawberry shortcake nightgown. I wasn't going to budge until the house was warmer. I'd wait all day if I had to for someone to have the good sense to lay a fire.

"No. Stop bothering me."

"Liza, it's a big old bear!"

Her breath was fogging up the window and she was rubbing away the moisture with the side of her fist.

"There is no bear out there. Leave me alone."

"Is too. Come and see before he goes back in the woods."

I was curious at this point, and with a lot of huffing and puffing, left my warm bed and headed to the window. I could not stand to show any interest in anything Elspeth had to say.

"I mean it, El, there better be a dam bear when I get there."

"Don't swear," she said.

"Dam is not a swear, it's something to keep the water from flooding."

I leaned in to the window and in the small clear patch that my sister had wiped away was the bear. He was huge, the color of wet ashes, and eating yesterday's turkey remains from our trash. He clutched the carcass in both hands and drove his snout into the whole nasty mess repeatedly.

"Wow," I said, unable to seem unimpressed anymore.

"Told you." Elspeth smiled. I still remember how beautiful she looked in that moment. "Let's go get some breakfast," she said.

"It's so cold. I don't think there's a fire yet."

"So, we can make one."

The thought hadn't occurred to me that at some point in my life I may be called upon to take care of my own needs. I was strangely excited about the idea that I didn't require a grown-up to see to my comfort. I followed my older sister of 17 minutes for the second time in nine hours.

It was Karl who greeted us at the kitchen table, hunched over a newspaper and a large mug of strong-smelling coffee.

"Good morning Karl," my sister said, in her faux grown-up voice. Very sugary. It occurred to me she may be trying to impress him, and I wondered if she had a crush.

"My little sister and I saw a very large bear in the back yard this morning."

"I'm not your little sister," I yelled.

"Well, I was born first so that means you are the littlest one."

Karl looked up from his paper. "A bear?"

"Yes," my sister said. "He was going through the trash."

Karl got up from the table and headed for the kitchen door.

"Where's my mother and Aunt Serena," I asked.

"They're sleeping in today," he answered, and smiled at me. The smile wouldn't work. I knew he was to blame for the troubles around here.

"Are you going to see the bear," Elspeth asked.

"Yes," he answered. "Bears shouldn't be hanging around the

house."

I started to cry. I was cold, hungry, and worried about my
mother and Aunt Serena. It seemed wrong that Karl and Elspeth
were more interested in what was going on with the stupid bear.

"You won't hurt it though, right?"

"Don't worry Elspeth, I won't hurt the bear." He touched the
top of her head. She turned to look at me, as though to gauge my
reaction to Karl's obvious affection for her.

"Why are you crying," she said.

It was too much. Being called out in front of Karl.

"I'm not! You're just stupid," I said. I ran upstairs. I planned
to wake up my mother and aunt and get things back to normal.
Before I made it to the third floor, Karl overtook me.

"Liza, I'd like to take you ladies out to breakfast and then maybe drive to Rexford to a movie."

"I want to see my mother!"

"Of course, but it might be nice to let her sleep and talk to her
later today. You must be pretty hungry."

I was pretty hungry, and I loved going to the movies, but I
could not be deterred from seeing my mother.

"I'm going to see my mom." I stared him down.

Karl nodded his head yes, and retreated. I climbed the last
flight of stairs and was overcome with a sense of dread as I approached the lavender door of her room. I almost let my visit go,
but settled on my path finally and knocked resolutely on the door.
She didn't answer. I knocked a second time a bit louder, and still,
no answer. As I was bringing my hand again to the door I heard
her say, hoarsely, "Go away. Please."

"It's me, mommy."

"Please." She was crying now. "Please go away."

And so, I did.

My mother had never told me to go away before. In that moment her image blurred together with my father's--one entered
and exited the other like a holograph. It seemed the only recourse
was to lock myself in the bathroom. I sat on the edge of the claw
foot tub and waited for the crying to stop. But I didn't want to
just cry. I spotted my mother's make-up on the edge of the sink.

The very make-up she'd worn to dinner the night before. She'd looked so glamorous. With her eyes shaded in orchid, and her lips painted in seashell pink—her cheekbones accented in a tawny cream.

Elspeth pounded on the door. I ignored it, and crossed the cold tile floor and reached first for the lipstick. I rolled the tube between my fingers until the pink tip of the stick emerged from its canister. It looked like a dog's thing. It seemed weird to put this to my lips, but I did. The taste was bitter, but my mouth looked full and womanish.

"We want to go and Karl won't leave you here alone. Hurry up," my sister yelled, and still, I ignored her. I felt like a queen.

I blotted my lips on a piece of toilet paper the way I'd seen my mother do, and reached for the cheek gloss. It was creamy to the touch, like frosting. It smelled like almonds. I carefully applied this silky stuff across each cheekbone, deliberately and slowly. I looked like a girl in a magazine. And finally, the crowning glory— the orchid shimmering powder for my eye lids.

"Karl wants to go!" My sister again.

"Since when should I care about anything Karl thinks? He isn't my dad." I yelled through the heavy oak.

"So what? He still wants to take us to breakfast and a movie. The Never-Ending Story."

My sister was the type who could be bought for French toast and a movie. She hasn't raised the bar very high since. She was excited when they opened a Denny's in Rexford. She just throws back the curtains and settles for whatever love from whatever corner it comes from. Good for her.

"No! I'm busy," I said. And I was. Diligently applying my mother's make-up made me feel better. My mother's words of banishment didn't sting so much now. I looked in the mirror and noted the heart shape of my face—the slightly pointy chin, so narrow compared to the width of my brow, and it was my mother all over again. I stroked the soft powder across my eyelids, but it was not dense enough and so I did it again. The left eye was now perfect.

I heard Karl's heavy boots on the stairs. For a timid sort, he didn't take care to silence his footfalls.

"Elspeth," he said to my sister. "We'll go another time. I'll make a fire and we'll have French toast here."

I did not need him to keep this house warm. I sprung on the door knob.

"Wait," I said, erupting from the bathroom. "I'm making that fire."

Elspeth rolled her eyes.

"What's with your face," she asked. "One eye is purple and the other isn't."

"So what," I answered. Elspeth shrugged.

Karl stepped back from the door and gestured for me to go first. I strutted down the stairs reviewing the steps of fire-laying in my head. I'd watched Aunt Serena do it dozens of times.

"Okay," I said. "Let me get down to business." I knelt on the pine floor and began to make balls from the stack of newspapers in the large wicker basket. Elspeth was humming a song direct- ly behind me that I recognized from a cassette my Aunt Serena played over and over. The words ten times round the seasons flashed in my head and I knew they'd be there all day now. But I stuck to my task and made at least 20 paper balls. I stacked them neatly in a pyramid and lay fine kindling in exes gently over the whole pile, finally adding 2 logs on the top. It was magnificent.

"Matches, please?"

Without turning around I extended my hand out to my side and waited for Karl to jump to it. To my delight within seconds a book was placed in my expectant palm. I'd seen Kyle light match- es when he snuck cigarettes in the cabana. I'd noticed how the match got placed on the little rough strip on the bottom of the book, the cover placed over it, and then the match was swiftly pulled out from in between the two in a burst of orange flame, fol- lowed by a dainty puff of funny smelling smoke. And this is what I did, and the whole thing was flawless. I flung the lit match onto my masterpiece and it crackled to life.

"Wow! You're a pro," Karl said. "It seems you've been making fires your whole life."

Elspeth actually clapped. She was not the jealous sort. Although I'd wished then that she was so I could gloat.

"What a morning! A bear in the backyard and a blazing fire on a dreary cold day," Karl said. The way he clasped his hands together whenever he wanted to relay genuineness drove me nuts. He had long arms like a gorilla, and it just made him look even sillier. I liked Karl no better for all of his gushing over my prowess with a match.

The fire had consumed my mountain of paper and began to fizzle—from a burst of color and heat to a low thrum of glowing cinders. This fire was no good. It was cold again. The euphoria of my first fire passed. I was stunned that I could have felt so good one minute and now so bad. I wanted my mother and aunt puttering around the kitchen in their ugly men's navy-blue underwear.

I wanted Aunt Serena's wistful music tinkling over the beams of the living room and floating to the floor in shimmering wisps of sound. I wanted my mother's sad eyes darting from the faces of her daughters and sister who loved her for hope and consolation. I did not want Karl's stupid French toast and there was no way I would go to a movie with him and Elspeth. My path was clear: go back to bed. I left them pondering the next moves of the garbage eating bear.

"Karl," I heard Elspeth say as I turned the corner on the second floor. "Let's name this big old bear Tomas. That was my dad's name."

Karl laughed. I couldn't stand these idiots.

Chapter 4

Snoutly kept coming around. The local wildlife and game folks urged us to shoot him. One in particular, Joe, was quite set on the idea. He was certain that it was a threat to the whole neighborhood that the bear came around as often as he did. It seemed an uphill battle to get the bear to leave us alone. First Karl got an electric fence, and when that didn't work he stored the garbage in bear-proof canisters, and when the bear kept visiting he finally buried those canisters in the ground. We were surprised that he still kept dropping by.

"We humans turn bears into problem bears," Karl said. We were chatting on the front porch with Joe who'd stopped by again for a bear update. It was a sunny April morning. The snow was melting and great rivulets of water traveled across the slant of our porch and down the front steps.

"I agree completely," Aunt Serena said. "What do you think Violet?"

"I'm not sure. I worry he'll hurt the girls, though." Karl slipped his arm around her and gave her a small hug. I'd noticed this sort of thing before and wondered what Aunt Serena thought.

"Bears think with their stomachs, but we can use our brains to live peacefully with wildlife," Serena said and smiled her come-hither smile at Joe. We'd heard her say this 1,000 times.

"This is dad!" My sister was sure that it was true. "His spirit is in that bear. It's so obvious!" She folded her arms across her budding chest and glared at Joe.

"Well, then Snoutly should buy me a bike instead of trying to dig up my table scraps." I crossed my arms around my non-budding chest.

I refused to refer to the bear as Tomas, and instead called him Snoutly. It was sort of cute when I was 9, but at 11 it was starting to seem like a dumb name, but it had stuck.

"That's not how it works. He's still a bear. It's transmigration."

"Don't confuse parables for truth," Karl said.

Elspeth scowled at him.

"Once a predator loses fear of humans shooting becomes reasonable," Joe added. "And the meat makes great chili."

"Losing predators is bad for forest health," Aunt Serena said.

"Guys! The real issue here is that this is dad! And we're not making chili out of him!"

Neither my sister nor I wished for Snoutly to be murdered. But for different reasons. I certainly didn't think my father was wrapped up in Snoutly somehow, but I did love animals, and had affection for Snoutly. He was a constant in our precarious lives. And I was pretty convinced that he could smile. I actually did think his visits were intentional, and more about his fondness for our family than his need for food, which had long been taken care of.

"Black bears are dangerous you know," Joe said. He lit a cigarette. "They can and do kill people. And they will end up being a real threat, even in heavily populated areas. Happened down in Portland just last fall." He exhaled, picked a piece of tobacco from his tongue and flicked it away.

"Portland? Really?" My mother looked up at Karl, as though he would have some authority to deny this.

"Yup. Spotted in a tree in a residential neighborhood. Warden service tried to tranquilize her but couldn't, so they shot her. Had no choice."

"Oh, I'm sure they had a choice," Aunt Serena said. Karl took her hand.

"Look, I don't know what you people don't understand here," Joe said. He took another big pull on his cigarette. The head of ash fell at my feet. "But bears are curious and wicked adaptable. They get accustomed to human activity and real aggressive about their food gathering habits. They've even been known to stalk people – following them or circling to approach from ahead. This isn't some cute bear in the animal farm."

"You think the bear is stalking us," Karl said. I couldn't tell if he was being sarcastic or not. I hadn't ever known him to be sarcastic though.

"He could be. And denning is over. He's going to be back now that it's April. Big time. Mark my word."

"I don't know what else we can do. We're as bear-proofed as can be," my mother said.

She leaned against Karl.

"I'm not sure you are," Joe said. He dropped his cigarette on the porch and stamped it out.

My Aunt Serena stepped in to him.

"What exactly are you saying? That you think we're feeding him on the sly?" Her ears turned bright red. I'd only seen that a handful of times, and usually when she was furious at a rude guest and was trying hard to be polite.

"Just remember," Joe said, "a fed bear is a dead bear."

"What's the next step," Karl asked.

"Relocation. But if he returns a third time, we'll have to shoot him."

"No one will shoot this bear!" Elspeth ran from the porch crying.

"Well I have to go folks. You have a nice day." He removed his baseball cap and bowed slightly to the women.

I watched Joe as he sauntered down the steps to his dusty white truck. He seemed in no particular hurry to get anywhere. My family went back inside without saying goodbye to him, but I did. It seemed to me that he was just doing his job. I'd heard my mother saying that to Aunt Serena a few times, and I agreed. And truthfully, I was a little afraid of Snoutly. In the end, he was a big black hungry bear.

I decided to look for Elspeth. Usually when she ran off in a snit

I found her in a patch of boggy woods behind the barn that was one of my favorite places too. I caught endless tadpoles there. It was one of many vernal pools that sprang up in March and April.

"El, where are you," I called as I headed through the pussy willows and sticky brush.

"I don't want to talk to you," she hollered at me as I approached.

"Why? What did I do wrong," I said.

I found a semi-dry spot on the banking by the large mud puddle that Aunt Serena had named Fairy Shrimp Spa. I loved the fairy shrimp and had written a paper on it for science class.

"You're on Joe's side!"

"I am not! I'm not on any side," I said.

"Well, don't you think you should be?"

Elspeth lifted her head off her knees and looked directly at me. Her creepy indigo eyes staring me down.

"Answer me! Don't you think you should be on our side?"

"Well maybe Joe has a good point. Snoutly is a bear. And bears can kill people."

"All sorts of things can kill people. I bet it's less likely that a person gets killed by a bear than dies from food poisoning."

"Hey, this is the first time we've been to Fairy Shrimp Spa this year!"

I'd perfected the art of changing the subject. It had become a survival strategy for me in the years we lived in Back Kingdom with the Fragile Sisters and Kooky Karl, names that my sister and I had made up for the trio of ersatz adults that infused our peevish lives.

"I know," my sister said. "It's deeper than usual this spring."

My tactic worked. It often did with Elspeth. She was easily derailed.

"Yeah, we had a lot of snow."

"Yeah," she answered, and lowered her head to her tender knees.

We sat like this for a long time. I'm not sure how long, until we were being called in for lunch. Maybe an hour had passed. My fanny was wet and numb when I finally stood up.

"I'm hungry, I said. "Let's go eat something."

"Okay," Elspeth said.

"Hey, speaking of food, do you think that Aunt Serena is secretly feeding Snoutly?"

I'd been worried about that since Joe had suggested it.

"Not even!"

"Okay," I said to appease my sister. "I was just curious what you thought."

"She'd never do that. She loves him too much to make things worse for him."

"Right," I answered. But I was not at all sure.

We walked to the back-kitchen door. Through the screen I could smell my mother's vegetable soup. She filled it with caraway. She told us she learned this from our father.

"I hope she made grilled cheeses too," Elspeth said.

"Absolutely."

I felt tired. I felt old. At least 14. I felt my breasts pushing through my chest wall, and my uterus stretching against my taut abdomen. I felt pubic hair sprouting from the soft bare vee between my legs.

It was a boisterous lunch. Not unusual in our house those days. The owners never did return from South America as expected. My aunt and mother with the help of Karl bought Back Kingdom Road House. Elspeth and I called it BK for short. But the place didn't keep us afloat. My mother took a part-time job in Rexford as a cashier at a Pick and Pay. Always there was a mist of doom descending on us. That and the knowledge that there was something odd about our family.

"I need some more ketchup," I said.

"Who puts ketchup on a grill cheese?" My sister put her finger in her mouth to signal gagging.

"I do. No different from eating pizza, and it's delicious. Try it. You might like it."

"Here you go," Karl said. He slid it across the table.

"Do you think Joe will come back," Elspeth said.

"Oh, you can bet on it!" Aunt Serena slapped the kitchen table.

"Maybe not," Karl said. He reached across the table and took her hand in his. My mother looked away.

"Why do you say that," Aunt Serena asked, and yanked her hand back.

"He says that because he asked him not to," my mother answered. She smiled at Karl. I wanted to telepathically send my twin a message: are you seeing any of this? I'd been noticing these gestures for months.

"Oh, Violet! Really! You think men like Joe will abandon their mission because someone asks them nicely? Who's more stupid here? You or Karl! I mean Jesus!"

Aunt Serena carried her soup bowl to the sink and let it crash to the bottom. She spun around, her long twirly bedspread skirt fanning around her bare legs.

"Joe just wants to kill stuff. That is what men like Joe are about."

"Why is it that you are an expert on Joe," My mother asked. It was rare for her to challenge her sister. Or anyone, really. I was proud of her.

"Violet, all he's wanted to do from the get-go is take this bear down. This beautiful sacred clever animal—this Native American symbol of strength, hard work, and love. You know, many tribes consider the "Great Spirit" to take on the form of a bear?"

"You mean God," Elspeth asked.

Aunt Serena returned to her chair.

"Yes. For the Native Americans the bear gave life to the land. The bear was a Mother-symbol."

"Do you believe in God, El," I asked. We'd never really had a conversation about God. Our family didn't belong to any religions, and we just didn't talk about this sort of stuff.

"I don't know," she answered. "What's for dessert?"

"I think there's some lime sherbet in the freezer," my mother said.

Karl got up. "I'll get it, you sit Violet."

"You know the Native Americans used the bear to explain the seasons. It rises up in the spring, waking up the earth." My aunt acted this out, rising from her seat at the table.

"As summer comes, its breath makes the world warm." She exhaled loudly.

"In August, the bear gets shot by hunters and her blood changes the colors of the leaves." She sort of crumbled her body until it looked broken.

"And in the winter, there is no bear and the earth is cold and lifeless." She sat back down with a thud.

"You don't believe that, though, right," I asked.

"I don't know, Liza. What do you believe?"

"Science," I said. And at that moment I came closer to knowing who I was, and felt excited to know what I believed.

"To believe in science gives you certainty. To believe in a God gives you hope," Aunt Serena said.

I wanted to ask my mother what she believed, but when I turned to her, her eyes were closed.

Karl was standing over me with a plastic container full of bright green sherbet. "One scoop or two?"

"None thanks," I said. I only wanted to go back to Fairy Shrimp Spa.

I caught my sister's eyes and gestured with my head to come on. She pushed her chair back from the table, wiped her mouth across her sleeve, and we were gone. I loved when our twin vibe was in sync. I felt grafted to her at those moments, and the rest of the world didn't exist. It was good.

We headed out the back door, and walked arm in arm to the spa where we resumed our spots on the damp banking. I wanted to ask her if she'd noticed the way Karl and our mother was acting. But she jumped in first.

"Our birthday is coming up," my sister said. "Twelve, I can't believe it."

"What should we do for a party this year?"

"I think we should have an actual party where we invite actual people. You know? Not just Kooky Karl and the Fragile Sisters and a bad homemade sugar free cake!"

"Like actual friends," I asked.

"Yeah, why not?" She plucked a piece of dead grass from the ground and rolled it between her fingers.

"We'd have to actually make some between now and May 24th."

"Very funny. We have a few."

My sister was much more optimistic than I was. "We do? Who?"

"Oh come on! There's Tyler, and Maggie and even Max."

"Tyler's stupid, Maggie smells like goats, and Max, well, I don't even know where to begin. I think he still shits in his pants."

"Don't be so mean." She glared at me.

I felt immediately awful for having said what I did about her friends. But they were her friends, and not mine. I was too self-conscious to hang out with the school misfits. I was misfit enough without singing it from the heavens. Better to go it alone.

"I'm sorry," I said. "I just think I'd rather do a family thing again."

Elspeth picked up a stick and began to carve concentric circles in the muddy banking.   It was by now mid-afternoon and the sun was slicing through the canopy of trees and creating a checker-board pattern. My sister and I were sitting in different squares—me in the shady one, her in sun. We were side by side, close enough to rub elbows, but we were in that moment a study in light and dark.

"Well, not me," she said and tossed the stick into the mud hole. "I will be hanging out with Goat Girl, Retard Face and Smelly Bum."

"You're that desperate?"

"Why don't you want anyone to come to our house?" She turned to face me and shook her head and raised her eyebrows.

"El, I think Karl is mom's boyfriend—not just Aunt Serena's."

"You're nuts," she said.

A jolt ran through me. Hearing myself just come out and drop it like that between us made my adrenaline surge.

"You didn't know that already," I said. It came out really sarcastic.

My sister turned her creepy snake eyes on me again, and laughed. I wanted to hit her—push her down on the cold wet patchy ground and step on her face with my muddy boot.

"What do you mean?" There was a catch in her voice, despite the laughter, like she might cry. And I wanted her to.

"I mean I've seen them. Mom and Karl. I've seen them kiss." I made a smooch face.

"How come you never told me?" She tossed her stick in the frog pond and screamed.

"Stop screaming. I didn't make them do it."

"But you never said anything." She was now on her feet, towering over me.

"One, I thought you knew, and two, it was too awful to talk about."

Elspeth plucked a pussy willow from the ground and ran her hand back and forth over the soft nodes. She was staring up through the trees.

"And what's even weirder is that I think Aunt Serena knows," I added.

"What can we do," she asked. She dropped back down to the banking.

I panicked. I should have an answer for this? My hands and knees were shaking.

"What can we do," I said. "I mean, he's the only man in town and I guess they're sharing."

"But that's gross," she said.

"You're telling me." I joined my sister in her square.

Chapter 5

The month leading up to our birthday party was busy with guests. Most of them were making their way from Maine to Georgia on the Appalachian Trail. We were well positioned to revive the tired hikers. It was exotic to me—to meet the hikers—most of whom were young. They collected in the evenings after washing the mud off. They sat in front of the big fireplace in the common room pampering their feet, eating their granola bars and drinking beer from the general store. They were kind to me and Elspeth, and some of the girls would play scrabble or cards with us. They were different than the occasional snowmobiler making his way to Canada along the tangle of trails across the gorges and lakes. The young nature babies, as Aunt Serena called them, were sexy.

But it was the afternoon before our party (to which I'd agreed and was looking forward to since I liked a boy named Travis in my class), that my sister and I made a plan to spy on some guests. We understood that it wasn't cool--both our mother and aunt had made that clear when they'd overheard us sharing the latest guest gossip. But on this particular day it was just too tempting—that taste of salty information about the strange goings on of boys and girls not much older than us.

Since our worrisome revelation about our mother, Aunt Serena and Karl, Elspeth and I had talked about little else, except our party--did mom and Aunt Serena take turns being girlfriends with Karl or did they even know about the other one? Was Karl keeping it all a secret from them and if that was the real deal, did we owe it to our mother and Aunt Serena to out his cheating? Thoughts about what was happening with the three gown-ups in our lives infused everything we did. Still, we'd worked ourselves into an excited knot of anxiety over our flight into normalcy—a birthday party where we'd have actual friends to our home to eat cake with sugar in it and open presents. A birthday party where Travis, the tall quiet boy who loved my project on fairy shrimp would attend, bearing a gift for me. But always the fear dangled over us that something would go terribly wrong. Our mother would start crying for no visible reason, or Aunt Serena would insist on dancing or worse yet, Karl would shine his love light on both of them in an obvious way.

It was that fear, we told ourselves, that called for an investigation of three guests who had checked in that morning. Maybe their behavior would reveal something about our mother and Aunt's behavior. The boy was maybe 20 and his two female companions were about the same. They booked a room with a double and single bed, like a family might do with a young child, and we were obsessed. This obsession was fed by the fact that the boy in question was quite a babe according to my sister. He was tall, some exotic blend of a few races with a wild head of dreadlocks, and not one, but two pierced ears. Most striking to me were his sad green eyes.

The two girls were quite different from one another. One was short, plump and tow-headed. She wrapped her long fine hair around her head in two fat braids, and her skin would get blotchy every time she spoke. The other was bony and taut, and her hair was almost entirely shorn, leaving a bristly faint black halo barely covering her large skull. She wore loose sleeveless t-shirts that revealed through the arm holes a completely flat chest. I found her quite spectacular.

Shortly after they checked in, they lay in a tangled heap on the braided rug in front of our big TV watching movies from the selection of used videos we'd accumulated. Elspeth and I were doing our homework at the picnic table in the kitchen, with one eye trained on this mysterious trio.

"The Big Chill!" The plump one exclaimed. She waved the video around her head. "I love this movie."

"Haven't you seen it like a trillion times?" The bald girl flopped onto the couch, defeated.

"So? It's a great piece of cinema."

"What about this?" The green-eyed boy examined Werewolves in London. "This is a trip."

"Whatever," answered bald girl. "I'm easy."

"We know," said the plump one. She popped in the movie, and the three of them arranged their limbs on the rug. It was difficult to know who was wrapped up in whom. It looked good.

"Do you think the blonde girl is his girlfriend, or the other one," Elspeth whispered.

"Well, he'd be crazy to pick her over the other one. At least I think so," I said.

"Really? The blonde's so much prettier."

I gestured to the backyard with my chin. It wasn't safe to have this conversation inside. My sister and I quietly headed out the back where the hammock had recently been strung between two spruces. We climbed in, trying not to tip over. I adjusted my weight.   It had swallowed both of us up in its netting, and I kept rolling into Elspeth and getting my legs tangled in hers.

"Anyway, I don't think the blonde is prettier. She looks regular. The other one stands out."

"She's so skinny, though, and she doesn't have any hair. Or boobs. She looks like a guy to me."

"Well maybe he likes tomboys. Not all guys like big boobs and long hair." I felt defensive of the tall bald one suddenly. As though she was my friend.

"I don't think that's true. Boys always like girls with big boobs and long hair."

"Well my bet is that she's his girlfriend, and the chubby girl is just their friend."

"So you think she's sleeping in the twin bed?" Elspeth's shirt rolled up and a thick slab of blubber rested on the tops of her jeans. I looked away.

"I think they couldn't afford two rooms, and that chubbers is sleeping in the twin bed. Yes."

"You know the only way to be sure is to investigate, right?" She sat up on her elbows and grinned at me.

"Let's put the finishing touches on our party before tomorrow," I said.

I usually loved an opportunity to spy on guests. It was always Elspeth who started off the investigation but I eagerly awaited her inspiration. I wasn't sure why this time it made me squirm.

"I think the party is in good shape. Everyone but Max is coming, and Aunt Serena is making a cool cake, and mom is getting the decorations from Pic and Pay. What's left for us to do," she asked.

"Will we all just sit around?" I was worried that the six or so of us who would be there would have nothing to say to each other, and no ideas about how to have fun. It terrified me. And especially because Travis was coming. I didn't want to look stupid, and I didn't want my family to seem too weird.

"Let's watch a movie," my sister said. "Like Flash Dance or something."

"That is actually the best idea you've ever had," I said. And I meant it. It would take the pressure off having to relate.

"Now that we've settled that, what about an investigation for the merry trio?"

 I didn't answer her.

"Liza, what's the deal? You never pass up a chance to get the scoop."

I wasn't sure what the deal was, so agreed to spy since I had no really good reason not to.

"Okay, but if we're going to talk about this let's head to The Spa. Out of earshot of the Fragile Sisters and Kooky Karl."

"Agreed," my sister said.

We helped each other out of the sagging hammock and headed to the woods. We assumed our usual places on the banking of the fairy shrimp vernal pool, which by now was swollen from winter run-off.

"Okay, Nancy Drew," I said, "what's the plan this time?"

"Well, the good news is that I looked in the guest book and they're on the second floor, so it should be easy to just look right in the window from Karl's ladder."

"Gee, Einstein, what if the curtain is drawn, or what if we're spotted on the ladder? I don't like it."

"We do it tonight. The ladder is already in the back yard, so that part's easy. No one will spot us."

"And the curtains?"

"We have to take them down. We just go into their room before they go to bed, and take them down. They probably won't even notice."

"And if they do?"

"If they ask about it we say we're doing a wash."

My sister looked at me and smiled. All her teeth showed. I noticed how white they were compared to mine. White teeth, not too tall, breasts, shiny hair, small feet. All the things I didn't have, because I looked like my dead father.

"We're doing a wash?" I snorted. "Puleeeze! That is the dumbest thing I ever heard!"

"Well, what's your idea?"

"The keyhole."

The old skeleton keyholes offered really good viewing, actually. Although sometimes you had to move a piece of furniture so that it was positioned in the right field.

"I don't know," my sister said. "I think it's too easy to make mistakes that way. I mean, you see some part of something, but not all that you really need. I think it isn't as foolproof as just looking into the window."

"Maybe," I said, "but I also don't think it's as risky as taking down drapes and climbing on a ladder in the dark."

My sister shooed a fly from her calf. "True," she said. "Okay. Key hole then. But one of us needs to make sure we can see at least one bed from there."

"That's a cinch, El. I'll bring in some towels and drag the double over a ways."

"Good," she answered. She slapped her thighs with the palms of her dainty hands, to signal the finality of our plan.

Later that evening when the merry trio were in their usual heap on the rug watching The Year of Living Dangerously, I delivered a bunch of clean towels to their room even though they didn't really need them. My sister knelt outside the door peering into the keyhole. She was to knock once on the door when I'd dragged the bed sufficiently away from the wall so that most of it could be seen through the hole. On my second try, the knock came. Our work was done. The only thing left was to hope they crashed soon so we could do the deed and get to bed before our mother or aunt caught us prowling the halls of the second floor. And then our birthday party would be here. In all of its glory, or all of its torpor.

"Okay," my sister said. "Let's get out of here." She yanked me from the doorway and gingerly pulled the door shut.

"Now what," I asked. I was relived not to be obsessing over our party. The investigation required my attention and offered the distraction I needed.

"Now we head downstairs and try to get them to go to bed," she said.

"How?"

She pulled me into an empty room and shut the door. It was now twilight, and the red glow that had infused the sky a moment ago had changed into silver. I thought it was so much more beautiful. So much easier to look at—the soft muted shades of silver all velvety and plush.

"Let's just set up a scrabble game or something in the living room and bug them."

I thought of the tall one. I saw her name in the guest book--Candice. The other one was Megan. Candice was such a much statelier name. The boy was Toby. I didn't want to bug the merry trio. I liked them. Especially Candice. But I agreed to the plan. Playing scrabble was a way to be around them. I wouldn't bug them though. But I wouldn't tell my sister this.

We headed down the front stair case, acting as nonchalant as we could. Elspeth was even humming.

"Want to play scrabble, sis," she asked in a voice much too loud. She never called me sis. I almost laughed out loud.

"Sure," I said.

She made much of retrieving the board from the shelves, set-ting it up on a lazy susan, and shaking the box to mix up the tiles. She shook it several times, and each time the noise was more irritating. I glanced over at the merry trio, and they didn't seem to register us at all. My eyes got caught up on Candice. One long tof-fee leg was wrapped around Megan, and one hand rested on Toby's dreadlocks.

"Let's see who goes first," my sister nearly screamed. "Pick a tile."

"I have a dee," I said, in an almost whisper.

"Oh my," she said in an old-maidish sort of way. "I have an ex, so I guess you get to go first, sis!"

After we made a few words, and my sister's antics didn't seem to be making any difference in the merry trio's viewing pleasure, I was about to forget the whole thing. To me they seemed engrossed in the movie. But then Candice disentangled herself and walked into the kitchen. I caught a whiff of patchouli as she passed by. I knew this scent, because my aunt wore it. On her way back, she stopped and looked at our board.

"I hope you guys don't mind if I kibitz?"

I didn't know what that was, but I didn't mind.

"That's fine," I said. I was fingering my tiles, looking for a word.

When Candy, as her travelling pals called her, pulled a chair up beside me to be my "kibitzing" partner in scrabble, she smelled like sweat and patchouli. When she was this close, I could see the fine black hair curling in her unshaven arm pits.

"You don't mind, do you? If I join you?" She smiled. Her left front tooth was chipped.

My heart was beating fast. "No. that's fine," I answered.

"Good," she said. She pulled her chair up closer to the table. "Because I love this game. I used to play with my little sister. You remind me of her a bit."

I scooted my chair closer to the table as well to accommodate her, and when I did, I knocked over the little ledge that held my letters. They clattered to the floor, and we both went down to get them but I was faster. I scooped up a handful of tiles, and on my way back up I struck my head, hard, on the table edge. Tears came into my eyes.

Elspeth laughed.

"Oh, my," Candy said. She leaned in to get a closer look at my head. "You're going to have a lollapalooza of an egg if we don't get some ice on it like now."

"No! I don't need any. I'm fine," I said. The tiles were getting damp in my hand. I was squeezing them too hard. "Let's just play."

"Yeah," my sister agreed.

"Candy is right," Toby said. "You really should ice it."

"You heard the lady," Candy said to her friend. "She said no ice, so no ice it will be."

By the time Candy and I skunked Elspeth with fez and scion, I was in love.

"If you scrabble whizzes are quite finished, let's crash," Megan said. "Movie's over and I'm in need of sleep, big time."

"Me too, actually," Toby added.

"Okay, it's time I guess," Candy said. "Thanks for letting me play Liza."

After the last goodnight was said, the merry trio headed up the stairs single file. Candy was bringing up the rear. Her cut offs slid below her Jesus hips. They jutted out like the wings of a bird of prey. Once they were all clear of the second-floor landing, my sister sprung to life again.

"Okay! It's time for our plan. We'll just give them a while to get into bed."

I had changed my mind. I knew them now and liked them. I didn't want to spy.

"Girls," Aunt Serena called from the landing. "It's 11:00 o'clock and you've got a big day tomorrow. Why don't you head off to sleepy bye?"

Elspeth mouthed the words sleepy bye and rolled her eyes.

"Yes sir, Auntie Mame," Elspeth saluted up at her.

"Very funny, you scallywag. Sleep tight beautiful girls." Aunt Serena's tinkling laugh trailed behind her as she made her way back to her room.

Elspeth and I straightened up the common area, as we were

expected to do, and ran a final wash of dishes. It was just past 11:30 when we managed to make it up to our beds. I actually was really tired, and even had less a desire to follow through on our plan than before.

"I think it's time, sis, for operation merry trio."

"El, I really don't want to do this anymore. I like them, and I'm tired."

"No fair. Just a peek through the key hole. Come on."

I knew my sister well enough to understand that she wouldn't back down. It seemed the best thing was to just get it over with so she'd get off my back.

"Okay," I said.

We tiptoed back down to the second floor. I heard the water running through the pipes and so it seemed at least one of them was in the bathroom. El heard it too. She pointed toward the bathroom door. I shrugged and gestured for her to go first. I kept watch on the bedroom door down the hall in case one of them came out and spotted us. My sister pulled her hair back, twisted it at the nape of her neck and bent forward, one eye squinted and ready to go. Within moments of adjusting herself for the best view, she spun around with her hand over her mouth. A look of both horror and shock, as best as I could tell in the dim light of the hall.

I took over her position. And there it was. Who was with whom? No question now. Candy sat on top of the sink, her long legs spread and naked from the waist down. It was Megan's head that was buried between them, her pudgy pink hands clasping Candy's thighs, her blonde bun unraveling from the back of her head as she ministered to my new crush.

"What are you guys doing?" It was Toby, a towel in his hands, heading toward the bathroom.

"We just wanted to see if anyone was in the bathroom," my quick-witted sister said.

I pulled my head away, stumbled as I got up from my low crouch, and ran past him to the stairs.

"Don't you just knock like everyone else," I heard him say to El. "Looks like spying to me," he said. "And that is not cool. I think you need to get out of here before I tell your mom."

My sister held her ground. "We weren't spying. Really."

"Whatever," I heard Toby say. "Just get out of here."

By the time she made it up to our room, I was already in bed with the blankets pulled over my head. Even Elspeth knew this wasn't the time to compare notes. I heard her saggy bedsprings creak and I lay there for hours trying to push the image of Candy's head thrown back against the medicine cabinet and her fingers clasped around the edges of the sink while her friend ransacked her nether parts with her tongue. The first birds were singing when I finally fell asleep.

"It's party day!" The voice outside our door was our mother. "And breakfast is on the table. Karl made homemade buttermilk pancakes!"

My eyes were barely opened when I recalled the events of the last evening. More than anything, I hoped they'd checked out early. More than anything I didn't want to face them. There was no way to know whether or not Toby told them, but why wouldn't he? Maybe they just laughed it off, or maybe they were really mad at me. It was me, after all, caught with her eye at the keyhole. I didn't think they'd told my mother, or she wouldn't have been so cheerful. That at least was good. But how could I ask my mother if they'd left without arousing her suspicion?

"Okay, mom. We'll get up. Do you need help stripping any rooms?"

As soon as I asked, I knew it was a dumb question. We only had the one set of guests and my only chores were the kitchen and common area.

"Do you mean the hikers?"

I pushed myself up on my elbows and stretched my legs. I'd slept in a knot.

"Yeah, I guess so," I added.

"Well that's very nice of you," she said through the door, "but they're still here. It's only 9."

"Right," I answered. "I'll be right down."

"Okay, sweetie. Bring her highness Elspeth with you please."

Check out at Back Kingdom was not until 11:00. Exactly when our party friends would be arriving. I had to avoid seeing any of the merry trio no matter what.

I pounced on my sister's bed. She was tough to wake up. I'd seen her sleep through massive thunderstorms, and once a guest had a screaming fight with her boyfriend in the middle of the night. Elspeth never stirred.

"Get up," I yelled, and pulled the covers from her. "Now!"

"What is your problem?" She yelled back at me, bleary eyed and tangled in the sheet.

"Mom wants us up, and the merry trio hasn't left yet. What if they tell mom?"

"Relax," she said, and sat up against the head board. "What if they do? She'll be pissed at us, but so what?"

"I can't face them, El. I just can't."

I was on the verge of tears.

"I am so embarrassed. I've never been more embarrassed in my life, and it's your fault. You made me do this."

"That's a load of crap! I in no way made you do anything! Did I hold a gun to your head?"

"I'm the one they caught, El. Not you. I'm the one that looks like a horse's ass."

I was in full-blown crying mode now. I couldn't stop. It was just too much to have Candy think of me as such a scum bag.

"Don't go downstairs until they leave," she said.

She pushed by me and crossed to our closet.

"I'll go down to breakfast and tell mom that you have a stomach ache or something. When they're gone, I'll come and get you. It's no big deal."

"It's a big deal if the party starts at 11:00 and they haven't checked out yet."

"Liza," my sister said, and spun around on her heels and stared directly at me. "Do what I say and everything will be fine. You're freaking out. Get back in bed with your stomach ache and leave it all to me."

It was comforting to believe that she could handle all this and all I had to do was lay in bed for a couple of hours. But I knew that I'd worry the whole time. I needed a distraction, so I grabbed my book. A guest had left it on the free shelf—*Fear of Flying*. My aunt thought it was too "racy" for me, but didn't take it away. I liked Isadora enough. I was titillated by the sex, and curious if the world of grown-ups was really like the grown-ups in this book. I thought, of course, of my own three grown-ups, and tried to understand them the way Isadora was trying to understand herself. And I suppose I was trying to understand myself a little as well. I wondered mostly if my own grownups worried about their freedom, and if this was the driving force behind their behavior. I even wondered if I would be like Isadora when I got older. I already thought I was maybe a little like her already—the over thinking, and the worrying. And then I fell asleep.

"Okay, coast is clear!" Elspeth was shaking me. "Merry trio on their way out, and far as I can tell not a word was spoken to the fragile sisters."

"Oh my God, really?"

"Really. But hurry up, cuz it's like, 10:40, and we only have 20 minutes before our party!"

"Did you see them?"

"Yes. And they ignored me. And I don't care. Get up."

I envied my sister that she just barreled ahead—left her cares in the dust.

I thought I'd feel this great wet rush of relief but I didn't. I hated what I'd done. I hated that I spied, and I hated what I saw. Not because I thought it was bad or wrong. But because I shouldn't have seen it. It was private. And even though I didn't think it was bad or wrong, it rattled me. I hadn't even had a first kiss yet. It was too much to see.

"Okay. I'll be down in a few minutes."

But I made no move to get out of bed.

"Well hurry up. Your boyfriend's coming after all," she said.

"He's not my boyfriend!"

Ever since I'd mentioned to my sister that I might like Travis she'd been goading me. And after last night's scrabble game, he'd faded to black. It was Candy I would think of now whenever I thought about love.

"Please don't ruin our party," were her parting words right before she slammed the door.

I took a 5-minute shower, pretty much all we got before the water turned cold anyway. I put on the same jeans and t –shirt as I'd worn the day before and slid my feet into my decrepit Reeboks. When I arrived downstairs, the place looked incredible—purple and green balloons, my sister's and my favorite colors, floated along the ceiling. Purple and green crêpe paper flowers burst out of drinking glasses. A huge lopsided cake with white frosting and purple and green letters spelling out happy birthday Elspeth and Liza sat in the center of the table on a silver platter I'd never seen before, and my mother, aunt and Karl were smiling at the sink.

"Is your belly better?" My mother smoothed my hair. "It wouldn't be very fair if you were sick at your party!"

"It's fine, mommy."

To my amazement I fell against her chest and let her enfold me in her brown freckled arms. I had not done this in a very long time. She hugged me forever. My aunt's eyes got shiny and wet. Karl walked out onto the back stoop.

"No sign of Snoutly this morning!" He hollered into the kitchen.

My sister was the first to laugh, and then a dam broke and we all began to laugh. Even Karl.   And then, our first guests arrived.

My sister ran to the door to welcome Max and Tyler. They were both carrying a Pic and Pay plastic bag that contained 2 small wrapped packages. Our gifts. Our gifts! I hadn't even let myself think of the fact that at birthday parties you get gifts. A little surge of excitement shot through my gut. On their heels was our third guest. Shellene. And she too was carrying a wrapped box-- quite large. I was hoping it was a microscope. Mostly what stood out was her turquoise party dress. It looked like a bridesmaid's dress that had been hemmed to pass as a regular dress. I felt sad for her. In a way that almost created a physical ache somewhere around my esophagus.

"Come on in girls and boys," my aunt chirped. The hesitant mothers at the door looked worn and threadbare. I could see them taking in my glamorous aunt, and buxom mother and kooky Karl with some suspicion, but my aunt thanked them for dropping their children off, reminded them of the pickup time, and saw them out to their cars. My mother took over and began offering our guests the little diamond shaped tuna sandwiches she'd prepared on whole wheat bread. I'd asked for white, but she'd said she just couldn't go that far. Max was the first to object, but Shellene reached for two.

I was watching the door for the others, especially Travis, my ex-crush, wondering what sort of gift he'd chosen for me and if it would hold any hints about what he felt. It was then that I noticed by the old mahogany desk we used as a reception area the army green faded duffel bag with the initials CG stenciled on it in black. Candice Greene would be returning. And I could not be present when she did. My mind raced. Could I casually walk over to the reception desk and pop the duffel bag out onto the porch for her to find when she returned to collect it? Could I somehow move the party upstairs or out into our muddy back yard? But it was too late. The screen door opened and in she walked. Her face was glistening with sweat, as though she'd jogged back here from wherever she'd been. It was likely they'd been either grabbing supplies at the general store or eating lunch down the street at The Trail Café.

She took in the scene of our little party unfolding. She hesitated, with one hand on the screen ready to leave. But she didn't. Instead, she walked deeper into the room. My mother turned to her and smiled.

"Hi," she said to our returning guest. "I'm glad you didn't get too far without your pack. I didn't even notice it."

Candy didn't respond to my mother. She came straight for me. "I thought you were my friend, Liza. What you did was wrong, and I think I deserve an apology. Meg does too. She's out on the porch."

She turned and called in Meg. And now they both stood before me.

"What's going on?" My aunt moved toward us from the kitchen, a pitcher of juice still in her hand.

"Your daughter was spying on us last night. Looking through the keyhole of the bathroom. And she got an eyeful," Megan said. Her face getting blotchy. Candice put her hand out to quiet Megan.

Candice was staring at me. She was composed and cool, but it was clear that she intended to get her apology.

"I'm sorry," I said.

She nodded, reaching for Megan's hand as they made their way out of Back Kingdom. As she approached the door, she turned suddenly.

"Happy birthday, Liza. Twelve is a hard year. Take good care." And she left.

I wanted to run after her and explain the whole thing. How it was my sister's fault that I was crouched at the key hole. How I'd really not wanted to do it at all. But how could I face her? And how could I face my guests? How could I be at this party, in this room, in this world?

And in a split second, it seemed, I took in the scene. Shellene, Max and Tyler sat like stones at the table, looking down at the floor. Karl had disappeared from the room altogether, and my aunt stood the closest to me, shifting her weight back and forth between her two feet. My mother gazed out through the window.

"Liza," My aunt said. "Go to your room!"

And so I left my 12th birthday party, the only one I'd ever had, in shame. The party went forward beneath me. I heard the music, and even the laughter. However awkward it seemed everyone felt, they got over it. There was cake to be eaten, punch to be drunk, and gifts to be opened. I wondered when I'd get to open mine, or if I even would. And with each passing second, I hated my sister, my aunt and my mother in that order. I did not leave my room that day. I wasn't told I couldn't, I just didn't want to see any of my family and dreaded when my sister would finally come to bed. I hoped that my mother would come to see me to check in. She didn't. And Travis never showed.

"I brought your presents up," Elspeth said.

She placed them softly on the floor by my bed much later that day. My back was turned to the wall. I wanted to look, but I didn't.

"I think you should open them. You probably got some cool stuff. There's a big one form Kooky Karl and the Fragile Sisters."

Her tone of voice was unusually low and gentle. But I didn't care. She could be as nice to me as she wanted, but I wasn't talking to her. Not ever. One thing I was good at was ignoring people. I could outlast the best, and I would. It was the silent treatment all the way for me. I wasn't a good fighter with words. My points were never as well developed as my opponents. And I gave up much too easily.

"Fine!" Elspeth said. "Ignore me."

And that is what I did. For three days. All of them. Until the letter came.

Chapter 6

When I got home from school a few days after the party I leafed through the mail in the basket on the front porch. I never really got any mail but I checked anyway out of habit. An envelope that looked like it was made from ragg paper was addressed to me. It didn't have a return address and I couldn't imagine who would write. I ripped it open, and was glad that Elspeth had not ridden the bus home with me that day.

A letter from Candy made it all worth it. The exquisite humiliation at the party, the spooky silence at school, the absence of a microscope amongst the ill-begotten gifts. The most ill-begotten from Travis that he passed to me at school—proof that he didn't understand me at all and likely picked out by his mother—a hot pink terry cloth head and wrist band set. Not even my mother and Aunt Serena managed to scrabble up a microscope. Karl at least got me a book about fossils.

But now here was this letter. In a handmade envelope that looked like it was formed from some sort of natural paper—almost like a big leaf. And I actually smelled her patchouli. I took the steps to my room three at a time, tripping once and banging my knee against the tread. I sunk into my bed winded and thrilled but also a little terrified. What if it said something bad? What if she was still angry about my horrible intrusion on her privacy?

I ripped open the envelope and then felt awful I didn't try to preserve it. But it was too late. The letter was written on stiff paper with no lines and the script slanted down. It was large and loopy. *Dear Liza, it began, I write this because I worry that you will wonder about what you saw, and maybe draw conclusions that will be confusing and even wrong. Even though what you did was not okay, I think I understand that 12-year olds do such things and mean no harm from them. So, I want you to know that I am not mad at you, should you have been worried about that.*

It's really hard to be an almost teen-ager and especially if you're a little bit different and then even more so in a small backwoods town like yours. I am different and I also grew up in a little town, but mine was in West Virginia. It was a lot like Westover and I counted the days to be old enough to leave. I did that, and I've never looked back. I hope this letter will help you. I wish someone had sent such a letter to me when I was 12.

Meg is my girlfriend. We are in love. I knew at a young age that I would grow up to love a woman. I met Meg four years ago when I was 16 at a summer camp where we both worked and she was and still is my first love. We hope that we can spend the rest of our lives together, although we know anything could happen. But that commitment to a mate is really special and anyone who finds it is lucky, I think. What you saw in the bathroom is an expression of our devotion. It is what two girls do to share physical love. I hope you know what I mean by that.

I am making a guess here, and I may be wrong, but I thought maybe you had a little bit of a crush on me, so I am reaching out to let you know that at least in my book, it is normal and natural. I don't want you to feel like a freak. Your mom and aunt seemed nice, and their friend Karl did too. But I don't know if you can really talk to them or not. If you ever need to talk, feel free to write back to me. I am starting grad school this coming fall in Cleveland. This summer I'm just bumming around, so I don't really have an address. As soon as I do, I'll send it. And my best and only advice about how to survive your teen-aged years up there in the North woods is to find something you absolutely love to do and throw yourself into it. As long as it's not bad for you (or anyone else!)
Love,
Candy

I read the letter at least 7 times, maybe more. I folded, unfolded, refolded and folded again. I placed it under my pillow, between my mattress and box spring, under my pillow again and then finally in a shoe box full of sea shells on my closet shelf. I would tell no one about this letter, nor would I leave a trace that it ever happened. As beautiful as the big leaf envelope was, I tore it into tiny shreds after copying down the return address in my journal and flushed them down the toilet. I recovered the sea shell box from the closet shelf, extracted the letter, folded it up into the most compact square possible, stuffed it into the sandwich bag I'd stored my acorns in and inserted it into the shimmering pink canal of my prized conch.

I then slid from the back of the house like a shadow and thankfully encountered no one. I ran for fairy shrimp spa. The April run-off had swollen the little vernal pool to twice its usual size. The muddy banking was soft and cold as I dug a hole with my bare hands. When it was deep enough, I buried the shell, and marked the spot with a hunk of basalt rock. "I'll come back for you," I whispered to the letter. I headed to my house. My aunt or mother had turned music on. Our manna is from heaven...the thick alto voice sung. And I joined with that woman's voice. I was like her.

But my manna was not from heaven. It was from Candy. Candy had given me my marching orders. And I would be a dutiful soldier. I would find what I loved and not look back; I would find the holiness in my life. Every day from the moment I read and re-read that letter would be a step closer to my life, because it wasn't here. I would immediately write back to her and hold tight that letter until I had her address in the fall. I would wear it around my neck like a scapula.

"Hey sweetie, how was school today?" My aunt tugged my braid as I walked past her.

I pulled my braid back and hurried by.

"Goodness," she said. "You're still doing the cold shoulder thing?"

I kept walking.

"I got to hand it to you—you sure can keep a thing going— shows great resolve. That will get you far," she called after me.

And for the second time that day I took the stairs three at a time, and this time I didn't trip. I bounded into my room and Elspeth looked up from her bed, startled. I was giving them all the silent treatment since being sent into exile on the day of our party so I resumed my composure and strode to my bed with as much cool as I could muster. It was hard. My adrenaline was surging and all I wanted to do was compose my reply to Candy.

"Hey," my sister said.

She smiled up at me. She'd been smiling at me a lot since the party—no doubt assuaging her guilt. "What do you think of the history project—I mean it's a lot to do between now and the end of the semester, don't you think?"

The history final project for the entire 8th grade class was to create a scrap book on the state of Maine. Our history teacher had just assigned it to us during last period. It was all anyone on the bus talked about on the way home.

I flopped on my bed, grabbing my notebook that lay on the floor on the way down, and turned to the wall. I cradled the notebook like a baby. It's where I would start my correspondence with Candy.

"Oh, sorry! I didn't know you were still not talking to anyone. How long are you going to keep this up? Didn't I apologize enough?"

Elspeth had in fact apologized enough. It didn't matter, though. I'd still been the one called out in front of our friends, and banished from the only birthday party I'd ever had. Not to mention caught in the act of spying on someone's private moment, and not just anyone's but Candy's. So yes, I was still not talking to anyone.

"Okay, ding-dong. Suit yourself."

Elspeth had taken to calling me ding-dong. I wanted to gouge her stupid indigo eyes out.

"Well, you can have our boudoir to yourself, princess cat-got-your- tongue. I'm going over to Shellene's."

Since our party, El and Shellene had become quite the bosom buddies. She slammed the door on her way out, and I was alone, finally. The thing with Shellene really did eat away at me. My twin and I had always been each other's best playmate. We bonded together like atoms—we made our own unique compound when we needed to, and that didn't happen anymore. The night we conspired to spy on our guests all that changed. But Shellene could have Elspeth. Shellene in her turquoise bridesmaid dresses. I didn't feel bad for her anymore. She had my sister now.

I reached for my green flair. The only thing that I really cared about was Candy. I wondered if she'd think that a green flair was too childish, and rummaged through my top drawer for a plain ball point in blue or black, but none of them worked. In the end, I thought a pea-green flair would demand her attention.

Dear Candy, I began, it was so lovely to hear from you. I thought lovely was an adult sounding word. Imagine my surprise when I found your letter waiting for me. I read it several times. Thank you for letting me know that you aren't mad at me for spying. I do understand it was wrong, but my sister made me do it and you are right that I can't really talk to anyone here about my thoughts and feelings.

You said you thought I might have a crush on you, and I do. I know you are way older and that is okay, because I am glad to be your friend. Maybe we could be pen pals?

I will try to take your advice about being happy doing stuff I love. I love the outside, like trees and ponds and insects and stuff like that. I will try to stay outside more, and maybe start a bug collection or a plant collection, like a botanist.

I am happy for you and Meg. Say hi to her from me.
Please please write back to me soon!!!!!

Your soon-to-be pen pal,
Liza April de Kooning

I spent close to an hour re-writing and re-reading, but settled on this. I thought it was a good idea to sign off with my whole name. It seemed to make the letter more formal sounding and it felt important for me to sound formal so that Candy would think I was smart. It seemed to me that smart people would not dance around their living rooms, or share boyfriends, or worry about magic bears. Smart people would be too formal for that. And Liza April de Kooning was smart.

Chapter 7

A few weeks before the end of 8th grade Elspeth and I were on the school bus heading to our house. I was sitting alone in the back. Elspeth no longer had much to do with me. I had gotten "increasingly weird" and she had gotten "increasingly trivial." That is how we described each other then. We drove into a massive black tunnel of heavy air. It had been a cornflower- blue- fluffy- white- cloud sort of day until we passed the covered bridge, and then pow—the rain came. Big loud sheets of it turning the tin school bus into a deafening chamber of sound.

The driver slowed to a crawl. It was a thrilling moment—the way it is when weather demands your attention. The sudden blackness was unexpected and eerie. I craved both. I was looking forward to the rain on our wooden roof. I'd moved up into a small room in the attic. Away from Elspeth. Just big enough for my single bed. It had no closet so I hung my clothes from hooks in the unfinished wooden walls. My only décor was a large elemental table on glossy paper hanging on the back of my door. The room smelled like saw dust and camphor. But my favorite thing was the sound of the rain so close over my head. I knew it would lure me to sleep. I'd taken to napping in the afternoons after school.

The bus downshifted as it neared our corner. I was hungry and planning my pre-nap snack of roasted soybeans and kelp. I'd become fixated on vegetarianism, and Aunt Serena joined with me in this quest for purity. Together, we created lavish meals that the rest of the family politely declined, with the occasional exception of Karl, who'd become a bona fide member of the family as the lover/protector of our aunt and mother. While no one explicitly labeled him as such, no one worked very hard to cover it up either.

Just as the bus rolled up to the front of the house, the rain came down even heavier. I could hardly see out the windows. The short trip from the yawning door to the front porch doused me completely. It felt good. Elspeth and I bumped into each other as we grabbed for the front door at the same time and laughed.

"Your mascara is running," I said.

"So I must look like Mrs. Allen?" My sister laughed. She made a Mrs. Allen face by pointing her nose in the air and sucking in her cheeks.

Mrs. Allen was our social studies teacher whose mascara never seemed to stay put.

"Only if I look like Mean Jean," I answered.

Mean Jean was our gym teacher. She was obese and had magnificent arm flab that swayed like hammocks during square dancing class.

Laughing with my sister filled me with longing for more. It had been a long time—since before the spying debacle.

We pushed the door open and shook ourselves off like dogs. Water sprayed off of us in silver pearls.   The house was quiet.

"Where is everyone," I asked my sister. Not really expecting that she'd know.

"No idea," she shrugged. "Ice-cream?" She pulled some butter pecan from the freezer, her favorite. "Oh, wait," she said. "You only eat bark and fiddleheads."

I wanted that ice-cream. Real Bad.

"I'll join you," I said.

My sister placed the back of her hand on my forehead, as though to check for fever.

"I'm calling the doctor," she said. "You must be sick, or something."

"Ha, ha, ha," I said. "That's so friggen' funny I forgot to laugh!"

We sat at the table each with a spoon and ate from the tub. The kitchen was dark, cool and quiet. The rain kept coming. The sink was gleaming. It was cleaner than I'd ever seen it. We were silent—eating our ice-cream in a trance. The twins. The de Kooning twins. Liza April and Elspeth April. de Kooning. A distant relation to a great painter. The back door was slightly ajar and rain was coming in. I crossed the orange pine floor and placed my open flat palm on the door and pressed it closed.

"Cookies?" Elspeth grabbed the hydrox—Oreos with no animal fat. Aunt Serena didn't like animal fat. We liked them fine. We thought the Keebler elves were cute.

We sat at the table and killed the whole package. It was chilly. It got darker and darker. We never got up to turn on the lights.

"Do you think they're all dead," Elspeth finally asked when the last cookie was gone.

"No."

"What do you think happened?"

"The fucking bear happened. The fucking bear ate everyone. That fucking bear that you think is the spirit of our dad."

"You know that's not true. You know creepy game warden dude relocated him."

"So what? He came back."

"I don't think Snoutly could do such a thing."

I stood up from the table and pounded my hands down on it.

"Grow up! Of course he could do such a thing. He's a wild animal!"

Elspeth began to cry. I didn't remember a time when she cried, since our dad's funeral, maybe. I felt awful.

"I'm sorry. Stop crying," I said. "I'm just kidding."

I wanted to go to her—put my arms around her and hug her or something. But I couldn't get my body to do it.

"What time is it?"

I didn't wear a watch, but Elspeth was addicted to hers. It was a knock-off Keith Haring. She still has it.

"Almost 7."

We sat some more. Elspeth stopped crying finally. At 8:15 Karl walked through the front door. He stumbled on the carpet where it curled up along its edge. He tried to find the light switch on the wall. I don't think he noticed us.

"Girls?" He shouted. I'd never heard him speak above a stage whisper.

"We're right here," I said.

He sunk down on the couch. He began to sob. Deep guttural sounds. He didn't sound human.

"Will someone please turn on a fucking light?" It was me who screamed.

To my surprise, Elspeth sprung from her chair and pulled the chain on the fluorescent sink lamp. It made everything a sickish blue.

"Are they dead," I asked, from my chair. I didn't think I could stand.

"Dead? No," he said. "Why would you ask that?"

I was suddenly freezing.

"Where's mommy, and Aunt Serena?"

"Mom's at the hospital. Your aunt is gone. She left."

Elspeth crossed to Karl and sat down beside him. She took his hand. She'd always liked him better than I ever had.

"Why is Mom in the hospital?" My sister was still clutching his hand. It made me want to smack her.

"Because she's so upset about Serena leaving."

I immediately understood. Our mother had gone crazy again. Our mother was a patient.

"I want to see her! Right now!" I was up on my feet. "Where is she?"

"In Lewisville," Karl answered.

Lewisville, I knew, was where crazy people went. And it was almost an hour away.

Both Elspeth and I pleaded with Karl to take us to our mother. But he said he couldn't. He said he needed to "try to find Serena." I felt like he was choosing our aunt over our mother. It was then I understood he liked Serena better than our mom. I wanted to gouge his stupid watery eyes out with a bobby pin.

"I'm going to sleep," I said, and hurtled over every third step to my attic hide-a-way. On my un-made bed was a note written in Aunt Serena's compact pointy script on her favorite stationary—

the stuff with creepy court-jesters dancing in a circle.

Dearest Liza:

> *I'm sorry I didn't say good-bye to you. The decision to leave was such an impulsive one, but one I know to be correct and true. Since Snoutly has been "relocated" (or murdered) and your mother has seemed stronger and better able to care for you, I realized it was time to go. Mom's love for Karl has grown, and this is also a factor in my decision. And of course, there is my history of growing bored and needing new adventures. I plan to head to the Denver area where I have a good friend. I'll be in touch. I love you, now and forever.*

> *Serena*

I ran down to Elspeth's room with the crumpled wad clutched in my hand. I pushed her door open and she stood by her window in the light from the moon reading the identical note.

Five days later Karl moved in. He took over Aunt Serena's room. He changed nothing, only added his old bulky stereo to the clutter of her many arcane objects. He asked Elspeth and me if there was anything we'd like from her room to remember her by. Elspeth sifted through every last item, and emerged red-faced with an armload of jewelry, small glass bottles and our aunt's entire collection of paisley scarves.

My aunt's stuff was all over the house. Her turquoise plastic sunglasses were still on an end table by the front door. Her orange slicker hung on a hook at the back door. Her Isabelle Allende books were on the couch in a stack, and the bathroom was brimming with her pungent creams and eyebrow pencils ground down to various lengths. I didn't need anything to remember her by.

I was curious why Karl didn't move into our mother's room. There was no other sister to placate anymore. I would have wondered if maybe it had always been in my imagination that he and my mother had a thing going on, but when she returned home over Memorial Day week-end I ran into him leaving her bedroom any number of mornings as I slogged through my going- to- school routines. I suppose I was happy for her. But her home-coming was anything but happy.

St. Marguerites in Lewisville decided mom was stable enough to be discharged the Friday of the long holiday weekend. We hadn't once visited while she was there, or even talked on the

phone. We'd asked Karl a few times to take us but he always had a
reason not to. My mother's grief was not the same color as it had
been over our father's death. It was blue then, a serene color. But
with her sister's abandonment it was fire-engine red. Her rages
were frequent and fierce. Like the evening she returned to us.

Karl had asked us to ride along with him to the hospital, and
perhaps we should have. We didn't want to, for different reasons.
Elspeth actually had a real date with Travis, the boy I sort of liked,
or would have if I'd "liked liked" boys. "I'm on cloud ten," she said
to me that afternoon on the way home from school.

I didn't want to go because I was mad at my mother for being
looney toons. I also had taken an Ursla leGuinn book out of the
library and stopped at The General to grab a slice of mushroom
pizza. This was my idea of a near-perfect Friday night to head into
a long week-end. So no.

"You're really not going to come to Lewisville to get your
mom," he asked. He had the car keys in his hand and was beating
them rhythmically against his thigh. I was just sitting down with
my slice and book at the kitchen table.

"I'm really not."

"Where's your sister?"

"On a date," I said.

"On a date," he said. I detected a snide tone that was so
foreign to Karl I had to look up from my book to make sure it was
him.

"On a date with whom?"

"Ask her. They're probably at the covered bridge debating
whether or not the Vulcans are superior to us."

Karl's car keys were really rocking and his blotchy face explod-
ed into a virtuoso of red.

"What is it with you girls? Your mom is coming home from the
hospital and you don't want to be there for her?"

"Correct," I said. And felt like I was 11 feet tall.

Karl and his keys jangled out the door. I was left in peace, for
a while. Until 6:48 that evening to be exact. Elspeth was still out
with Travis someplace. I was still at the couch with Ursula, feet
up on the coffee table which by now was littered with pizza crust,

Werther's originals candy wrappers, and a few empty Moxie bottles.

And the storm that was to be my mother her first month home arrived with gale force.

"This place is a fucking disaster. Don't we have guests on the books for tomorrow? What the hell. No one obviously did shit while I was rotting away in a snake pit full of bat-shit crazies. Get off the couch Liza! Pick this dump up. And where's your sister?"

And before I could get off the couch her rant sprang from a well so deep and frigid that I felt I was taking on water.

"Answer me, Liza! Where's your sister?" She bent down so her face was in mine. Her eyes were puffy and the little blue capillaries spread out under her bottom lash.

"Where's yours," I said

"Liza, I think that's enough," Karl said.

"You know what, Karl," I stood up for effect, "no one is talking to you, and what's more is that you are not my father."

My mother grabbed the back of my t-shirt as I was heading toward the front door, to go where, I don't know.

"He's your father now, missy, and don't you forget that."

My mother had called me missy about three times in my life. Once when I bathed a cat we had in Vermont with bleach and once when I snuck out of the house in College Park at four in the morning to swim in the Johnson's pool. I detested the sound of missy— so old-fashioned and musty. Missy smelled of dead papery moths and spirals of wet dirt and dog hair. I spun around and pushed her. Karl darted between us and my mother struck him, intending to strike me, likely, across the face. I bolted out the front door and down the porch steps where I disappeared into the ball park across the street.

I looked for my sister and Travis, but didn't find them. The General had closed already, and Westover offered no place to go. I didn't like fairy Shrimp Spa in the dark—it was just a big wet hole when the sun wasn't out. I walked up and down Main Street, spun around the gazebo a few times and was about to give up and head back home when a car slowed down, rolled down a window and called my name. I was shocked to see my sister and Travis in a car with two older kids from high school. Shocked but thrilled.

"Liza? What's going on," my sister asked.

"Mom's home," I said.

"Say no more," she said, and pulled open the back door. "Get in."

A guy named Josh and a girl named Chelsea, both sophomores, were in the front seat. Elspeth and Travis were in the back, and now I was a third wheel. Neither my sister nor I had ever driven around in a car with high school kids. We were just finishing 8th grade. Josh, it turned out, was Travis's cousin. He stuffed an eight-track in, cracked it up really loud and lit up a Marlboro. It was the first time I'd heard the band *Yes*.

We drove over the covered bridge that spanned the Ellis. We parked and waded out to a large sand bar in the middle of the narrow river. Hundreds of stars glowed above and the moon was full and bright. The days were longer now, so although dark the warmth of the sun lingered still. The flutter of breeze carried the scent of lilacs. Chelsea, a thin and quiet girl with straight red hair pulled a joint from a Sucrets box. She lit it and passed it around. My sister took a toke, pulled in the helix of smoke, held her breath, did not cough and passed it along. She'd done this before. What else did I not know about Elspeth? The joint came to me, so I tried to be like Elspeth, but with less success. I coughed until my eyes watered.

"Don't worry," Josh said, and chuckled. "You'll get used to it."

"Yeah," said Travis. "You'll get used to it."

"Yeah," added Chelsea. "You will."

June came on strong. It was hot. I spent many afternoons alone at Fairy Shrimp Spa writing crazy letters to Candy. I never sent them. Instead I folded them into ragged sailboats and dropped them into the silty waters of my vernal pool. Elspeth and I had grown closer again; I don't think we could navigate the landscape of pain. I know I couldn't, and so we turned to each other. But she remained attached to her new friends--she and Travis were inseparable and I was jealous as fuck. Occasionally, when he wasn't around, we'd take long walks out of town to Richardson Lake and smoke Josh's weed, which Elspeth seemed to have plenty of.

My mother's rages remained frequent and fierce. We couldn't read the signs, so couldn't avoid being caught in the maelstrom. It was a day when Elspeth and I bounded up the few steps of the listing front porch to grab bathing suits for a dip in the chilly Ellis at the Covered Bridge when Karl asked us to have a seat. He sat on the plaid worn couch that was still piled with Aunt Serena's stuff, as though she were away for a few days and coming back for it. My mother, rumpled and red-eyed perched on the edge of the couch looking like a lonely and hungry drab little bird.

"Why do we have to sit down?" I'd had enough sad news lately and I thought if I didn't sit they couldn't parse out bits of rancid tidings from the dark side.

"It's nothing bad. You don't have to sit if you don't want to," he said. My mother looked out the window.

"Just tell us then," Elspeth said. She also remained standing— arms across her chest and one hip thrust to the left.

"Your mom and I have decided to get married."

"This is some sort of twisted joke, right?" But I knew it wasn't. Because that's just how things went in our lives. Nutzoid people made horrific decisions with no thought whatsoever about how anyone else in their lives may feel. Like me, or Elspeth.

"It is, isn't it?" Elspeth was actually shaking—like she did when she forgot to eat all day.

"Mom?" I said.

I wanted her to burst out laughing, the way she did once when Aunt Serena used Lestoil in a cake by accident. But no belly laugh—just a dead-eyed glance at us. But what a glance. It seemed a tumid glance—had I been able to stick it with a hat-pin salty water would have run up my arm into my sleeve.

"No, girls," Karl said. "It's very much happening. We've picked a date and booked the grange hall—July 16th, and we'd love for both of you to be in it."

"Like bridesmaids or something?" I was the one who let loose a belly laugh. Me, in a pink frilly dress and straw hat. Elspeth in a sky-blue matching dress and hat.

"Sure. Something like that," Karl said, and smiled at us. A

big toothy happy yellow lab smile. I actually felt bad for him. He was so clueless and utterly out of his league. I didn't want to hurt his feelings, as much as I despised him at this moment, so I just shrugged as if to say maybe, half smiled, and walked up stairs to get my bathing suit. Elspeth followed. I stopped off on her floor and joined her in her bedroom. I hardly ever spent time in her room.

"So, what now?" I plopped down in her faux-suede second hand bean bag chair. A book lay face down on the floor. I reached over and smoothed out its pages.

"Herman Hesse? This is one of Aunt Serena's books."

She snatched it away and stuffed it under her pillow.

"I like it."

"That's fine by me, I was just mentioning it."

"They'll want to get rid of us, you know," my sister said.

"Are you loco?"

"Maybe, but newlyweds want time alone, and we're pains in their butts. We're just warts on the ass of progress."

"Do you think that's true El?"

"I don't know. No. I don't think so, do you?"

"No. I think they care enough about us to want us around. Don't you," I said.

Elspeth didn't answer. She just lay in her beanbag. I needed to change the subject. It was too strenuous to think about who wanted us and who didn't and her room stunk like rotting feet.

"Do you think mom can do it without Aunt Serena?"

"Maybe not," Elspeth said, and shook her head and her eyes welled up.

"Let's go to the spa," I said, and grabbed her hand.

Fairy Shrimp Spa was still the best place to go to have a serious talk out of earshot. Although out of whose earshot was the real question. Mom was in bed most of the time and Karl worked all day. He brought grill cheeses and pickled eggs from the general store when he got home. Elspeth ate the eggs by the handful. I couldn't even be in the same room when she ate them.

We plopped down on the wet bank, and because of the recent rains the little pool was swollen and the tiny pink translucent shrimp wiggled all over the place.

"I bet they just want to get married for us. Maybe they think it's the right thing to do. I don't think they'll try to really get rid of us," Elspeth said.

My sister was making mud balls and dropping them into the water.

"If they offered us to be flower girls or something, would you?" It was such an Elspeth question. She looked for the light in everything. I reached down to tie my sneakers. The end of my nice new white laces were wet and brown.

"Would you?"

I wasn't sure what I hoped Elspeth would say. I thought it could be sort of cool in some ways to be in a wedding.

"I guess it depends on what happens with mom. I mean if she can't act normal pretty soon, I don't know if Karl will really want to marry her, and no one will take care of us then."

We fell into silence. We had a lot of unanswered questions. I thought of the big cool house in College Park and the lemony smell of the front hall with the potted trees. And then there was Spud. But could I live with Uncle Doug?

"You think Snoutly is okay?" Elspeth stared directly into my eyes.

My sister worried about him often. She no longer thought he was our dad, but seemed to think he hadn't really wanted to be relocated and was positive that Aunt Serena and he had some sort of "magical connection."

"There's no way in hell that the forest ranger guy won't hunt him down and kill him," I said. And I believed it.

Elspeth began to cry. I put my hand on her shoulder. She was heaving so much it slipped off. I put it on her shoulder again, and pressed down a little harder. She leaned into me. I wasn't sure what to do. It seemed I should hug her, but I really didn't want to. I don't know why. I just let her weight fall against me and sat there. It was starting to get dark. I figured it was about six. The time Karl usually appeared with pickled eggs and grilled chesses.

"Let's go. I'm hungry."

I stood and pulled her to her feet. She leaned into me as we walked back to the house.

Chapter 8

Karl planned the whole wedding, and even sprung for the grange hall. So much disappointment and strangeness curdled in the corners of our ersatz home. Just me and Elspeth and long hot empty days. She and Travis had been cooling down, so we were hanging again, with little else to do other than ruminate over what our bleak future would bring.

"Do you miss Aunt Serena?" She leaned toward me from the edge of her bed, her nose only a few inches from mine. Her breath smelt like Good and Plenty.

"Every minute of every day," I said. "I thought she'd call by now and at least give us a phone number or something."

"Yeah. I know," Elspeth said and fell back on her mattress. "So, I guess we're getting a step-daddy."

"Yeah. I guess so."

"I think mom needs him to take care of us," she said.

"But I'm getting sick of grilled cheese and pickled eggs," I answered, and dug myself deeper into the bean bag.

"Let's ask him to get frozen pizza," she said. It was so earnest and heart-felt that it made me laugh, and I couldn't stop. It was hard to catch my breath and I began to gasp and cry at the same time. Too make it worse, she said, "So I guess you thought I was kidding?"

I grabbed her straw rubbish basket and tossed my lunch.

The day of the wedding was sticky hot. The ball field, which was next door to the grange, was overflowing with kids playing a pick-up game. We stayed home and cleaned up the house for our rich New Jersey relatives who apparently deigned to come to this freak show. The grange hall was booked for 3P.M. and our cousins were expected by then. Karl wrote some vows and asked us to "speak" at the "celebration." It was enough for me that we'd agreed to give our mother away. I passed. But Elspeth wrote a poem. The only town folk coming were Shellene and her mom and dad. Elspeth didn't want Travis there. She wouldn't admit it but I think she was afraid there'd be some sort of fiasco.

I had just scrubbed hair out of the bath tub drains when I heard some commotion in the street. I ran to the big second floor front hall windows and there it was. My Uncle Doug's huge blue suburban. Elspeth ran out to meet them first, the broom still in her hand. I watched for a few more minutes. First Uncle Doug hopped down from his driver's seat, and then my chest-nut haired cousins spilled out from the back, except now they were blondes and their hair was no longer coiled into top knots. They looked bored and disgusted.

I was waiting for Aunt Kitty. Uncle Doug walked around the front of the car and opened her door for her. It seemed an unusual act of kindness for him. When Kitty was helped out of her seat, I noticed how thin she was—even more so than before. Without her deep suntan and fancy clothes and jewelry, she looked quite plain. Almost like the moms around here. She was washed out; graying and wearing rumpled lose beige clothes.

From my vantage point at the window, I felt safe and almost smug. I could look down at them all, size them up, get in their heads and imagine what they were thinking of us hiding out in this old behemoth of a house at the other end of Appalachia. I was in no hurry to greet them. But I knew I must. I knew I could not give them any reason to think we'd turned out peculiarly under the care of Aunt Serena and mom. I knew Uncle Doug didn't have much use for either of them, and was coming only out of a sense of duty and because Aunt Kitty probably badgered him to do it. All this knowing was grueling.

I took a deep breath and foisted myself off the window sill.

"Liza? They're here!" It was Elspeth. She sounded excited. Maybe she was. Maybe I should be too, I thought. But I wasn't. I was scared, and not sure why.

The screen door slammed. "Liza! Come down!"

I ducked quickly into the open bathroom door and glanced in the mirror. Who would they see? My once sandy hair was turning a dull dishwater blonde, and hung in a flat braid that was coming apart. My ruddy complexion was even more uneven with the heat. My striped orange t-shirt was faded and sneakers raggedy. Not only was I not beautiful, I was dressed in someone else's cast-offs picked from the free box at the What-Not shop in Rexford meant for a larger girl.

"Liza!" Again, my excited sister. I wished I could be excited too.

"Chill! I'm coming."

Chill was my new favorite word.

I paused at the landing to take one last look at the five people arranged at the table in the lobby of Back Kingdom. Two snotty thin girls with poofy hairdos, a sallow husk of a woman, a mean paunchy man with my mother's eyes, and my smiling idiotic sister.

"Beam me up Scotty," I muttered under my breath. Another new favorite phrase, courtesy of Travis, a Trekkie.

My sister looked up. "There you are. My God, what were you doing?"

"Cleaning the bathrooms," I answered with a forced assertiveness, as if to say I am great, and this is a proud moment. And in that instant I did feel proud. I could do something my cousins likely couldn't. But then I caught a look between them. And I was sure I could hear their thoughts, and that their thoughts were rife with repugnance for me. But I continued down the stairs and joined them at the table.

Aunt Kitty spoke first. "I am so so very sorry girls about your Aunt leaving like that." She reached across the table and placed both of her spotted thin hands on ours—the right one on mine, and left one on Elspeth's. Elspeth drew hers away, but I liked the cool dryness of her hand on mine.

"We all are so sorry," she continued, and gestured to her family with a tilt of her head, but none of them met my eyes.

"Where's your mother?" Uncle Doug crossed to the sink and poured himself a glass of water.

"Getting ready," El said.

"So she's marrying this Karl character?" He turned to us and leaned against the sink. "I heard he was Serena's boyfriend." He made a face like he'd smelled dog shit.

My white-hot hatred for Uncle Doug flared. There was something primitive about him that made my skin actually shrink when he was around. All my alarms sounded every time he walked into the room. I thought he had tremendous capacity to harm people, in all sorts of ways.

"Nope, Mom's boyfriend," I said. I wanted to piss him off.

"Violet's boyfriend? I'm confused."

"Well, he was both of their boyfriends," I said. "Until Aunt Serena ran away from home."

"That's sick," he said and tossed his glass in the sink.

The cousins snickered and Aunt Kitty shot a look at both of them. A shut-up look.

It is true that I intensely disliked my spoiled bratty twig-like cousins, but at the same time, I had a sort of twisted reverence for them for managing to live with their father. And I was jealous that they still had a father, but had my choice been a dead father or Uncle Doug to come home to after school, the choice was clear.

"Doug," my Aunt said, "please."

He shook his head and returned to the table.

"Well, where's this wedding?"

"Across the street at the Grange hall," my sister said.

"This guy and your mom are getting married at a Grange?"

"Doug, what difference does it make to you? Leave it alone," Aunt Kitty said.

I wanted to take him on. I wanted to be a bad ass. My Aunt Serena said more women should be bad asses. I never got to ask her why. But now I thought I knew.

"Jesus Christ, I feel bad for you girls. I really do," Uncle Doug said.

"Why? Our life is just fine," I answered.

Aunt Kitty placed her hand on his arm, to head him off from coming back at me.

A car door slammed and I knew it was Karl's Dodge dart because the door never caught the first time on the driver's side. He always had to slam it again, and harder the second time. Aunt Serena had said that men never quite get around to making even the smallest changes in their lives, including fixing the car door. She'd said she thought it was because they liked things to stay the same, even if they were broken. She said she thought this was true because they hadn't needed to adapt as much in-utero.

My father, Karl and Uncle Doug. One dead, one brain-dead and one should be dead. These were the men in my life. Karl. Well, Karl meant us no harm, and in fact only seemed to want good for us, although he had no idea how to wrap us up in the love and guidance we needed. Perhaps we wouldn't have accepted it. I am sure I would have pushed back; it was and still is my nature. But I hold him accountable for not having tried; although I am fairly sure he didn't even know he should.

Karl struggled to open the front door with both arms filled with bags of ice for the reception. I held the door open for him.

"Oh," he said, and his face turned a deep crimson in blotches that spread up from his throat, engulfed his left ear and faded around his eyes. And I noticed for the first time that his pale whitish hair had edged back away from his cheekbones. "Let me get this ice taken care of and I'll properly introduce myself."

His stoop was more pronounced than usual with an armful of ice. I felt protective of this man who was an hour out from promising himself to my mother for the duration. After placing the bags in the freezer, he strode over to the table and extended his ice cold red hand first to Uncle Doug who clasped it in his meaty way and nodded and grunted out a tepid hello.

"And you're Kitty?" Karl once again thrust a red and cold hand out, which my aunt clutched in both of hers and squeezed.

"Karl, has anyone mentioned that you're a dead ringer for Violet's deceased husband?"

"Yes. I've heard that Doug. But please excuse me, I've got some last-minute details to attend to at the grange. It was nice meeting you all. You too girls."

I almost followed him out the door, ready to feign some sort of task that I needed to take care of at the grange. But I also needed to shower and change. My mother then appeared at the bottom of the stairs in her best dress. In the days that had passed since her sister left us, including the days she'd been in the looney bin she'd lost weight. Her favorite periwinkle silk dress used to hug her breasts and rest on her hips but now fell straight from her shoulders to her calves.

It was Kitty who sprung up and wrapped her arms around my mother. My mother flinched--seemed surprised and maybe even uncomfortable with this demonstration of affection, or contrition or whatever it was. I think it was love.

"Violet, you look so pretty."

"I don't know what to do with my hair," my mother said. Her heavy black shiny hair was pinned behind her ears with two oversized plastic clips. Twig one and Twig two, which I'd decided were apt names for my cousins, looked embarrassed. For what or whom I wasn't sure, but I could easily imagine they were embarrassed for their raggedy looking mother throwing her lot in with my even more raggedy looking mother, and for a flash I felt akin to them.

Aunt Kitty pulled away to examine my mother's hair and I could see the damp look of her blue eyes, rimmed in red. Uncle Doug got up with a lot of fanfare and crossed to the sink where he filled his glass with water for his wife.

"Shall I give you a French twist, or chignon?"

"You can do that?" My mother smiled.

"Absolutely," Aunt Kitty said.

"I'm sorry that I wasn't here to greet you," my mother said. She looked first at her brother and then back to Kitty.

"Don't even give it another thought," my Aunt Kitty said. "It's your wedding day. You have things to do." She reached for my mother's hand and led her to the table where she began to fiddle with my mother's hair. I excused myself. Elspeth followed suit.

"It's almost 3:00 girls. Try to go fast like little bunnies," my mother said.

Elspeth, who'd been so quiet almost knocked a chair over on her way to the stairs.

"Yes! Let's go Liza!"

She yelled this as though we were a baseball team warming up for the big game.

My Aunt Kitty continued to twist my mother's hair in some elaborate knot while the twigs sat looking morose next to their father who cleaned under his nails with a matchbook. Once upstairs I headed Elspeth off and snatched the first shower. Karl must have returned from the grange and gotten into the downstairs shower because my water got weak and thready. It would be cruel to leave my sister with nothing but a cold and sporadic drizzle. I climbed over the lip of the lime-stained tub and left the shower running for her, wrapped up in a towel and opened the door, where, per usual, she waited with her favorite vanilla shampoo.

Just before 3:15 we all fell into a crooked line and filed out the front door. Elspeth at the head, Karl at the rear and the rest of us shuffling along in the middle somewhere, all stiff like spent soldiers. All I could think was what a morose and random family we all were, and especially so when we walked past the playing field next to the grange that was filled with picnicking families, kids on the swings and see-saws, and gathered at the big pine tree whispering secrets to one another. I should have been with them, even though they likely would have shunned me.

The grange smelled musty and the mismatched Formica tables, some with legs propped up on phone books, were strewn haphazardly throughout the homely room. The only personal touches were a framed picture of a mother doe and her fawn, and an embroidered American flag attached to the paneling with one thumb tack. And this is where we collected to give our mother away to Kooky Karl, the king of pickled eggs. We waited silently for others to show, and as expected, only Shellene and her family arrived.

The sight of her in a stupid turquoise prom dress, the same one she'd worn to our birthday party, made me want to smack her. Hard, with the back of my hand, right across her pale freckled face. I glanced over at the twigs who were giggling, and I knew with the certainty of the stars coming out at night that they'd go back to Maryland and laugh with all their friends about our hillbilly wedding. It made me hate Shellene even more for giving them yet another reason to make fun of us.

"Hi guys," Shellene said. She crossed first to my sister and gave her a hug. Her mother did as well. I watched as Elspeth squeezed both of them back. That pissed me off too.

"I'm sorry about your aunt, Liza," Shellene said. She stepped in closer but there was no way I was going to let her hug me. My sister may not have been embarrassed by her coal miner's daughter thing, but I secretly hoped that the grange would explode from a gas leak and we would all die.

"Yeah," was all I said.

I was trying to figure out where I could sit to be away from the whole crowd and heard the screen door swing open. I turned to see who could possibly have decided to come to this sorry rendezvous and as if it couldn't get worse, the game warden strode through the door. The one who thought my Aunt was one ply short of a roll and who relocated Snoutly, or worse.

My sister gasped. Karl, forever the gentleman, approached him with his hand extended. The game warden clasped Karl's hand and they had a nice shake. My mother looked at her feet.

"Well," Karl said, "why don't we proceed?"

He motioned for Joe to take a seat, which he did, alone in the back by the door. I chose to remain standing off to the side. Karl walked up to the front of the room and took his position next to the local Justice of the Peace—an obese woman named Dora in yellow, too much red lipstick and poodle curls. This was Elspeth's cue to switch on the CD player with our mom's favorite Segovia CD. The music really was beautiful and did the grange wonders. My mother entered through the door of the grange and Elspeth and I walked her up the aisle to the waiting Karl in a three piece suit that smelled like it had been packed away with sweet pipe tobacco.

Dora, in her yellow flowered dress delivered her wedding spiel in a loud clear voice, much like a high school elocution teacher might, and it was time for vows. Karl began: *"Violet has a great spirit, generosity, and wit. She cares deeply about her lovely daughters, Elspeth and Liza, and all creatures, great and small. Truly a gentle soul...*" He stopped. His face blotched up and his eyes filled with tears. It struck me for the first time that this man had lost his girlfriend. For all I knew he was really in love with her. For all I knew he might have felt about her the way I felt about Candy. And now he was marrying the other girlfriend. And maybe he was genuinely in love with her too. And even loved us. He didn't have to ask her to marry him.

"*Violet wants us all to live happily ever after. She often tells me what she dreams of for all of us and how happy she is that she and her daughters have a beautiful and quiet place to live and grow. I am thrilled to be spending the rest of my life with this amazing woman and her beautiful children.*"

I looked at my mother who was quietly weeping, and Elspeth who had gently placed her own hand on my mother's back. It seemed that I should be there, pressing my flesh against theirs, but I couldn't.

"*I send us off into this new stage of our lives with hopes for adventure and deep love now and into the hereafter.*"

And then he did something so un-Karl like that it didn't seem possible. He blew a kiss into the stale air of the grange hall to my mother, bowed his head to us and turned the floor over to his bride.

My mother's vows: "My dearest sweet man. I am forever grateful for your presence in our lives. You, and you alone, are who I want. Your patience, kindness, steady hand at the helm and acceptance of myself and my darling apples is more than I could dream. Thank you for choosing us as your family."

It was Elspeth's turn to speak. She faced the guests like a queen. She too seemed un-Elspeth like in this moment. I was impressed by her poise. She looked pretty too. Beautiful, in fact. In a lilac colored sun-dress and her long hair in a French braid. Her voice was a little shaky when she spoke.

"I have a poem about my mom. *The darkness of boredom never bothers my mother. She lives as if time doesn't matter, and if her minutes aren't filled, she basks in the space between them. I wish she could understand her life more than she does—that she is not crazy, and that the earth knows her. In another time and place, she would be a healer of hearts. I love the coolness of her thick black hair, her smell of warm wood and how hard she tries to live. I love you mom."*

Silence. I could hear the ping of a leaky faucet from the kitchen behind the swinging green saloon doors. I counted nine pings. My sister sat down like a ballerina on her rusty grange chair. And I can tell you this, I was jealous. Jealous of her beauty, poise, lovely poem, and mostly, jealous that she so willingly accepted our bizarre lives.

And at that moment, the grange ladies appeared on cue from behind the saloon doors with platters of finger rolls and congo bars. Solemn, shod with sensible shoes and hair nets in place, they quietly deposited our luncheon onto the folding tables and departed swiftly back into their haven of the kitchen.

I actually wanted one of the tidy little tuna rolls. I liked the way the tuna was mashed into a paste with little flecks of celery--the thrill of the inconsequential crunch amidst all the mush was exactly what I longed for.

"Why are you here?" It was my sister Elspeth. I turned with tuna in hand to find her in the warden's face, hands on her almost womanly hips, the ones I didn't have.

"To pay my respects to your mom and step-dad, that's all." He backed away from Elspeth, though I noticed he was eyeing the congo bars.

"You hate us. Were you even invited?"

"That's not so. I don't hate nobody. I was trying to keep you and your neighbors safe from an animal that had no business in town."

"What's the problem here," my Uncle Doug asked, inserting himself between the warden and Elspeth.

"No problem, sir. I was just leaving." He turned to go. I felt sort of sorry for him. It seemed like a nice thing to do, to come to the wedding. He didn't have to. I grabbed a congo bar and followed him out.

"My uncle is an asshole," I said. "He doesn't really give two shits about us, and he actually hates my mom."

I passed him the congo bar. It was still warm and the chocolate chips were melty and luscious.

"Here," I said.

He looked surprised, and sort of smiled. He plucked the congo bar from my hand.

"I really didn't mean to cause trouble," he said, and stuffed the congo bar in his mouth.

"Right," I said. "Well, good luck hunting bear," I added before heading back to the grange.

"Everything okay?" It was the Brianna twig.

"Yeah," I answered.

"Who was that guy," she asked.

"He's the game warden. He killed Snoutly. Maybe. Or he just moved him."

"Who?"

"The bear. The bear who Aunt Serena loved."

"Jesus. I don't even know what to say."

"Few do."

"Yeah. I guess."

We stood there. A beam of sun held her exactly in its path. Little nebulae floated around her head and with the light directly in her eyes, I noticed a brown fleck in her blue iris. She was not perfect.

"No offense, but what do you guys do around here?"

I laughed. I thought I might like her. "We hang out at Fairy Shrimp Spa!"

"There's a spa in this town?"

"Want to see it?"

"Sure!"

And with that, Brianna and I slipped away. As we headed towards the back of the house into the damp woods, she stopped dead in her tracks.

"Liza, where are we going?"

"To Fairy Shrimp Spa! It's right over there," I said. I pointed to the vernal pool that had shrunk to a big mud puddle over the past few days.

"I don't get it," she laughed.

"It's a frog pond. Aunt Serena called it Fairy Shrimp Spa because it's filled with fairy shrimp. Little pink spiny fish like guys."

I sat on the cool moss. I was surprised that my cousin did the same, even in her white pants.

"Do you miss her?"

No one had asked me that but Elspeth. No one had talked about her leaving at all. I started to cry, and Brianna scooted over and put her arm around my shoulder.

"I know," she said. "It sucks. My mom is sick. She's maybe going to die."

"Is that why she looks the way she does?"

"Yup."

"What's the matter with her?"

"Her liver's crapping out. I think it's because of all the booze."

I hadn't thought of my aunt Kitty as an alchy. But I could see why she may have tried to drown her troubles.

"She's on a wait list for a liver, but they don't want to waste livers on boozers, so I don't know if she'll get one."

"Jesus, now I don't know what to say."

"Well, we could just both sit here and plot our get-a-ways. And call me Bri. Brianna is a sappy name."

"I'll take Morocco," I said. "Bri."

"Istanbul," my cousin added.

"That would be my second choice!"

I sort of liked her. We sat in silence. Bri picked up a stick and began to swirl it in the water. I watched the circles within circles expand outward toward the edges. And then we returned to the grange to join the fun. And later, when Elspeth sat between my mother and Karl at lunch, as though they had secretly formed a family without me, I knew I must go.

Chapter 9

Several months after the Maryland gang left us to writhe in our own agony, and our mother seemed to be filling up from the inside with her old juices, becoming more recognizable than she'd been in months, I wrote a letter. Maybe I was buoyed by what seemed mom's constant inflation, or the deepening of the green-ness of a Maine summer, or just the loud ticking of time, but I was instilled with the courage to write to Candy.

I told her everything that had happened—how our aunt ran away, and how Snoutly had been carted off by the game warden so he could no longer bother the good people of Westover, and of course, how my mother married her sister's ex-boyfriend, and was now enfolded in his arms all the time, and how I had made a friend with my cousin. I told her that despite the seeming return of my mother to some sort of normalcy, I still felt like I was living in a displaced persons' camp. And within a few days of dropping this letter in the box, our phone rang. I was relieved it was me who answered it.

"Back Kingdom Road House," I said into the phone. "Liza speaking, may I help you?"

"No, but I think I can help you," the voice on the other end said. And I knew it was Candy, with just that slight hint of coun-try in her voice.

"Hi!" My heart was beating too fast. I felt like someone had turned up the treble in my body. I sat down on the bottom step.

"First, let me say that I am sorry to hear about your aunt. It's totally bizarre and totally horrible. And I am really truly sorry. No one should have to deal with all you've been through."

"Thank you," I squeaked out of my tight throat.

"I'm at work so I need to talk sort of fast. But you need a good friend, and if that friend can also be someone connected to you by blood, even better, I think. Cousins can be awesome supports. What if you lived with this Bri you talked about in your letter? Would they let you go there?"

"Live with my Uncle Doug?"

"Yeah," she said. "Could you?"

"He's an asshole," I answered.

"Oh. Well think about it. It may be worth it. Look, I have to go, but really, think about it. It might be better or maybe not. You'll know if you tune in to your higher intelligence. I'll write soon Liza. Bye."

She hung up. My higher intelligence? I didn't know what that was. I thought maybe Karl would know. He was a smart guy. I'd ask him.

That night we all managed to gather at the dinner table, our battered family. My mother actually made us all halibut and string beans. The halibut was swimming in a milky butter with black pepper, and the string beans were crispy and salty. It tasted like a five-star meal to me. We'd been living on P and J on English muffins and sausage pizza from the general store.

As we all sat, I gazed around the table. My mother looked pretty in a blue and green flowy dress, and had even done up her eyes with some purple eyeliner, making them more striking than usual. Karl was clean shaven and looked like he'd slept well and my sister sort of glowed. None of this made sense to me. We were devastated, weren't we?

I wondered what they saw when they gazed at me, if they did. The hair badly in need of a shampoo? The blotchiness of my skin? The puffy eyelids from crying myself to sleep? And then it just came blurting out. As though riding on my exhalation. "I think I'd like to move in with Uncle Doug and Aunt Kitty," I said.

El looked up first. Fork held aloft like a conductor's baton signaling an upbeat.

"What?"

"You heard me," I said, with a resolve that I was proud of.

"Are you for real right now?"

"El!" I said, "What is the reason, pray tell, to stay here with all you freaks?"

Elspeth scraped her chair back with such force it fell over. She bolted out of the house, slamming the screen door as she went.

My mother began to weep and I suddenly felt like the scum on fairy shrimp spa. Worse. I felt like dog shit.

Karl stood up. He pulled my mother to him and hugged her.

"We'll talk about this later," was all he said, and led my weeping mother away.

I hadn't had a chance to ask Karl about higher intelligence and it seemed like a really bad idea now. I needed to know, and had no one to ask. Everyone was pissed at me. My sister had likely fled to the woods, probably sitting at the edge of Fairy Shrimp Spa hating me for ruining her good vibe and my mother was crying into her pillow, and I made her do that when she had seemed finally to feel good.

The one person who might have known what my higher intelligence had run off to Denver. But her books were still spilling over from all the shelves. And so, I started to look. In the span of an hour I found one that seemed promising. It spoke of tuning into an inner voice that knew what was right for us on some intuitive level—a place that lived outside of our brains. At least that's how I understood it. Sort of a gut feeling that could guide us if we could get in touch with that power we all had to know the right answers. It sounded wacky to me, but I was desperate. So, I followed its advice, and I thought hard about my question: should I move to Maryland if they'd have me?

I went upstairs and burrowed under my bedspread, naked. I went to sleep repeating my question over and over, so that I could dream on it and have an answer in the morning. And I did. The answer was I had to go. I knew this was the answer because in my dream I was sitting in the crook of a big tree looking down on Back Kingdom. I started to fall and was hanging on to a skinny branch that should not have been able to hold me, but it did. I thought this branch was Aunt Kitty.

I lay in my bed, in my own room that I had grown to love. Its warmth, tucked in the attic's eaves where birds nested and sang songs to one another. The slant of sun in the morning and evening that left a river of light across the length of my whitewashed floor. And now that it was August, the passage of light was a slow crescendo and diminuendo that left me breathless. Could I leave this for Maryland? What would the light be like there?

I could hear my twin stirring in the room beneath me. I could smell bacon wafting from the kitchen window four stories below. I had a long lazy summer day unfurling ahead of me that I could spend in any way I wished. Unencumbered by responsibility and left alone, I could hang at fairy shrimp spa, read a book, collect rocks or walk over to the Ellis River for a swim.

Breakfast would be tense after last night. I wanted to avoid it, but I was starving. I got dressed and took my chances.

"I'd like to talk with you for a bit," my mother said. She sat at the table with a mug of tea. Again, she looked pretty. Like my old mom.

"Okay," I said. But my knees began to tremble.

"Let's take a walk," she said, and got up from the table. Her feet were bare.

"Sure," I answered. It was odd that Elspeth and Karl were not in sight.

My mother led the way. Once outside, she made a left away from the village and toward the Ellis. Our walk to the river's edge was brisk and silent. She sat first, under the big tree where the tire swing hung.

"What's going on?"

"What do you mean," I asked.

"Why do you want to leave us? For Uncle Doug, no less. Who I know you can't stand?"

I knew that the Ellis would still be cold this early in the morning. But it was still and iridescent. And I thought how lucky I was that I could come to such a place anytime I wanted to. And I wondered where I would go in Maryland when I needed to slip away to nature. But it seemed that I'd made up my mind and I couldn't retrace my steps—couldn't see a clearing to jump from the train I was on.

"It can't be worse than it is here," I said. I wanted to hurt her.

My mother laid her hand across her stomach.

"Can you tell me what is that bad? Here, I mean?"

"You need to ask?" I was enjoying my power. I dug my naked big toe into the cool moss on the river bank and flicked a green chunk into the river.

"Liza, why are you doing this?"

Her stupid violet eyes were all over my face, like she would find some secret code just under my skin that would spell out the answer.

"Doing what, exactly?"

"Liza, who has hurt you so bad that you'd leave us. Was it me?"

Was it me? Was it me? Did she really just ask me that? If I'd had any pang of sadness that I was hurting her feelings, it was gone. Not only was it gone, but I now felt completely vindicated going for her throat.

"When parents have kids, they're actually supposed to love them and take care of them. Not just when they feel like it, but all the time. All the time means all the time."

I stretched out my words like taffy and opened my hands and extended my arms to either side as far as I could.

"You missed that part altogether. You only took care of me until Daddy died. Then you turned in your mom badge, so I'm turning in my kid badge. I gotta go," I said, and made great fanfare of standing, shook my hair out like a komodo dragon puffs up their neck fins, and sighed as if it was just all too sad. I felt fucking great. My work here was done.

My mother put her hand up to her mouth, and I walked away.

Chapter 10

Aunt Kitty arranged for me to start ninth grade in College Park. Karl drove me to the Greyhound in Portland and I boarded a bus to Baltimore. I carried all my earthly possessions in Karl's step-father's army rucksack from WW II. The name Peterson was stenciled on it in faded black block letters. It smelled of male cat spray. But my stuff fit just right.

I had four novels, mostly Ursula Le Guin stuff, but one by John Irving that a guest had left at the road house. I had all of my clothes but two shirts I left behind, and one skirt I vowed I'd never wear again, and a pair of shoes that I'd outgrown a couple of years ago. At the last minute I tossed a photo album in of old family pictures from before my father died. And that was that was that.

The bus pulled out of Portland at dawn, switched in Boston, again in NYC, again in DC, and finally, I was in Baltimore, but not before a fight broke out on the bus between NYC and DC.

"Don't be scared, hon," and older woman with orangey hard looking hair said to me from across the aisle. "Happens all the time. Bus driver will take care of it."

I hadn't known I looked scared. I'd been trying to seem impervious to the whole thing. The bus driver did stop the bus and kick one of the guys off at an Arby's. My heart was racing and I felt light-headed. I wanted Aunt Serena. I wanted her to assure me that there were more good people in the world than bad.

I fell asleep somewhere in Pennsylvania, but woke up as we pulled into the depot in Baltimore. It smelled salty and old. But I thought the ocean was magnificent and while it was sickeningly hot an odd little tickle of a breeze sent a trill up the back of my neck.

"Baltimore," I whispered to no one, as I trudged off the bus. "Feed me."

I had eaten my six P and J sandwiches on homemade oatmeal bread. My mother packed them. My mother who acted more like a mother between that fateful day at the Ellis (and my Day of Leaving on August 1) since my father died. And when she pleaded with me to stay that morning I left, I told her she was a day late and a dollar short.

El was furious with me, and wouldn't come for the ride to the station even though she'd been planning to, as had my mother. She didn't end up coming either, but for different reasons. I think she was just too reamed out. I looked back at the roadhouse as Karl pulled out of the driveway, but just for a second. I wondered if Candy had given me bogus advice, but was pretty sure she wasn't capable of doing anything wrong.

"Liza! Over here!" It was Bri! Waving at me from the big suburban. I was relieved to see Aunt Kitty behind the wheel and not Uncle Doug.

I half trotted to the car with my borrowed rucksack dangling from my shoulder.

"Hello hippy girl," my cousin said and then she hugged me.

Aunt Kitty was grinning like a jackal. I climbed into the high back seat. The AC was blasting and the leather seats were shiny and smelled like cantaloupe. I was happy to be in this car with these two women. I thought Aunt Kitty looked better. She had more flesh on her body and her eyes were not as vacant. I was hoping she was getting better, but didn't know how to ask that question. I would just have to watch closely.

"I'm sorry Courtney couldn't join us Liza," my aunt said. "She's a lifeguard at a summer camp in the Alleghenies."

Bri rolled her eyes. I wasn't sure what that meant. Either Aunt Kitty was making up an excuse for Courtney, or Bri was jealous of her sister's cool job. Another thing, I thought, that I'd have to pay close attention to as I wormed my way into the folds of this family. And I had no idea about where the Alleghenies were and was too embarrassed to ask.

We all fell into silence. I was relieved. My head was buzzing from all the hours zipping down 95 with screaming little hellions and their crotchety parents. I closed my eyes, inhaled the cantaloupe fragrance that baffled me, since our car smelled like old feet and ass, and let the cool midnight blue leather hold me like a baby.

I fell back to sleep, because I missed everything between the depot and our arrival at the big brick house. The first thing I noticed was the same gleaming gigantic door knockers from that steaming day five summers ago.

"Hey," I said to Aunt Kitty, "Do you still have your little dog?"

She turned to me and smiled. "We do, honey. He's old old old. He's a bit cranky and forgets to pee outside, but yes. We still have him."

"That's awesome," I said.

I really wanted to see that little dog. Spud. The first several weeks after we left Maryland for Back Kingdom, I plotted to get one of our own. One just like him. But despite many promises of later, it never came to pass. Snoutly was all we got.

"Oh, Honey," Aunt Kitty said. "I just want to prepare you that Courtney's reception of your joining the family may be a bit frosty. But just go about settling in, okay?" She turned to me and smiled and pulled her keys from the ignition. They seemed to stick, and she appeared slightly baffled by what to do next.

Frosty, I thought, was a description of a cold drink, or the name of a snow man. I had never heard this word used in this way, and I liked it. I turned to Bri, smiled and shrugged, as though to say, bring on the frost. I don't care.

Bri grinned and popped out of the big suburban with the grace of a dancer and leapt to her mother's door and opened it for her. I couldn't tell if this was something she always did, or if it was new since her mother got so sick. But it was nice.

My aunt's belly was protruding. It was bizarre in her skinny frame. I figured it had to have something to do with her liver stuff, and tried not to look below her shoulders. Bri put her arm through my aunt's, and so I reflexively put my arm through her other one, and the three of us ambled with no urgency to the big front doors with their shiny silver sea shell knockers.

Uncle Doug was at work and Frosty, my new name for Court-ney, was somewhere perched in her lifeguard chair in a tight one-piece bright red bathing suit toasting up to a light golden brown. I did not tan. Thanks to my father. I blotched, burned, freckled and peeled. But there was the doggie. A little grey around his snout, but still bouncy and shrill. He made a bee line right for me.

"He remembers you Liza!" My Aunt Kitty said.

I knew this was really unlikely, but it made me happy that she said it, and I loved her even more for it.

"Let's get your stuff put away," my cousin said and she led me to her room. Bunk beds had been installed.

"Top or bottom," she asked.

I'd always wanted to have bunk beds and I'd always wanted the top. "You don't care if I pick?"

"I wouldn't have asked you if I cared!"

"Top then!"

"Okay, top it is. We got this dresser too," she said, pointing to a white ornate dresser with lots of scrolly wood. "And there's closet space as well."

"Thank you," was all I managed, because I felt like I might cry if I said anything else.

"Okay," she said. You unpack and take a shower. Because you stink a little, and then we can do whatever."

"Oh shit," I said, sniffing my pits, "I actually really stink?"

"Yup!" She laughed. "But a day on the bus will do that."

"Can I ask you something about Aunt Kitty?"

"Sure," she said, sitting on the bottom bunk.

"Is she going to be okay? Her stomach looks weird."

"Yeah. That's fluid. It's normal I guess when your liver craps out. If she gets a liver, she'll probably be okay."

"This must suck so bad for all of you."

"Big time sucks," she said and walked out of our room.

I was tired. I climbed up my bunk. The room was cool and smelled like fresh sheets and lemon pledge. I wanted to sleep, but I wanted to shower more. I was not in the habit of wearing deodorant. I didn't even have any, and so I would need to make sure I managed to get some. Or maybe I could borrow Bri's for now.

I slid down from the top bunk and walked into my cousins' bathroom. It was huge and white. I opened a cabinet that was filled with shampoos, conditioners, and two rows full of toothpaste, band-aids and toilet paper. I peered into the tub--no green and rust colored stains from hard water. No chipped enamel or hair in the drain. I slid open the drawers in the vanity counter. They didn't stick. They were brimming with white folded velvety towels and face cloths. I pulled open another drawer and there I spied the coveted deodorant sticks. I smelled them after pushing up the little tube of waxy stuff. Cotton candy and pink. Another drawer was clotted with hair doo-dads, a blow dryer and a straightening wand.

It seemed like a store display to me. In my house, we bought things when we ran out, and never more than exactly what we needed at the time. Sometimes we ran out and still didn't even have the stuff we needed right away. We improvised, as my mother called going without. We used coffee filters for toilet paper, or toilet paper for paper towels. But this house was the planet of plenty. Where cabinets were loaded to ensure that no ass would go unwiped, and no armpits would go unscented. And in that moment, it made all the sense in the world to me. And after a shower where the water just kept coming and the temperature never leapt from scalding to frigid and back, and with plenty of cotton candy gunk under my arms, I lay my body down on rose petal pink cotton sheets and fell asleep to the thrum of central air, and didn't wake up until the next morning.

August 3rd, 1984, began my new life in one of the affluent noveaux riche sub-divisions of College Park. I mostly loved it, for all of its glitz and bravado. And I was completely impressed by the manicured bright green lawns of the university. Each time we piled into the big suburban and drove to the mall I ogled all the students lolling on the steps along Baltimore Avenue. This and all the turquoise lagoon shaped swimming pools in all the back yards in our sub-division were enough to have me grinning like an idiot most of the time.

"Oh," Bri grunted, "It is so damn hot, and it's what, like 7:30 in the morning?"

She peered over the edge of her bed at her watch which lay on the carpet right next to her pillow that she always threw to the floor in the middle of the night.

"How can you tell it's hot?" I asked. "It's always cold in here!"

"The AC sounds different. The hum is higher and faster when it's hot."

"You're so weird," I said and dangled my arm over my top bunk and fake swatted at her.

Six weeks had gone by and Bri and I were now inseparable. When Frosty returned from the posh Allewhatsies summer camp somewhere in West Virginia, I thought Bri would forget about me. School started the Wednesday after Labor Day, and Uncle Doug picked Frosty up the day before. The counselors had to stay and clean up the place. I dreaded her return and kept fantasizing that there'd be a terrible accident. But then again, it was also possible that we were tight enough to withstand any attempts at separation.

"You guys are stapled to one another's asses," Uncle Doug said, in a friendly way. I think he approved of us.

"So, it's fine with you if we don't want to make the drive to Kiawana," Bri asked at the Labor Day Picnic.

"Sure, why not. You need a day to get all gussied up so you can set that high school on fire!"

"Girls," said Aunt Kitty, wrapped up in a lavender blanket in a chaise lounge, "I am so sorry I can't take you to the mall for school shopping."

Aunt Kitty was now pretty high on the wait list for a liver, and we were all hopeful. But every day she apologized to someone about something she wasn't able to do, and some days she apologized multiple times for the same things.

"Mommie dearest," said Bri, stretched out in the lime green chaise next to her mom, with her Dr. Pepper in her hand clad in a leopard print bikini, "enough already. You do know that they have these new-fangled driving machines called busses?"

Both Uncle Doug and Aunt Kitty laughed. Uncle Doug walked away from his station at the hibachi where he rotated skewers of scallops and ruffled Bri's hair.

"You're a little pistol," he said.

No one had ever ruffled my hair and called me a little pistol.

"Hey, I've got a keen idea," Uncle Doug said, and sprayed his skewered scallops with a plastic water bottle filled with his "special" marinade.

"But is it peachy keen daddio?" Aunt Kitty said.

Bri laughed, belched and laughed harder. The day had not been what I'd expected. Uncle Doug was so easy in his skin. I'd wondered if this kinder Uncle Doug was the result of his wife's illness.

"Oh, yes! It is peachy keen," he said. "How about I drop you girls at the mall? And then you'll just need to bus back."

"That would be groovy, and we accept," Bri said.

"You're quiet today," Uncle Doug said. "Are you worried about school, Liza?"

"No, I'm good," I said.

"Don't worry about anything. You and Bri will have everything you need for a day at the mall. You can get all gussied up too," he said.

I don't know how this happened, but I got a big lump in my throat and as hard as I tried tears just sprang up out of nowhere.

"What'd I say?"

Uncle Doug just stood there with spatula in mid-air dripping fat on the slate patio. He looked like a large sad orangutan.

"Nothing, Dad." Bri said. "You're fine, really."

He walked to the cooler, retrieved a diet Fresca, my new favorite soda, and handed it to me. And then he ruffled my hair.

Uncle Doug didn't let us down. He passed us each a crisp $100 bill and delivered us to the mall. I didn't even know how to begin school shopping. I wasn't even sure of my size. Bri kept piling things up in my arms and commanding me to try them on. Lots of Madonna and Cyndi Lauper type stuff that I'd never pull off. I was more comfortable in the men's department. Several oversized t-shirts in greens and blues and lots of horizontal stripes, some jeans, and a bulky sweater or two. I wouldn't mind a jean jacket and a puff parka for when it got cold, if it ever did.

She pushed underwear on me too. "I've seen your bloomers, and they're ridiculous," she said.

I had no idea how underwear could be ridiculous.

"Why," I asked. "Because they're white, cotton, what?"

"All of the above," she said, and passed me an armload of padded lacey numbers in pastels.

By the end of the day I'd blown through the whole wad of cash, and probably a little more than fifty percent was stuff I'd likely never wear, but my cousin was happy. I did have a new jean jacket, a pair of Reeboks, two sets of Levis and some flannel pajamas. The punk-slut stuff and pastel underthings were an oddity that sort of delighted me in a strange sort of way. Picturing myself in them made me giggle out loud.

We'd also eaten piles of greasy mall Chinese food. No Chinese food, in Westover, so my stomach rebelled. I started to feel queasy before leaving the mall. By the time we'd waited for the city bus, I knew it was coming—from one end or the other, and possibly both.

"Liza, you look a bit green," my cousin said.

I sat in an aisle seat with one foot sticking out to make it easier to bolt from the door at whatever stop would be next, just in case.

"Well," I said, "you know what Kermit says, right?"

I clutched my bags to my chest, closed my eyes and used Aunt Serena's trick for queasy bellies—breathe in, breathe out --slowly and mindfully. We'd barely pulled away from the curb when my mouth filled with saliva. I opened my big plastic GAP bag filled with my new jeans and let loose. Food was coming up exactly in the shapes and sizes and colors it went down.

I glanced over at Bri, between convulsions, trying to signal with me eyes how sorry I was but she was looking out her window. And why wouldn't she be? People in seats around me were fleeing. By the time we got to the next stop I had nothing more to give, and thankfully it all came up rather than down.

I rolled the bag up, preparing it for the closest trash bin, when Bri turned to me, smiled, and said, "Don't get mad, get Glad."

If there had been any question as to how deep my feelings ran for this bleach blonde cousin, they were all put to bed with that one comment. I went from one of the most humiliating moments of my life to complete rapture. She pulled baby wipes from her purse and handed them to me to clean up.

"Why do you carry baby wipes in your purse?"

"They make awesome make-up removers. And puke picker-uppers."

"I have to throw all my GAP stuff away."

"Fuck no you don't! That shit is going in the wash. You can't throw all that away you silly goose."

"I love you Bri."

"Sure you do, but don't talk to me right now. Your breath stinks."

A few hours after we got home, and my new clothes were spinning around in the bright red dryer, Uncle Doug's Saab pulled into the driveway and two car doors slammed. Frosty had arrived. I was trying to figure out the best way she could find me—to make an impression. But I couldn't land on what impression I wanted to make. Should I be languorously draped over the couch in the den reading a novel? Which novel? Or, should I be scrubbing the sink in the laundry room, or maybe napping to avoid her all together?

These three options would say very different things about me—I don't care what you think, I care a little bit about what you think, and I sleep a lot. I went for the novel, but now I had to decide what sort of novel. Was I an intellectual? Did I read the same sort of crap as her mother? Aunt Kitty had only one small bookshelf in the entire house. It was tucked away in a corner of the rumpus room in the basement. Down I went for my perfect prop. Danielle Steele, Maeve Binchy and Ann Tyler, something about a tourist. I'd never heard of her, so why not?

The only thing left now was The Drape. My legs are long, so perfecting The Drape was not a stretch for me. I decided on the big white suede chair in the picture window. The sun in my hair would be a nice touch. Like a painting. I assumed my pose just as the front door opened. I feigned utter fascination in my novel. I read and reread the first paragraph three of four times.

Frosty stuck her head in the living room and said hello to me. She was absolutely a knock-out. She looked like a supermodel—tall, lean and deeply tanned. Her hair was loose and long. Curly and dark blonde.

"Oh! Hey Courtney! You're home!"

I put the book down on the end table, smiled my best smile and walked toward her. I wasn't sure what I planned to do, but then it didn't really matter because Frosty put her arms out to me. Her hug was strong and she smelled like chlorine.

"How's it going," she asked.

"Oh, you know, it's going," I said.

"Well, I've got a summer's worth of laundry to do before school starts. I'll catch you later."

All this anxiety about a pretty girl who gave me a hug and smells like swimming pools? I sort of hopped to the bedroom to try on all my new clothes. Even the stupid stuff. Frosty was sorting through the dirty clothes she'd dumped on the floor.

"Frosty, what do you think," I asked about one particular arrangement of clothing. I'd been so used to referring to her as Frosty that it slipped out.

Frosty looked up from her sorting. "Frosty?"

"Oh, I'm so sorry. That was my best friend's nick-name back home."

I thought I'd done a masterful job of saving my ass, but Bri tossed a balled-up page of her notebook at me and said: "Tell her the truth, cuz!"

"Tell me the truth about what?"

"Go on, Liza," Bri said.

I shot her my best death stare but she just cocked an eyebrow and giggled.

"Okay, guys, what's going on," Frosty said.

I sat on the edge of Bri's bottom bunk and took a deep breath and just blurted it out.

"So, I sort of nick-named you while you were at Kiawana."

"You nick-named me Frosty? Why Frosty? That's a hoot," she

said.

"You're not pissed," I said.

"Well, I don't know. It depends why you picked Frosty," she answered.

"Because you're so beautiful, sort of like an ice-queen," I said.

Bri looked up from her notebook where she was doodling eye-balls, and looked directly at Frosty.

"Yeah, like an ice-queen," she said with her most serious face.

"I like it," Frosty said. "Keep calling me that. It has ring to it."

After a few more variations of outfits I compromised with both my cousins about my first- day -of -school attire. A decision was made that I would wear my new 501s from the GAP, good as new after a spin around the washing machine, donned by one of my punk-slut lacy black shirts and all finished off with blinding white reeboks.

"Well, it's original," said Frosty.

The next morning, we all hopped in Frosty's blue Pinto and headed off to school. We pulled into a freshly paved parking lot and I thought my new high school was brilliant. It was huge and clean and state-of-the art. Had I been in Westover I'd be in the same building as I'd been in for all my years there, except in a dif-ferent wing—an old building erected in 1954 on an arid plateau of ledge. Now I was in a high school with as many students as in the entire population of Westover.

And there she was, in home-room. Gemma Goldstein. Edgy. I liked that. She wore a lot of black and circled her eyes with heavy dark liner. Patti Smith was splattered across her tight t-shirt. No one compared to Gemma. She was as tall as me, about 5'10", but much sturdier, like a brick house. I'd decided I was a breast woman. But how would I ever be able to talk to someone as cool as she was? I'd have to get the scoop from Bri.

Gemma hadn't turned up in any of my classes that day. It would be a home-room thing, if it happened at all. And she was probably straight anyway. The bell rang to signal we could head off to our first period. I had my schedule stuck into my trapper-keeper which listed ELA as my first class. Room 220-B. My home room was

312-A. What the AB thing meant I didn't know, but there was Bri, trotting down the hall to catch up with me.

"Hey," she said, "Maybe we can swim at Kyle's after school. It's supposed to be like 88 degrees today. That way you can see Kyle. I know you're all about Kyle!"

I wasn't actually. My cousin didn't know anything about my feelings about girls. It was more apt that I was all about Gemma than Kyle. But I liked Kyle, although mostly I liked to swim.

"Bri, he's a 12th grader!"

"So, since when has that stopped anyone from having a crush. Strange thing is I think he sort of likes you too!"

"Yeah, right," I said and changed the subject. "Where's 312-A?"

"Third floor in the front. See you at lunch. Meet me in the ladies' room across from the caf," Bri said and fluttered off.

I got through three blocks with no humiliating fuck-ups. I didn't drop my back pack, forget my name, or start my period. Most kids just ignored the new girl but some nodded in my general direction. After science came lunch and I made excellent time arriving to the girls' room to meet Bri. When I passed into the cool white bathroom, I was alone. I stared hard at myself in the mirror to see what my new school mates could maybe like. My hair was sort of pretty. Dark blonde, pin straight, even silky since my cousins had turned me on to conditioners and straightening wands. My eyes were an interesting shade of pale blue, but for the most part, what I noticed was the bridge of blackheads across my nose, the translucent skin under my eyes that seemed to show all the veins in my face and the three crooked bottom teeth right in the middle of my mouth.

"Are you staring at yourself?" I had not heard my cousin pad into the bathroom behind me.

"No!" I said. "I have something in my eye."

My cousin laughed. "Yea, right! You were trying to see if you were pretty enough for Kyle!"

It dawned on me that it might be a good idea to play along with the crush thing so I could pass for normal.

"Okay," I said. "I do sort of have the hots for him."

"Hey! I've got a great idea!" My cousin sat on the toilet in a stall, left the door half opened and peed. It was at first unnerving that she would do this with such ease in front of me, in a public bathroom no less, but she did it at home all the time. "Let's get a bunch of us to go to Ghostbusters this week-end. We can ask him!"

Other girls were streaming in now. I jumped in the stall and pressed my cousin's stall door shut. She beamed at me from the toilet.

"Look," I said, "I highly doubt a senior would have any reason to go to the movies with the likes of us."

"I'm a sophomore, my love, and we all grew up together," she said, and wiped herself. "He would definitely go."

I had mixed feelings about the whole idea. I had mixed feelings about my mixed feelings. I liked Kyle. He was a person of substance, I thought, and had a lot of scruples. I thought he was cute. But I didn't lose my breath when he walked into a room. I didn't fantasize about the moment when he'd finally proclaim his undying love for me the way I had with Candy. And the way I thought I might with Gemma.

Chapter 11

Things started out well that morning. Aunt Kitty got some good news about her place on the waitlist for her liver. She'd kept all her meetings with her social worker at the hospital and remained on what she called "the nice girl list" because she wasn't drinking at all, and had convinced all the right people that she was committed to sobriety. I barely knew what that meant, but I knew it was a good thing. On top of that happy news, the heat wave broke and that Friday morning had an astringent feel to it as ocean air wafted up the Chesapeake. And finally, we were all going to see *Ghostbusters* that night. Me, Bri, Kyle and some friend of his. A guy named Will who I had only seen in the halls once or twice.

"Are you psyched?" Bri asked after the last dinner dishes were put away. We were all helping Aunt Kitty a lot these days.

"Bri!" I tossed my dish towel on the counter for dramatic effect. "I really need you to stop."

I really was annoyed that she kept pushing Kyle on me.

"Sor-rry!" She laughed. "Just make sure that you don't have any spinach in your teeth!" And with that she tossed her own dishtowel at me.

There was something about the playfulness of the moment that made me dizzy. I had to sit down and bend over as though I was examining my toes. It reminded me of evenings around the kitchen at Back Kingdom with Aunt Serena, and even my mom on those rare occasions when she acted normal and forgot she wanted to die. For the weeks I'd been in Maryland, my campaign to forget my weird life had worked pretty well. So enamored I was of fluffy towels, and drawers full of hygiene products that forgetting was easy. The new life for the old. Wax on, wax off. But suddenly, all I wanted was to be enveloped in purple velvet arms drenched in patchouli.

"Earth to Liza!"

Bri stood over me waving a red plastic spatula dripping with water.

"Move it! We got to go!"

"I hope you girls have a fun time," Aunt Kitty said.

She was leaning against the counter, wan and yellow, with her belly protruding. So completely unlike my bear-loving aunt. But maybe almost dead. Unless the phone rang soon with news of a fresh liver untainted by vodka and gin waiting at Johns Hopkins in a picnic cooler.

We hugged her good bye, grabbed our denim purses and headed out into the salty Maryland evening.

I was the first to spot Kyle and his friend Will in front of the theatre. I wanted to be going to the movies with Gemma. I was a freak, I knew, but then Candy didn't think so, and I didn't think she was a freak either, so I wasn't sure.

"Well, I guess it's me and Will and you and Kyle. Frosty pulled a Frosty," Bri said.

"Do you even like Will?" I really didn't think she did. She never mentioned him at all.

"Well, you know what the song says, love the one you're with!"

"I guess," was all I could come up with.

We approached the two boys. Someone smelled like he'd had too much garlic bread and I hoped it was Will.

"Hey," Kyle said, and was at my side. I was pleased to smell Irish Spring.

"Is that a moustache?"

The minute I'd said this I realized I'd made a stupid comment. But the smudge over his top lip caught me off guard.

"I'm trying," he said, and laughed, and I was immediately at ease.

"Goobers?" Kyle asked after we'd bought our tickets.

"Good and Plenty," I answered.

"Oh. You're one of those," he laughed. "I should have known!"

"One of what?"

"A licorice lover."

He smiled at me, and I wondered if I could like him like him.

"Hey guys, we're sitting in the balcony," Bri said. "Catch you after the movie."

I hadn't thought I wouldn't be sitting with Bri. Now it really felt like a date and I wondered what I'd do if he slapped the moves on me.

We settled into seats in the back, and shortly after the previews Kyle slipped his arm over the back of my chair and let his hand drop over my shoulder. It was no big deal, really, so I ate my candy and laughed at all the right places and bided my time until the lights came up, and they finally did.

"Like the movie?" Kyle asked.

"Yeah, it was good."

I really didn't think so. I thought it was sort of stupid. I wasn't a big comedy fan.

We met up with Bri and Will. Bri was all bubbly and talking nonstop about how funny Bill Murray was.

Will finally broke in. "You guys want a ride home?"

"Sure," Bri answered, but I wasn't so sure.

Will led us to his dad's car, a big boat of a thing, and I slid in the back next to Kyle. He put in a Red Hot Chile Peppers cassette. No one spoke. Not even Bri. Ten minutes or so passed, and even though I didn't know the area that well, I knew we weren't heading in the right direction for Uncle Doug's. I leaned forward and asked Bri quietly where we were going.

"To the lake, I think."

"Lake?" I asked.

"Yeah. Artemisia."

I sat back, not sure what to do, a little shaken up. These were older kids. What would they have in mind? Would they want to make out? If Kyle tried to kiss me or touch me, what would I do?

Was it stupid that I'd left Back Kingdom where everyone left me alone?

We pulled into a parking lot at the lake. It was huge and shimmering under a harvest moon. It reminded me of home. The way the moon looked over the Ellis River by the covered bridge. Aunt Serena had taken both of us there more than once to look out the windows of the old bridge into the moon-trail on the black river.

"It's so beautiful here," I whispered more to myself than any of the others.

"We aim to please," Will said, and pulled Bri into his arms and put his garlic mouth on hers.

"Don't worry," Kyle said, "You're in charge."

I started to cry. He placed my head on his shoulder and we sat like this for the next thirty minutes while Bri and Will disappeared into the seat.

Chapter 12

The fall pushed on and I was relieved that by October the weather was more like Maine's. Trees changed color as well—it was not the Vegas extravaganza, more like a community theatre show, but dazzling in its own subtle way. Pumpkins were showing up on stoops and porches, corn cobs were hanging from maroon front doors, and purple and yellow mums were all over the place. That was outside. On the inside of the Chabot household life was ratcheted up as the tension surrounding Aunt Kitty's ailing liver infused every moment. Nothing was banal anymore; it was all ominous.

"Mom," Frosty said one bright Saturday morning around Halloween. "I'm running a load of laundry today. If you want to give me your blanket, I can wash it for you."

We were eating toast. I made it and it was a little burnt. Aunt Kitty didn't eat much and Bri had slathered apple butter all over it to try to fatten her mother up. Aunt Kitty politely nibbled on one crust, wrapped in her lavender blanket.

"Thank you honey, but I don't think it needs to be washed."

Frosty shot one of those what-the-fuck glances at Bri and me. Aunt Kitty's blanket was a menace to society. We couldn't fathom how our fastidious mother/aunt hadn't got sick from the smell of her blanket. Aunt Kitty's body emanated a sweetish smell of rotting food most of the time, and at other times, like a jar of old pennies. But her infantile connection to her blanket was such that none of us ever wanted to force the issue. We spent a lot of time around her breathing through our mouths.

That morning, after our burnt toast and laundry duties, we all left together in Frosty's car for a mall trip. We decided it would be a blast to do a massive decorating thing for Halloween. After tucking Aunt Kitty in with her fetid blanket we were out the door. Uncle Doug was, as most men in suburbia that day, raking piles of leaves from our maples and oaks.

"Going to spend all my money ladies?"

We all said yes in unison. Unrehearsed and completely organic. And we cracked up—even Uncle Doug. I glanced back over my shoulder before getting in the car to sneak a look at my complicated uncle. He had paused in his raking and was looking up at the perverted zaftig clouds. He was smiling.

Just after pulling out of the driveway, Bri fished a pack of Camels from her purse. This was a new habit ala Garlic Breath. Both Frosty and I abhorred this nastiness, and Frosty refused to let Bri smoke in her beloved Pinto. She kept it clean and shiny.

"Bri," Frosty said, "put that nasty shit away."

"The window's down, for Christ's sake," Bri said.

"I don't fucking care. You know the rules."

"It's a Pinto. It's not a Porsche."

"It's a Porsche to me, Bri."

"It's a Lamborghini to me," I said.

I often found myself in the role of the funny girl who ran interference between the cousins. I loved this new found skill I'd never known I possessed.

The first store we hit was Spencer's for cool Halloween stuff. We'd decided on a vampire theme. We'd all shared Anne Rice books and I was especially obsessed with them and had crushes on all the girl vampires.

"Guys," I said, "look at this lamp."

A raspy voice said from behind me, "Cool, isn't it?"

I startled, turned around, and The Gemma stood behind me in full regalia, but it was those laced up high-heeled combat boots that slayed me. They must have made her six feet tall.

"Oh! Hey Gemma," I said. Seven weeks in home room and nary a word. Now, I was actually speaking to her.

"Here for a costume for the party?"

I had no idea what party Gemma was talking about, but I didn't want her to know that I was such a dweeb that I couldn't stay on top of the cool events at school.

"No," I answered, "just getting stuff to decorate the house. You know, for all the little kids in the hood."

"That's sweet. I figured you were that type of girl. You have the aura."

Aura? This was the sort of stuff Aunt Serena talked about. She once said mine was orange.

"Yeah," I said. "It's orange."

Gemma burst out laughing. Apparently, she thought I'd made a joke. So, I went with it, and laughed too. Then she waved and disappeared down the aisle.

I stared at the lamp a few minutes. The cousins were nowhere to be seen. The lamp was calling to me. It was tall and slim, like a dancer's body. It was black, maybe wrought-iron, and its feet were in the shape of claws. Its shade was also black with small red beads dangling from the bottom. I had to have this lamp. This was a lamp that Lestat would own. Or maybe Armand. I turned it over and looked at the price tag—it was $24.99. I had enough, but just enough. This lamp was mine.

I found Bri and Frosty at the check-out. They each had stuff to decorate the house, and I only had something for me. I felt guilty, so I said we could put the lamp just inside the front door on the little table where we threw keys and mail, so the trick-or-treaters could feel like they were going into an old Victorian scary mansion. They bought my story. We walked around for about an hour, and decided to get some bagels since the burnt toast had been sort of a bust.

"Hey, you know that Gemma girl?"

"You mean the Goth chick in the boots," Frosty said.

"Yeah, you know her?"

"Not really. She's so fucking weird," Frosty said.

"Why do you say that?"

I didn't want to hear what she had to say. Dumping on Gemma was not okay with me.

"I know why she says that," Bri said, between bites of her huge everything bagel. "Because she walks around like her shit doesn't stink and has never worn anything that isn't black since 8th grade."

"So, what's the problem with black?" I hadn't touched my bagel. I didn't feel hungry anymore.

"I don't have a problem with black. It's just a color," Frosty said. "But I do have a problem with people who are starving for attention and then act pissed off when someone notices them."

"Well, she said something about a Halloween party."

"Oh, that," Bri said. "Some of her Goth friends have a party every year. I think it's at this kid Adam's house."

"Did she invite you," Frosty asked, bagel held aloft and staring at me with huge eyes.

"No. She just mentioned it."

"Well, if she invites you, don't go," Frosty said. "Those kids are bad news and really fucking creepy. They're all obsessed with death, and half of them are starving themselves."

All I could think of was Gemma's spectacularly strong body. She was certainly eating something. Wheaties and spinach, it seemed to me. Their warnings did not perturb me. If Gemma invited me to hell, I'd go.

A light feathery snow fell in Maryland that December. It made me miss home. I had exactly six letters from my mother. Usually about the weather, and occasionally Elspeth would indulge me with a little story about school. My life was so very different now in the burbs that I sometimes couldn't pull the faces of our old school friends up in my brain. Since the strange night at the lake where garlic breath guy made out with my cousin, they'd fallen in love, so I spent much less time with Bri, and Frosty was out of my league all together—so popular and so frosty.

My aunt had progressed to end-stage liver disease, and although she remained on the transplant list, the phone hadn't rung. Her quiet presence and strategically raised eyebrow at the right moments kept us in check most of the time. If we walked away from a littered dining room table after killing a bag of chips and a liter of Dr. Pepper, the left eyebrow went up. If Bri dropped the ef word, the right eyebrow went up. But now she spent most of her time in bed wrapped in her pungent lavender blanket. All in all, the happy feelings of my arrival were fading to black.

It was Gemma now. Although we'd not said a word to one another since Halloween shopping at Spencer's, she colored my dreams. I hung on her every inflection, read the horror novels she carried around at school, wanted combat boots and gave up meat again (because I'd heard her tell another kid in homeroom that she was a vegetarian) which incensed my Uncle Doug. But how could I tell this girl that I was in love with her? I had a week or so of vacation time over the Christmas holiday to lay low and rest my muddled mind.

A few nights before Christmas, Bri was out on a date with Garlic Breath. I was bored out of my mind, and channel surfing for a Christmas special. Rudolph would have been nice. My own family was popping into my head and I was wondering what Aunt Serena would be thinking about the bizarre turn of events of my living with her nasty big brother, whom she despised. And then the phone rang. And it rang and rang, and no one was picking it up, which was odd given that we were all waiting for The Call. I grabbed the phone in the hallway just in time. It was Johns Hopkins. My aunt's liver had arrived.

"Aunt Kitty! Uncle Doug. Come to the phone, now!"

"Is it the hospital?" Uncle Doug appeared from the bedroom at the top of the stairs where he spent more and more of his time watching television cop shows. His hair stuck straight up and his eyes were bloodshot.

"Yes!"

He took the stairs two at a time and grabbed the phone from me. All he said was yes, over and over.

"Get your cousins," he yelled. As though I could make them materialize. But I didn't want to fail.

"Okay," I answered. "I'll find them."

My uncle vanished back into the bedroom where my aunt lay wrapped in her lavender blanket in a peach velvet sweat suit.

"Kitty! Get up. We have to go."

"Where," I heard her say.

"Just grab your bag."

I ducked back into the kitchen and tried to figure out how to find my cousins. I should run over to Kyle's. He drove and he'd know where to look. I headed out the back door and across the yard to a small hole in the fence, crawled through, and was pounding on his door in seconds. When he answered, I leaned against him.

"What's going on?"

"My aunt," I said. "Her liver is here. I have to find Bri and Frosty."

"Let's go," he said.

Kyle and I spent the next hour looking for my cousins. We unearthed Bri and Garlic Breath at the lake, but couldn't find Frosty.

"I'll drop you guys at the hospital," he said. "I'll track down Courtney." Kyle had not adopted my nickname for my cousin.

"Good luck," Garlic Breath shouted from his steamy window as we ran to Kyle's car.

"You're a mess," I said to Bri.

"So? Who cares?"

Bri was a little pissed at me these days because she'd wanted us all to be a happy foursome. She rode me hard for being too much of a "priss" to go out with Kyle.

We jumped into Kyle's car and she smoothed her hair out and wiped her smeared lip gloss on her coat sleeve. We raced to the Greenbelt and drove in silence.

"Can you come in with us?" I wanted Kyle to keep me company.

"No," was all he said, but hugged me. "I need to find Courtney."

Bri grabbed my hand and pulled me up the walk toward the entrance.

"I don't want to go," I said. My heart was beating too fast and my legs were shaking. One aunt had already disappeared.

"Bullshit! You have to go."

"Bri! Please. I can't do this."

"Liza! After all my mother has done for you? Are you fucking kidding me?"

She stood under the halo of the big outside lamps. My gorgeous cousin with her rumpled hair and wrinkled coat. Her high heeled burgundy leather boots that she loved firmly planted on the concrete. And all I could think was that she looked like a 12-year-old in grown-up clothes and I loved her in a way I have loved few since. For being my friend, and for saving me from Back Kingdom.

"Okay."

"It will be fine," she said and pulled me into the white light of the lobby. Frosty arrived an hour later, Kyle found her at the mall. The three of us sat up all night drinking V-8s from the vending machine and waited for Uncle Doug to appear from some inner sanctum we knew nothing of. It was after five in the morning when he appeared with a huge smile, almost bouncing on his toes.

"She's good!"

Frosty and Bri ran to him and they all hugged. I couldn't do that, but I did go to his side.

"She's going to be okay, Liza," he said and then he hugged me. I wasn't sure what to do, but it seemed I should hug back, and so I did, and he started to sob.

"I'm sorry," he said, still crying. "I'm sorry for all of it." And then he let me go and turned quickly back down the shiny corridor to his wife.

"Dad, when can we see her," Frosty called after him. But he didn't seem to hear her in the din of hospital clatter and kept trotting.

"Let's go guys," Frosty said, "I'm toast."

I wasn't sure that would be the appropriate thing to do, but I was relieved when Frosty brought it up.

"Are you sure?" Bri seemed to have read my mind, and I was glad she asked her big sister the question I didn't dare to ask.

"Suit yourself," Frosty said. "But I see no sense in sitting in a hallway."

She turned away and strode down the hall. Bri fell in line, and then me. So many sad and tired looking people slumped in the plastic puce chairs in the waiting rooms we passed. I probably would have run for the gleaming revolving doors if I hadn't been following my cousins.

We waited for Kyle to retrieve us that dark snowy morning, as twinkle lights flickered in the majestic sycamores outside the donut place across the street from Hopkins. I didn't think they were as beautiful as the pines back home. Frosty sat alone. Bri and I sat together at another table. Only five others drank coffee that morning. I snuck side-ways glances at their haggard faces. One was a girl who appeared about our age. Her hair was matted and her clothes were smeared with grease. She was tiny and didn't wear a coat. What wicked goings-on had befallen her? What trouble was she in? What amongst her stories brought her to this abject moment in the snow? God, I wanted to sleep.

When Kyle pulled into the parking lot, I walked down the aisle past the tiny girl and it was all I could do to keep walking—such was the urge to reach out my hand and gently tug her off with us—not leave her sitting in the chilly coffee shop that smelled of stale pop-corn. I wanted her—she seemed to me a cricket on the hearth. If I could clean her up and protect her, she'd bring me good luck. It made no sense, but I couldn't shake off that feeling.

"I have an idea," I said to my cousins when we walked in the house, "let's see if we can find a Christmas show."

I yearned for my bed, but sleep seemed unlikely.

"Actually, that's a great idea. I'm too keyed up to sleep anyway," Frosty said.

"I'm in," Bri said. "But PJ's first."

"Like a slumber party," I said, and a trill spiraled up my spine. I'd never been to one.

When we gathered in front of the TV clad in flannel, Frosty commanded the remote. Bri's eyes met mine and we commiserated in code: our Frosty was large and in charge. For once I didn't mind, because I couldn't stop my brain from lingering on the tiny dirty girl in the donut shop. Whatever Christmas Classic Frosty chose to lull us to sleep in our hog pile under Bri's big white puffy quilt was fine by me.

"Guys, did you notice that girl in the coffee place? Maybe about

14, with the matted up hair?"

"What girl," Bri said.

"She was sitting toward the front. She was really petite."

"I didn't see her," Bri said.

"Did you, Frosty?"

She fiddled with the remote. "Nope. Hey, what about Frosty the Snowman?"

"How apropos," Bri said.

And then it was all over—all we could do was laugh. Big fat peals of laughter, replete with snorts, snot, peeing our pants, and choking—even some tears. I didn't think about the cricket girl again, or much anyway.

We still didn't have a tree, and Christmas was only five days away. It was my idea to surprise Uncle Doug. He was mostly at the hospital, which made plenty of sense and none of us minded. It was fun to live as though we were three twenty something roomies even though none of us was even 18. Uncle Doug had naturally left us with a reservoir of cash for anything we might need in his absence. We had almost two hundred dollars. We picked the time and place we'd get our tree and Bri brought all the Lucite tubs filled with decorations in from the garage.

"Wednesday is a half day," Frosty said. "Let's go straight from school."

"Sounds excellent. Let's meet at the auditorium exit," I said. I liked that exit best because Gemma was in the Drama Club. I'd occasionally see her hanging out there by the band room.

We drove straight to Belaire's, the biggest green house in the county. It was the place for the largest and most spectacular trees. Apparently, they came from Canada. Frosty was cranky that day. As an eleventh grader she was shopping around for olleges, and so the first argument that afternoon was between her and Bri.

"What even makes you think you could go to a place like Harvard," Bri said.

"Duh. My 3.9 GPA? My extra-curricular activities? My participation in student government?"

"I wish you could hear yourself right now," Bri said.

"I can. My hearing is fine," Frosty said. "I think you're worried that I will get into Harvard, and you'll be lucky to go to University of Maryland."

"Fuck you," Bri said, and stabbed the on button of the radio with her knuckle. It was so loud that we all jumped.

"Jesus, Bri," she said, and stabbed the off button with her index finger.

"I'm not the one that had it up that high. Don't get pissed at me," Bri said.

This inane shit continued all the way out to Belaire's—almost forty minutes. The piney winter smell of Westover was everywhere. It was my favorite smell in the world, but it was making me sad. I just wanted us to agree on one of the fat blue spruces and get away from the parking lot forest.

"Hey guys, check this beauty out," I said.

" It's huge," Frosty said.

"It's gorgeous," Bri said.

I stepped into the tree, wrapped my hand around its stout sticky trunk and pulled it loose from its corral. I straightened it so my cousins could swoon at its majestic grandeur and we could just go home. I was also starving. I was cold too, and the elastic of my panties was cutting into my thighs.

"Alright. Let's get it," Frosty said.

The second fight was about where to get lunch—the bagel place or the taco place. Bri won that fight, so we all had tacos. I'd actually hoped Frosty would prevail. I wasn't a fan of fast-food tacos. It was curious that neither ever asked me to weigh in on their stupid spats, but also a relief. I was not a fan of choosing sides. And then we were pulling into the driveway with our magnificent blue tree tied to the top of the Pinto. We cut the tree loose of its twine with my exacto knife. We'd been making linoleum prints in art class, so it was in my back pack.

"You carry a knife around," Frosty said. "That's sort of fucked up."

Was she trying to pick a fight with me? It wouldn't work, because I didn't like fights.

"It's for art class, dumb ass," Bri said.

They went at each other for a few more minutes. I ignored them and focused on pulling the tree into the house. I'd almost made it to the front door when I sort of tripped and toppled down with my face was wedged between two boughs, and for a second I couldn't breathe. I got myself unstuck but was covered in needles. They were in my eyes and nose. I shook them out of my hair.

"Are you okay?" Bri ran over and pulled me up. Frosty got back in her car and drove off.

"What's that all about," I said.

"Who knows? She's been a bitch for days.'

We made hot cocoa, put a Jim Nabors' Christmas cassette in and wrangled with the tree which was too big for the stand, but we finally did it. When the sparkly glass balls were hung, and twinkle lights and white garland strung, dusk fell. We plugged her in and gasped at our masterful work.

"What about the topper," I asked, and plucked a big silver star from the Lucite bin.

"Dad gets to do that," Bri said.

Within the hour Uncle Doug returned from the hospital. We were both stoked for his reaction. But I could tell by his foot falls that he may not be in a mood to appreciate the tree.

"Where's Courtney," he said. "And you better both tell me the truth!"

"I don't know, really," Bri said.

He looked at me.

"I don't know either. We got the tree after school and we thought she was coming in the house with us to help decorate, but she took off instead. And that's all I know. Truly."

My uncle glanced at the tree, mumbled something about it be-ing nice, and headed back to the front door. Just as he reached for the doorknob, he spun around.

"So help me God if I find out you girls are lying to me there'll be hell to pay around here. And if she comes home before I do, you best make sure she stays home." And out he went.

"What the hell is that about?" Bri flopped on the couch.

"I don't have a clue, but I'm putting that star on this tree."

"Go for it," Bri said. "How about you don't get your head stuck in it again, though."

"Righty 'O," I said, and headed to the garage for a ladder.
When I returned Bri was asleep. I pulled the plaid wool throw over
her thin body. I was overcome by a surge of emotion I didn't expect—a sort of weepiness. In that moment she was the cricket-on-
the hearth girl in the donut place. I sat gently next to where she
lay and pushed a chunk of hair from her face. She said something.
I thought it was thank you, so I said you're welcome. I climbed Uncle Doug's paint splattered old wooden ladder. I wondered about
all the splotches—what had he painted? The star fit perfectly over
the leader. My work was done here.

Whatever was going on with Frosty wasn't going to ruin my
gorgeous tree. I inhaled its citrus aroma. I sat on the burgundy
Persian with my back against the couch where Bri gently snored—
more like a purr, and gazed at my blue spruce. An hour or so
passed, and no Frosty or Uncle Doug. I left Bri sleeping and went
to bed. The sheets did not feel as smooth or cool and smell like
they did when Aunt Kitty was home.

I woke up around three in the morning to the raised voices of
Frosty and Uncle Doug in the kitchen. I wasn't able to catch every word, but it seemed as though Uncle Doug got a call from the
school about a ton of absences, failing grades, and possibly a guy.
Frosty never mentioned anything to us about any of the above. Occasionally she was hard to locate, like the night Aunt Kitty got her
liver. One thing Uncle Doug said, or yelled, actually, was quite
clear: "How could you do this to your mother, of all times?"

That is when Frosty clomped away to her room, and I could
make out muffled crying through my wall. I waited till I heard my
uncle's footsteps fade up the stairs. I wanted Bri real bad. I padded in my bare feet across the cold tile of the kitchen and the soft
plush of the Persian rug.

"Liza?"

Bri was sitting up, still fully clothed from the night before on
the edge of the couch. The blue and green tiny lights from my tree
cast a wintry glow. She looked like a painting of an angel.

"What was that all about," she asked.

I sat next to her on the couch. "I'm not sure. I only got bits and pieces," I said.

"Well, I got the whole thing. Christ. What's wrong with this family?"

"So, what's going on," I said.

"Did you have any idea about Frosty?"

"Idea about what," I asked.

"She basically hasn't been at school—like hardly at all, and she's failing this semester. Someone told the principal that she's seeing some older guy. Like a lot older, it sounds. He picks her up every day like nine, and brings her back at four."

"Wow. That's insane."

We sat there in the blue glow. The pendulum of the grandfather clock heavy in its glass cage.

"There isn't one present under the tree," she said.

"Yeah. But that's okay," I said. "We've got each other."

"Who are we? The fucking Waltons?"

"What's wrong with the Waltons," I said.

Bri cracked up. "I love you, Liza. I really do."

She got up from the couch and grabbed my hand. "Let's raid the fridge."

"It's empty," I said.

"No, I think there's some leftover tuna salad."

After we scraped the silver mixing bowl clean, we climbed into our bunks and slept.

We woke up late that Thursday. It was the day before Christmas Eve day. No school, no errands, no nothing. It did occur to me that we may want to buy a few presents for at least each other and maybe Uncle Doug. Maybe some food for Christmas dinner? Neither of us professed to know the first thing about cooking a turkey, but I didn't think it could be that hard. I'd watched Aunt Serena cook holiday meals before.

By elevenish we'd decided to wake up Frosty. We wanted to visit with Aunt Kitty, and pick up a few groceries and trinkets to wrap up. I missed my family, hard, for the first time. But I didn't talk about that. I didn't want to bail on this family.

Bri came out of Frosty's room and sunk into a kitchen chair.

"She's gone," she said. "But there's a note. Here."

I wouldn't read it. I'd had my share of notes.

"Just tell me," I said.

"Well, the bottom line is she's left. With a guy named Gregg, with 2 g's no less. Who's married, with actual kids," she said. "It seems he's from the summer camp."

"Should we tell Uncle Doug?"

"Hell no."

"But he'll worry. And what about Aunt Kitty?"

"I haven't gotten that far yet. Let's just stick to our plan for today."

"If it's all the same to you I'd like to get out of here before your dad wakes up," I said.

"Let's roll," she said.

"Would you mind if we asked Kyle to join us?

Bri winked at me. "Not at all."

By 11:45 we were showered, dressed and knocking on Kyle's door. He answered in Spider man PJ bottoms and a wife-beater. I must say he was yummy. Even from my perspective. Then there was his St. Christopher's medal. This kid was actually into being Catholic.

"Hey! To what do I owe the pleasure?"

"So sorry, but would you like to join us today? To do a little shopping, and other stuff?"

"Other stuff has my interest," he said.

"Kyle, yes or no," said Bri.

"Let me change and I'm all yours," he said. "Come in out of the cold."

"God, he gets better with age," Bri said. "Does he not?"

I ignored the question. He appeared in no time flat with a huge Atlanta Braves hooded sweat shirt over his PJ bottoms, and bright blue Nikes on his feet.

"I assume I'm driving," he asked.

"You assume correctly," I said.

Kyle drove an ancient Austin. I thought it was the coolest car I'd ever seen. He bought it off some old hippy who'd advertised it in the penny saver.

"Where to," he asked.

We directed him to the Bread and Circus, and the K-mart. We grabbed Christmas fixings and presents. I bought silver hoops for Bri, and a black leather wallet for my uncle. For Frosty, should she return for Christmas, I bought a powder blue hoodie that said Harvard on it.

"Should we tell Kyle," I said

"I don't know. Do you want to," Bri said.

We were standing in a long check-out line at K-Mart. Kyle was waiting in the car for us. I thought it would be a great idea to tell him. I wanted to tell someone.

"I do, actually. I think he can be trusted."

"Then go for it," she said.

I got in front next to Kyle, and just blurted out that Frosty had sort of run away from home, with an older guy named Gregg.

He didn't say anything. He just kept driving. After a few strange and empty minutes, he put in a Pat Metheny cassette, tapped along on the steering wheel, started to speak, then stopped, coughed and tried again.

"I know that," was all he said.

Bri leaned forward from the back seat. "You know what, exactly?"

"That Courtney split with some older dude. He was the photography instructor at that summer camp. They looked at each other and something happened. Seems to me like they're really in love."

"When did she tell you this," Bri said.

"July," he said.

"July? She wasn't even home in July," Bri said

"Correct. I drove over there to see her."

"I don't get it," Bri said.

"What's to get," Kyle asked.

"Why didn't you tell us?

"Bri, it wasn't my place."

I finally chimed in. "Is she with him now?"

"What do you think?" Kyle pulled into a Dunkin Donuts. "Coffee anyone?"

The next couple of days leading up to Christmas were some of my saddest days in Maryland. Frosty had called home to assure us all that she was well and safe, but would not be home for Christmas, and had no plans at this time of returning, "anytime soon, if at all."

We avoided visiting Aunt Kitty, because neither of us could bear telling her, and Uncle Doug, when he was home, was more a ghost than a ghoul. Our money had run dry and neither Bri nor I had the guts to mention this to Uncle Doug. We wrapped our few feeble gifts and placed them under the tree, and on the afternoon of Christmas Eve opened up some cook books and planned a dinner for the next day.

"I love this recipe," I said. "It uses dates in the yams."

"That's gross, and we don't have any dates anyway."

"Are you pouting," I said.

"Yes, and I plan to pout and sulk all fucking day. Because this is the worst, the very worst Christmas ever!" Bri said.

"Speaking of which, I need to call home," I said.

"Knock yourself out."

My hand trembled a little when I picked up the receiver. What would I say about our situation down here? I wouldn't give them the satisfaction of knowing that we Maryland folks were maybe even more fucked up than they were. On the third ring Elspeth answered. "Back Kingdom Road House, Elspeth speaking, may I help you?"

"Yes, my name is Gretchen Bullcox and I need a room for me and my walrus."

After the smallest of pauses Elspeth laughed and said, "So sorry, Ms. Bullcox, but we have a no walrus policy. The last time we had a walrus here he ate all the crumpets."

My heart fell on the ground. This is the sister I wanted right now. Not my fill-in sister Bri, although I loved her.

"Is the tree up?"

"We dragged it in just yesterday from the back 40."

"Mom there?"

"She and Karl went into Rexford for provisions."

"But everything's good?"

"Everything is copasetic."

"The boyfriend?"

"He's a dick."

"What? Why?"

"He cheated on me with Shellene."

"I want to get that picture out of my head," I said. "Say hi to the newlyweds."

I wondered why I was about to dress a turkey with Bri and not Elspeth. The pull to go home, for the first time since I'd arrived in August, made me ravenous. But I'd run away from one family and wasn't going to run away from this one.

"How are they all down there?"

I sat on the stool at the sticky marble island and leafed through The *Joy of Cooking*, but felt no joy. "Oh, you know," was all I said.

A few hours later we had amassed quite a number of side dishes, and with Jim Nabors singing in the background the house felt a little Christmassy. My tree, of course, was more spectacular every day. I don't know why—it just seemed to preen for us. Maybe it knew.

Uncle Doug trudged into the kitchen around four. He looked like a hound dog. Everything drooped and he needed a haircut.

"Smells good in here ladies," he said and tossed a pile of mail on the kitchen table with other piles of mail that remained unopened.

"Any word from Courtney?" He asked this every time our paths mingled.

"Nothing new," Bri said. "Dad, are we doing mid-night mass, and opening presents in the morning and stuff?"

"Sure, we can do that if you want."

"I know it won't be the same without Mom. How's she doing, by the way," Bri said.

"You girls should go visit her and find out for yourselves. I need a shower. Chinese for dinner?"

Bri ran to her father and hugged him. I wanted to, but I didn't. I kept chopping a carrot into little nubs for our home-made stuffing.

We had that Chinese food. After my ordeal at the mall I was a little on guard, but my belly held out just fine. Check. We dropped by to see Aunt Kitty, who was tearful and apologetic about not being able to make a "nice Christmas" and Uncle Doug had warned

us to say "nothing of Courtney's disappearance." Check. (The excuse for her not being with us for our visit was that she was home
cooking!) It sort of pissed me off since I'd cooked all day, and
still had more to do after mass and even in the morning. Bri, as it
turned out, didn't shine in the kitchen. And then, we walked into
the cavernous, dark and sweet-smelling Cathedral of St. Francis of
Assisi where somber organ music in minor cords wafted from the
balcony. Check.

We'd gotten through the entire eve of Christmas with all the
skill and panache of opera stars. And now we slid into a deeply
oiled walnut pew. I spotted the Johnson clan, Kyle at the center of
his family, a few rows up and across the aisle. He was wearing a
suit. I relaxed into the pew.

I'd never been in a Catholic church, although my mother had
been raised in this very one. Had she sat in this pew? The music
and the incense from the burners swinging in the arms of a robed
and bejeweled priest filled me with longing for my mother. This is
a moment I'd like to have shared with her. I could reach over and
squeeze her hand. I could let her know that we were one in the
spirit and one in the Lord. Did I think that was true?

I rose Christmas morning a little after six, started coffee for
Uncle Doug and popped some frozen waffles in the toaster. While
things were percolating and toasting, I leaned against the door
jamb between the kitchen and living room and gazed, once again,
at my tree. The room was shrouded in the half-light of an early
grey morning. The tree was alone, but dazzling and happy. I heard
the pop of the toaster and returned to putting breakfast on the
table. Frosty was standing at the sink with a glass of grapefruit
juice.

"Hey," she said.

"Hey," I said back.

"There's an enormous turkey in the fridge," she said.

"Well, I thought Gregg and the kids might come." As soon as I
said it, I wanted to not have. But, it was too late.

"Fuck you," she said. But she was smiling.

"These monster birds take like forever to cook, you know. We
gotta get this monster in the oven," I said.

"What is it, a pelican?"

"Yes," I said. "Yes it is."

Frosty finished her juice and held open the oven door while I slid in my gorgeous stuffed bird. I felt so grown-up. I was proud. I'd even pre-heated it when we got back from church.

Then came Bri. She chose not to acknowledge her sister. We ate waffles in silence. I put a few more in the toaster for Uncle Doug.

The grandfather clock was chiming. Uncle Doug appeared. He went first to the coffee maker, and didn't see Frosty. Then he turned to join us at the table. I placed his plate of waffles before him with butter. He didn't like maple syrup.

"Jesus! Courtney! You're home?"

"I am. Gregg wanted to spend the holidays with his wife and kids."

"I don't ever want to hear that piece of shit's name mentioned in this house ever again," he said. His face was getting purple.

"That's just fine with me, Daddy."

Chapter 13

Several days after Christmas Aunt Kitty was still in the hospital, but had been moved to a regular room where it was easier to visit. She still looked awful though, sallow and thin, and her face sort of caved in on itself making her wrinkled and old looking. She kept up a good patter about our lives at home without her and even made a few jokes about what state the house must be in. But mostly she was upset that she'd "abandoned" us at Christmas.

"I want you girls to make up for it at New Year's. I don't know if I'll be home or not, but I give you my blessing to have one heck of a party."

"You didn't abandon us Mom," Frosty said.

"Ya, really, Mom," Bri said.

I felt I had to say something too.

"Aunt Kitty, we hardly worried that you'd forgotten us! We were busy being worried about you."

I thought this was pretty good, and I actually meant it.

It was closing time and her nurse shooed us away. I was actually a little relieved we could make our exit. It was weird being at her bedside with all the bells and whistles hooked up to her skinny yellow body.

"A party?!" Frosty laughed, once we were out of earshot of Aunt Kitty. "That's a first! Dad will have a shit fit."

We waited in the lobby for Kyle to come and get us in a cold grey drizzle and started planning. The only thing I really cared about was making sure that Gemma was on the invite list. And Uncle Doug was not at all pleased about the idea. We were lucky (and happy) that Aunt Kitty did make it home in time for New Year's Eve. He could hardly say no to his wife at such a time, so he relented, but was snarling at us all day as we assembled party platters and hung up decorations in the rumpus room.

"I want to have one of those veggie assortments," Bri said, and yanked three bags of carrots from the crisper.

"What for a dip, though?" Frosty asked.

My two cousins got into a heated discussion about dip, and I had one of those moments where my heart pinged for my family, who never worried about dip, and I needed to call them. I slipped into the small den off the kitchen, which Uncle Doug called his office, although I never once saw him doing any work in that room. I wondered what my mother, Karl and Elspeth would be doing on New Year's Eve. I tried to picture them sitting in front of the big fireplace and wondered what sort of plans they'd have. I was sure there'd be no parties, though, and didn't know if I thought that was a good or bad thing.

My mother picked up on the second ring.

"Back Kingdom Road House," she said in a sing-songy voice.

"It's me, Liza."

"Oh. Liza. I was so sad I missed your call last week." I almost hung up; her timid voice irritated me so.

"I just wanted to say Merry Christmas and happy New Year and all that good stuff."

"When are you coming home?"

I could hear Elspeth prattling in the background to Karl. I was trying to hear what she was saying. The tone was pressured, and I was sure she was trashing me.

"I don't know. I just called to say hi. How are you?"

"I'm okay," she answered. "I'm talking to somebody and it's helping a good bit."

"Talking to somebody? Like a professional, you mean?"

"Exactly. A therapist. And I like her a lot and she's smart and funny and she's making me talk about everything. It's really hard, but I'm getting better at it."

"Oh," was all I could say. So, my mother was officially nuts now. She had a therapist.

"How's Aunt Kitty?"

"She got her liver. She's home."

I was glad to have been derailed from thinking about my mother's therapist.

"Give her a hug for me?"

"Sure. I have to go. This is long distance and I don't want to run up their bill."

"Of course. Come home Liza."

I hung up. And got to work on making dip with my elegant dip-eating cousins.

By eight the rumpus room was all set up for our party. Bri hung tinsel from the fake beams and Frosty pulled all the best cassettes from her collection. Aunt Kitty's colorful pottery bowls were strategically placed on all the surfaces for quick access to a staggering variety of chips and dip. All we had to do now is put a *Talking Heads* tape in and wait for the doorbell to ring. And I felt like I would not be able to relax until Gemma walked in the door.

An hour or so passed. About twenty people were quietly milling, and eating up all the chips. One of them snuck in booze so several were getting shit-faced, but you couldn't describe the party as very exciting. And none of them was Gemma. At ten or so I was ready to call it a night. A few more girls had straggled in and at least a few people were dancing and laughing. The drunken group was drunker and provided some entertainment being drunken shits. And then the doorbell rang again and since I was heading upstairs to crash, I answered the door.

"I'm at the right place? All these little boxes made of ticky-tacky look the same to me."

Gemma and two of her friends, both of whom were pierced, be chained and sporting mohawks, stood in the door.

A ripple ascended my spine. "Yeah, this is the right place. Come on in."

"You're the poor relation," said the green-haired skinny guy with a face full of zits.

"Sam! Not cool," said Gemma.

The girl with the magenta spikes in her hair never looked up from the floor, and Sam slunk his arm around her shoulder and muttered something under his breath. Gemma led them to the rumpus room as though she owned the place, and I took up the rear. The surly trio flopped onto couches and chairs and immediately looked bored. I wanted them to stay, because I knew Gemma would split if they did.

"Can I get you a drink," I asked. I had no idea where I would get them a drink. We didn't have any booze in the house because of Aunt Kitty. Frosty once told me that Uncle Doug had a secret stash someplace in the garage.

Gemma looked at me and smiled. Her face was so different when she wasn't scowling. She tucked a heavy piece of thick blacker than black hair behind one ear.

"What d'ya have?"

"I'm not sure, but word on the street is there's booze in the garage someplace."

"Well, what's keeping us?"

Gemma got up and linked her arm through mine. And the two of us headed out the back door of the rumpus room and made way to the garage. It was cold out, and neither of us had coats on. I pushed open the back door of the garage and fumbled around with various light switches until the correct one bathed the place in hard blue fluorescent light.

"This light isn't good for us vampires!" Gemma laughed.

I was trembling a little and felt unsteady on my feet.

"So, poor relation, where's Uncle hide the good stuff?"

"No idea, but between the two of us we'll find it, I'm sure." I wasn't at all sure, but I was feeling cocky all of the sudden. Like maybe I could do this. Maybe I could pull this off.

Gemma and I pulled open cupboards, turned over wheelbarrows and looked behind piles of tarps, and there it was. A bundle of single malt scotches, according to Gemma, whose father, she reported, was a "professional drinker."

"I don't want to share this; it's expensive shit," she said. "Let's you and me have a private party."

My dreams were coming true, but it was cold in the garage.

"You're not freezing?" I asked.

"We can get in the car!"

And so, we did. Gemma unscrewed the bottle. "This is called Laphroaig. Uncle has good taste. Smell it!"

"It smells like wet burned wood." That was a smell I knew well from my bon-fire days in Maine.

"Taste it!"

I did not love the taste, although it was exotic and warm.

"So, poor relation. What's your story?"

And I told her, one swig at a time. And of course, it was not long before I slipped into that murky half-light of reason. And somebody kissed somebody. And somebody licked a nipple, and somebody, and I believe it was me, said I love you to somebody.

"You don't love me," she said. "You're just happy to get some girl love. Bet I'm your first?" Gemma slipped her hand into my baggy fatigues and set the silky butterflies in my nether parts free.

"What the fuck," she rasped into my ear. "You're gushing. You're an exciting girl."

I slid down into the pliant leather of my uncle's backseat and let Gemma tug my pants down. I was trying to control my breathing, and it felt like my chest might burst open and spew confetti against the steamy windows.

"I'm going to kiss your honey pot. Is that okay? I want you to taste the wonderful saltiness of you."

Gemma's head popped up from between my legs, and I could see the gleam of her white smile in the semi-darkness of the garage.

"That's okay." It must have been a whisper, because she still looked at me, expecting an answer. I said it again and she descended.

This is what I'd seen Candace and her lover do in the bathroom at Back Kingdom. I'd thought about what it might be like and now I knew—it was like being a wave in the ocean. I felt a sound somewhere deep and growing, and then convulsed.

"Charming girl, you are," Gemma said and gently kissed me there. She moved her strong warm body up the length of my body until her mouth was above mine.

"Open your mouth, baby. I want you to taste yourself."

I did, and she placed her tongue on mine and fondled it with hers, and I tasted myself. I was tangy. I was good.

"Now, would you like to lick my honey pot?"

I nodded yes. She pushed her hands up under my sweater and flicked at my nipples. It hurt, but it didn't.

"I'd like to do one more thing to you first, if that's alright?"

"Yes," I said.

"Oh, you're such a good girl. Roll on to your tummy for me, baby," she said.

She kneeled behind me and placed her knee between my legs, and bent over enough to place her tongue in my butt. I began to rub myself against her hard thigh, and the faster I did, the faster her tongue penetrated me. And I convulsed again.

"You are so orgasmic. It's so much fun to fuck you. Now it's my turn."

She got herself under me and pushed her pants down around her ankles. She took my head between her two hands and gently placed it in her crotch. I began to lick and nibble and kiss, and she groaned. It seemed I was doing this right. I kept at it, and she clasped my head tightly between her legs and pushed herself up against my face. I could hardly breathe, but it was so warm and wet. She smelled like ivory soap. I reached my hands up to her breasts and rubbed them. She grabbed my head and thrust herself up to meet my mouth and then fell back.

"Well," she said. "Aren't you all that and a bag of chips." We stayed like this for a while. My head rested in the crook of her thighs, and she stroked my hair. And then the car door swung open.

"What the hell's going on!" My uncle Doug towered above us as the dome light blinded me.

"Shit!" I sprung from Gemma's sopping thighs.

"Get out of here. Get out of my house," Uncle Doug yelled, and grabbed Gemma by her jacket collar and dragged her from the car. "Liza?"

It was then I realized he hadn't known it was me prostate and sweating on his back seat with my pants around my ankles. But I could only think about Gemma, who by now was running out the back door of the garage.

I was trying to sit up and cover myself, while screaming for my new girlfriend when he hit me, open palmed across my cheek.

"Get out of here, Liza. Crawl back under the rock you came from. Get your stuff and go. Tonight."

I was sick to my stomach. It came over me swiftly and mercilessly. And I vomited on the floor of his new Saab.

"Jesus!" He grabbed the garden hose and began spraying the

ice-cold water onto the cranberry carpet. I made my way out
the opposite door, ran out the back of the garage and didn't stop
until I got to Kyle's, but all I wanted was Gemma. The third time I
pounded on his window, he pulled aside his curtain. I wasn't sure
he'd be home. He wasn't at our party, but he could have been anywhere on New Year's Eve.

He beckoned through his closed window for me to come around
to the front. When I got there, it was open and he stood waiting
in his warm golden living room. Dylan was playing from somewhere.

"Are you alone?"

"Yes." He moved aside to let me in. "Your face is all red. What
happened?"

I sunk into a deep velvet pumpkin colored chair. "Uncle happened. Do you have a phone book?"

Kyle didn't push me for details. And I even loved him more
then. He passed me the phone book from the kitchen counter and I
found lots of Goldsteins.

"You happen to know where Gemma Goldstein lives?"

"Yeah. Two streets over. Chestnut, I think."

There were several. One was a doctor. It seemed right, so I
picked that one.

"May I use your phone?"

"Of course."

I was grateful that he walked away. I dialed the number and
got an answering machine. "Hello. You've reached Dr. and Mrs.
Goldstein, and Jacob. Please leave a message at the beep." No
Gemma? I tried the second Goldstein on Chestnut. It rang and
rang and rang. No answering machine at this number.

"Take this," Kyle said. He passed me a bag of frozen corn.

"I'm not hungry," I answered. I had no idea what this bag of
Birdseye corn was for.

Kyle laughed, so I started laughing. "It's for your face silly
girl!"

It sunk in, and so I sat back with the bag across my cheek.

"I'm gonna try that last number again."

"Keep the corn on. I'll dial it for you."

Kyle picked up the phone book. I watched his fingers rifle the pages. They were unnaturally long, and very white. They seemed to belong to a woman's hand, but there was a faint blonde hair on the knuckles. The nails were chewed and ragged, but an alarming sea-shell pink.

"You have really pretty hands."

"You're shit-faced, Liza!" He laughed and picked up the receiver and passed it to me.

I nodded. Was I shit-faced? I didn't have anything to compare it to, but I realized that I probably was. If I moved my head quickly, I felt a little spinny. The phone was ringing someplace on Chestnut street.

"Hello?" An out-of-breath Gemma answered.

"Gemma! It's Liza."

"Oh. Liza I'm sorry, but this whole thing is just too weird for me. Let's forget about it. Really sorry. You're awesome, but we're a bad idea."

She hung up.

"Liza, I think you need to just crash here tonight. Let me put you to bed."

"What time is it?" I was trying not to cry. And I did want to sleep. My head hurt and I wanted the spinning feeling to stop. But I wanted to say Happy New Year to someone.

"It's almost midnight."

"I don't want to miss New Year's."

"Okay. You won't." Kyle stood up and pulled me gently from the chair. He took the corn along with us as he led me to his room. "You'll sleep in my bed. I'll sleep in the guest room."

He lowered me down to the bed and covered me up. It felt so good to be horizontal and warm under the weight of his tangled blankets that smelled of Irish Spring.

"I have to make midnight," I said.

"Liza, can I ask you something?" He sat at the foot of his bed.

"MMMhmm."

"Are you and Gemma more than friends?"

"For a few minutes," I said.

"Oh. I thought maybe."

"Do you think that's gross?"

"Not at all. Why would I?"

I was drifting off, but determined to be awake at midnight. I think my drunkenness buffered me from feeling so mangled; so humiliated. So utterly fucking devastated.

"Liza, I'm going to bed now." Kyle got up.

"Stay with me 'til midnight."

He stood with his hand on the doorknob. Light from the hall backlit him. He looked so sad.

"I love you Kyle."

"I love you too Liza. Happy New Year."

The next morning, a little confused by waking up at Kyle's, I knew exactly what I had to do. It was odd; there was no doubt at all. I thought about how everyone at the party probably had a good enough time, rung in the New Year with Johnny Carson, and went home by 1:00 to their respective beds in the 'burbs with no event. But not me. I killed the better part of a bottle of expensive booze in the back seat of Uncle Doug's Saab with a girl's head between my legs. And now, I had to go.

The little clock by Kyle's bed said 7:15. My head ached, and my tongue felt like it was taped to the roof of my mouth. At some point someone from next door would want to find me. Maybe not Uncle Doug, but probably Aunt Kitty and Bri—maybe even Frosty. And I didn't want to see any of them. The thought of it made me nauseous.   I really had to go. I got up and padded down the hall as quietly as I could to the guest room, pushed open the door and found Kyle, wide awake.

"Please take me to the bus."

"Now?"

"Yeah. Please. I need to go home."

"You want to take a bus to Maine?"

"I do, but I need to borrow money. I'll send it back to you as soon as I get there. I promise."

"What about all your stuff?"

"Just stuff. Don't need it."

"What about Bri and your aunt?"

"I'll write them. Maybe you can give them a letter."

Kyle got up. He still had his boots on. He grabbed a sweatshirt and tossed it to me.

"Let's go then."

By the time we arrived at the terminal, I'd written a letter on some notebook paper Kyle had in his car. It said good bye, thanks, and don't worry about my things, I don't need them. It wished Aunt Kitty a speedy recovery, and Bri and Frosty a good 1986. Kyle waited with me until the 8:40 bus on New Year's Day pulled out.

"If I liked guys, you'd so be the one," I said, and boarded.

He smiled and saluted as the bus pulled away from the curb. I chose a seat in the back, dropped into it and sunk my hands deep in the pockets of his hoodie. I felt paper, and pulled out a fifty. Maybe he didn't realize it was there, or maybe it had been intended for me. But it bought me several root beers, a few quarter pounders and as many cinnamon donuts. I could have made a call to Back Kingdom. Twice I'd had the receiver in one hand and the other poised to dial at our roadside stops. I just never got around to making my index finger work until I had no choice, and Westover was an hour away.

Of course, there was a ton of snow. As soon as we'd hit Connecticut it started, and by the time my sneakered feet hit the pavement in Maine a good old-fashioned Nor'easter was bearing down. So unlike the trip I'd made in August, full of hope and Technicolor fantasies of life in the burbs with the well-to-do pretty cousins. I wanted to brush my teeth. And I was tired. Oh, so tired. The seedy station lobby was greasy with brown slush, and a line had formed at the one pay phone on the wall. A blonde girl about my age, her mascara ringing only her right eye, was crying into the phone.

"Please? Please Mom?" She repeated it several times before hanging up. And then she bowed her head into the wind through the heavy glass door and was gone. But that wouldn't be me. My mother would come. The lobby was cold; I bounced from foot to foot to keep my toes from throbbing. Three people to go and the phone would be all mine. I dug my change from the back pocket of my jeans. I had seven quarters, two dimes, and a nickel. Certainly, enough to call home. It hit me that the Maryland gang knew I was gone. They'd absolutely called my mother. Kyle more than

likely had informed someone over there that I was heading home.
Wouldn't my mother ring up Greyhound and get the schedule?
Shouldn't she have already figured out I'd be in Lewisville today,
just now, in fact? What the fuck was wrong with these people.

"It's your turn!" A fat woman in a dirty pink parka nudged me
from behind.

"Sorry." My hands shook as I inserted coins.

After I steadied them enough to feed the coins in the phone it
rang and rang. What would I do if no one picked up? Would I have
to spend the night in this rancid depot across the street from the
strip joint? It was called the Mistletoe, and everyone in the state
of Maine knew it was the gnarliest place around. I sat back down
in a hard orange plastic chair encrusted with the dirt of 100's of
wrung out asses.

"Maybe they'll pick up next time," a man sitting next to me
said. He had a long salt and pepper pony tail and several teeth
scattered in his mouth. They looked like candy corn. His breath
smelled like the grey fluid at the bottom of a garbage pail left in
the rain. I almost gagged.

"Yeah. Most likely," I answered. I didn't know if he was just
being friendly, or if he was up to something. I wished I'd had a
book to read.

"Lots of snow out there, and weather man says more is coming.
Hope your people don't live too far away."

"No. Not too far," I answered. I was worried that he'd keep
talking to me. The depot was tiny, and there'd be no getting away
from him unless I left.

"We're lucky we're in central Maine. We aint getting as much
as up North. But Western Maine sposed to get hit the hardest."

"Oh. Wow," I said. But now I was really worried. Westover
was right along the NH border, about as west as it gets. Maybe
they'd lost power? Maybe phone lines were down? If it was snow-
ing that hard at home, why weren't they inside staying out of the
storm?

"I'm going to try again," I said, and left my new friend sitting
alone. But still no one picked up. I went into the ladies' room,
hoping that he'd be gone when I returned. The depot had emptied

out. We were the only two left, and it was late. I doubted any more buses were coming or going tonight, and I wondered what I'd do if they closed before I could get home. I sat in a stall for at least 30 minutes, and a knock came on the door.

"We're closing up!"

I came out and was relieved to see that the guy was gone. Only me and the man who worked the window remained.

"I couldn't get a hold of anyone at home."

"That's rough," the man said.   His nametag read Chris.

"Where should I go?"

"That depends. Do you have any money for a hotel?"

I had about 30 bucks and I told him so.

"They got rooms to let over the Mistletoe. That's about all you'll get with short money."

"May I call again one more time?

"Okay, but make it quick."

Once again, I dropped in my coins and dialed.

"Hello?"

"El!! El. It's me. Please. I'm at the bus in Lewisville. Ask Karl to come and get me. Please."

"Karl!" I heard my sister explain where I was.

"Liza, I'm on my way," Karl said. "The roads are terrible. It could take a couple of hours. But I'm coming."

He hung up. I turned to Chris who was looking sort of pissed that he wasn't on his way home at 11:00PM on a snowy Sunday night.

"Where should I wait?"

"Not much is open. The Mistletoe is."

"I'm underage."

"Do you think they actually card anyone over there? It's your best bet."

He ushered me out the door. It was freezing and the wind was picking up. Chris turned left and walked up the hill away from his little window, and I stood gazing across the street at the flashing yellow and orange neon sign that blinked Mistletoe into the blustery January night. Three days ago, at this time I was making out with Gemma, and hoping for a great New Year. Now I was about to head into the stench of a seedy strip joint and have a drink. If they'd actually serve me, I was going to ask for a laphroaig and silently toast to Gemma.

The first thing I saw was an old woman dancing. I could tell she was old from the way her lackluster flesh fell from her thighs and breasts. As though it took all she had to shake her boobs around. They were heavy and droopy. Her hair was frizzy and orange. Her blue eye shadow had been unevenly applied—much heavier handed on the left eye than the right. All she wore was a hot pink sequined G-string and matching stiletto heels.

Six men sat at the bar, and a young college aged couple was drinking beer at a small table in the back. As Chris had said, no one asked to see any ID. My entrance into the bar was barely noticed. I was hoping I could sit quietly over by the couple, and bide my time for an hour or so. Through the window on the door I could keep an eye out for Karl's decrepit Dodge Dart. It was at least warm, and the lights were low—restful in an odd sort of way. I did feel sad for the old woman, but I didn't have to watch her dance.

"Hey! Is that you?"

The guy from the depot slid off his stool and headed my way. He pulled out a chair and joined me, lit a Tiperello and introduced himself.

"I'm Claude," he said, and flashed his seven teeth. He then extended his hand to shake.

"I'm Tessa." I'm not sure why I said that. Perhaps I thought it made me less real.

"Pretty name for a pretty girl. Can I buy you a drink?"

"I'll have a laphroaig."

"I don't know what that is. How about a Coors?"

I didn't know what that was, but I said sure. And they kept coming. The old red-headed dancer finally got off the stage some-where around the third beer. I didn't like the taste of them at all, but the floaty feeling was good. A younger, prettier olive-skinned tall girl stripped to a slowish Joe Cocker song. I couldn't take my eyes off her. She reminded me of Gemma—swarthy with heavy eye lids.

"You like her?" Claude lit another Tiperello.

"She's a good dancer." I didn't want him to think I was imagining touching her body.

"Her name's Michelle. She's a half breed from the county. I can introduce the two of you if you want. You'd be good together."

"You know her?" I wasn't sure what he meant by good together. Did he know I liked girls? Could he tell? Did he care?

"Yeah. I manage this place. I hire most of the girls. You could work here if you wanted."

Wow. There I was with Claude, encircled in his sweet smoke and hearing all about Michelle, the beautiful "half-breed" exotic dancer.

"I picked her up in the bus station, just like you. She ran away from her dad in Aroostook. That was two years ago."

"Well, I've got a ride coming. My mom's boyfriend is on his way. So, I can't dance here." I wanted to be polite. But I was getting a little afraid of what was around the corner. It seemed this man was not in the depot for any other reason except to find fresh meat.

"Everyone's mother's boyfriend is coming to get them, sweetie. But by last call and no one shows, we've got food and a warm room upstairs for girls just like you."

Despite the three beers, I was conscious of time. I looked down at my watch and it had been a little over an hour since I'd called home. Karl warned me it would be slow going, but he'd be here by last call so my eyes were on the depot.

"I'll have Michelle join us after her set. You'd like that, I'll bet."

"Why do you say that?"

"I can tell when girls like boys and when they like girls. Makes no never mind to me. I like people all the same. They nice to me, is all that I care about it."

Claude scraped his chair back, flashed his seven teeth again, and headed to the bar where he grabbed a couple more beers, and then made his way to the platform where Michelle was gyrating against a pole. She wore a feathered headdress and fringed stilettos to resemble moccasins, and fringe was pasted to her nipples and suede G-string. When the blue spot hit her just right, I could see an old bruise turning yellow on her thigh. I ran out the door.

It was freezing, and Kyle's sweatshirt and my canvas sneakers were no match for the Nor-Easter that was sinking its teeth into Lewisville.

As far as I could see through the thick slant of snow nothing was open. I could wait under the awning of the depot and freeze, not to mention be a sitting duck for Claude, or I could keep moving and lurk in alleys where I could keep the road in my sight. I headed down the hill toward the big bridge over the Androscoggin. Just shy of the river between the old Bates Mill and Ward Brothers was the perfect crevice to wedge myself into, and there, I'd see Karl as he came to my rescue.

It had been two hours since I'd called. I let my mind wander. I imagined that Claude would come looking for me and force me to dance, or maybe the beautiful Michelle would be on her way home and see me shivering in the alley and invite me to her attic room on the other side of the tracks where she would make me orange pekoe tea and share her single bed piled with musty quilts. I imagined that Karl drove off the road in a white out somewhere between Westover and Lewisville, and that he'd leave his car, get disoriented and freeze to death in a snow bank because of me. I imagined that hypothermia would slowly descend and that I'd be found all hard and blue at first light by a snow plow guy and that he'd have nightmares forever because of me.

My toes were stinging. My fingertips were too, even in the pockets of Kyle's hoodie. My face felt stiff and numb. I decided I must generate body heat like in the movies and began a series of jumping jacks. I sang Joni Mitchell songs under my breath that Aunt Serena used to play so my mind would stay alert. I was starting to think my only choice to keep from freezing to death was to return to Claude at the Mistletoe. "Fifteen more minutes," I said to myself. And I started to count. Car lights were coming from the top of the hill. Not the direction Karl would be approaching from. Who was driving around this late on a Sunday in the middle of a Nor'Easter? I craned my neck out of my crevice to find a police car coming into view.

"Shit," I whispered to myself. "It's slowing down."

The cruiser glided into the drift along the curb and stopped. I hadn't done anything wrong, had I? I did have booze. That was against the law. Maybe they were going to arrest me? But how would they know. Maybe Claude reported me missing?

"Are you Liza de Kooning?"

"Yes," I answered, and my heart began to thrash in my ribcage like a wild bird.

"Are you in some sort of trouble Miss?" The driver, a large red-faced man, was doing all the talking. His face was kind.

"Just waiting for a ride."

"From Karl Pulsifer?"

"Yes," I emerged from the shadows into the glow of the high beams. "Is he okay?"

"Why don't you get in the cruiser? It's warm in here," said the younger guy in the passenger seat. He looked like a kid.

"Is Karl okay?"

He was dead. Just as I'd thought. Because of me. My mom lost her husband, her sister, and now her new husband, because of me.

"He's okay, but he's not going to make it tonight, and you can't stand in the alley or you'll catch pneumonia, or worse," said the kid-cop.

I opened the door in the back. It smelled of car heat and onions and felt like a sauna. Kyle had one at his house, and we all went in there one damp November evening that seemed like a million years ago instead of a month ago.

"How'd you know who I was waiting for?"

"We responded to a car off the road, and it was Karl's. We found him walking toward the Super 8. He told us that you were waiting at the Depot." The big one was doing all the talking now.

"He's not coming for me tonight?" It was too much. I could feel the lump in my throat forming already.

"The roads from up your way are impassable. He made it to Turner and had to abandon the vehicle. He'll collect you in the morning after his car gets dug out. It's supposed to lighten up soon."

"Collect me? Where?"

"It's okay, Liza," the kid said. "You can hang out at the station house. It's safe and we can give you a blanket and some food and you can catch a few zzzz's."

"No!" I was yelling. "I came all the way from Maryland, and I want to go home!"

"I know Liza," the kid said. "Just not tonight."

They pulled out and headed to the police station. When Karl picked me up in the morning, I ran to him. I'd not felt this way—like a small helpless child—possibly ever. But of course, I didn't really know. Maybe at one time I'd been that child. He picked me up and lifted my feet from the floor. "Let's go home," was all he said.

We pulled up to Back Kingdom that morning and snow was everywhere. The branches of the huge red pines in front were laden with its weight. I pushed open the back door of the old Dart and it would not give way against the three-foot snow bank, so I crawled across the seat to the opposite side. I stood in the middle of our street and turned in all directions. Our little village of Westover looked like the North Pole. The several farm houses along this stretch of road, the general store, and the Congo church were all sparkling in the morning sun.

"Liza," my mother, from our porch, yelled. El stood next to her—her long dark hair ablaze with glistening flakes. I ran up the snowy steps into their arms, and they pulled me through the door to a crackling fire. Karl remained outside shoveling the walk.

"Where's the tree?" It was a strange first thing to say to my mother and sister whom I hadn't seen since August.

"We took it down," El said. "We always take it down on New Year's."

"I know, but I really wanted to see it."

"Let's go get another one!" My mother dashed out the front door to where Karl was bent over his shovel. "Karl! We need your help. We have to go get a tree!"

And so, the four of us trudged off into the deep woods behind Back Kingdom, past Fairy Shrimp Spa, Karl with axe in hand, and we dragged home a perfectly conical seven foot Eastern White. We decorated it all day to my mother's Johnny Cash Christmas album, and drank hot mulled apple cider.

"It's grander than last year's," she reliably said. We left that tree up through Ground Hog day.

Chapter 14

A relatively peaceful life unfolded. I was content in Back Kingdom. For a while. And I hung onto those shining dangling threads for as long as I could. I did make up stories in my head to convince myself how lovely and serene it was to be back in my hometown, a slash, a crater in the granite, surrounded by jagged peaks, and swallowed up in snow nine months out of the year. I did say pleasing things to my mother, my twin, her pseudo-grunge gang of red-hot chili peppers wannabees, stoners. I did feign interest in Karl's quiet and monotone prophesies about the end of the world as we knew it if we all continued to shower so much.

My mother was quiet, mostly. Medicated, but I guess, as she said, "In a good way." I may have eased into my predicament of hating where I lived, and hating most of the people who surrounded us in our odd life in the big peeling yellow failing road house since Aunt Serena had left, but I ultimately didn't. The little bit of business we'd once had died down. The house wasn't cleaned often enough, and so eventually guests just dried up. With the exception of a hiker or two who really didn't give a rat's ass if the linens matched, or dust bunnies lolled under the bed, we had no one.

I may have just good-naturedly bided my time, maybe go to college somewhere, or work at the 4H camp Candy ran. We were in touch, in a careful and controlled way. Her letters were sisterly, kind and encouraging. She seemed to think I was her Eliza Doolittle, and constantly suggested books I should read, thoughts I should think and opinions I should espouse. And I usually did. I may have just done what I needed to do to survive the next couple of years in Westover as a young gay woman terrified to come out, if Trinka and Matthew had not showed up.

It was me who answered the phone that night. The slightly greasy, avocado green phone that hung on the kitchen wall and smelled slightly of curry for reasons I never understood. We mostly existed on general store food—ham hoagies, tuna subs, chicken fingers and pizza. It was Tuesday, because that was the day my mother had therapy in Rexford. I remember that. And it was early spring—or as we call it in Maine, mud season, because I looked down on the kitchen floor as I picked up the receiver to see that I'd managed to track in globs of it on the bottom of my boots. I'd been out to fairy shrimp spa to write to Candy.

"Hello, Back Kingdom Road House," I said

"May I speak with Violet deKooning?"

"I'm sorry," I said. "She's not here. May I take a message?"

"My name is Trinka. Trinka Lovejoy." The voice was low and soft. She spoke in a halting way, like she was reaching for the next word. The name rang a bell, but I didn't know why. She gave me her number, thanked me, and said goodbye. No one really called any of us. If the phone rang, it was usually for Elspeth, or occasionally Karl—someone from the West Paris Academy reminding him of a faculty meeting. Mom didn't get calls. Later that evening, when she came home from Roxford with Karl, I passed along the message. She grasped Karl's wrist and I recognized That Look. The one that heralded her dysregulation, that flipped the switch to her amygdala, that made my stomach lurch.

"It's okay, Vi," Karl said.

"What do I do?" My mother sunk into the couch.

"What's the deal?" I wanted to know. I'd decided when I moved back from Maryland that I'd not abide secrets. Karl answered: "Trinka and Matt are the folks who used to run this place. Your aunt's friends. It's where she went when she left."

I wasn't sure why this information alone would create panic in my mother.

"I'm not calling them back," she said.

"Oh, really Mom? Well, I am."

"The call was for your mother," Karl said. "You will not call them back."

I think it was the first time Karl commanded me about anything.

"Fuck you," I said, also a first, and walked toward the phone where the message was pinned on the cork board. Karl blocked my way. I knew he would not, ever, lay a hand on me. El walked in the house, high, as usual. Our mother and Karl seemed never to notice, or care. Her usual big eyes, now a slit, darted from me to Karl.

"What the hell is going on?"

"Karl doesn't want me to call Trinka Lovejoy back."

"Who's Trinka Lovejoy?" She opened the fridge.

"The Colorado people. Aunt Serena's friends. You know, the ones we got this place from."

El pulled a left-over slab of frozen lasagna from the back of the fridge and popped it in the microwave.

"Nice," she said.

"You're so fucking stoned," I said, and moved for the phone. Karl didn't budge.

"I want to know what's going on. I'm sick of this shit," I said, and reached over Karl's head to grab the receiver, but he deflected my arm with his shoulder.

"Did you really just stop me from making a call in my own house? It's probably about Aunt Serena!"

"The call was for your mother, and your mother will return it when she wishes."

"Woe, I'm not getting into this shit," El said. "Goodnight." She tossed her plate in the sink and disappeared up the back staircase.

"Karl," my mother said, "I'll call Trinka."

I expected that I'd feel relieved, triumphant. But my hands and feet went cold, and my mouth tasted metallic. Of course, I knew that this was not a mere call from what for us was a total stranger. I knew that if Trinka Lovejoy, the woman with whom my aunt was staying since she ran away from home, was calling my mother, it was with bad news.

"Don't worry about it, Mom. Really. It's okay. You don't have to call. I'm sorry."

She brushed past me with deadened eyes. The only life in her face flickered around her mouth, a twitch where her lips met in the corners. I wondered why I'd never noticed this before, and thought that maybe it was new tic—special for just this occasion. I wouldn't stay in the kitchen for this call. The back staircase, rarely travelled by any of us for its steepness and stupidly small steps as though designed for a child's foot, that had just moments ago served my sister's egress was now my get-a-way as well. I took them three at a time, palms flat against the opposite walls for ballast. My heart thudding when I reached the third floor.

I heard El sobbing from my room. "What are you doing in here?"

"She's dead, you know. This time she really is."

"Shut up. You're high."

"It doesn't change the fact that she's dead."

From the kitchen, three floors below through a heavy oaken door, it came up—at first a low -frequency rumble. The power of that sound grew as it got closer to us, like the call of a blue whale.

"There it is," El said. "The Scream number two."

Three days later they arrived.

Chapter 15

My mother returned to her bed. But unlike when my dad died, she occasionally appeared. An effort, at least, was made to attend to what El and I needed—she would ask us each morning how we were doing; she just didn't wait for us to answer before she skulked away. It was Karl who was uncharacteristically absent. He didn't go to work, feed us general store dinners, drag a broom across the kitchen floor every evening or bring in the mail. El was a total train wreck. She sobbed all day, and, I think, even in her sleep, or at least what there was of sleep. I tried crying, but it didn't work. For me, it was a relief when the Lovejoys finally appeared with Aunt Serena in a Wal-Mart bag.

We assembled on the couch at 2:00 that Saturday. Trinka had said they would land in Portland around 11:45, so we figured by the time they rented a car and got here it may be around two, and we were nothing if not ready for horrible news. I had worked out the conversations we'd have in my head over and over for the week between the phone call and this, their arrival. I had the whole sordid scene committed to memory—had even practiced my indignant outrage that they'd let her die. These utterly grotesque and brain-dead losers living their squalid and ridiculous lives "off-the-grid" as though this somehow elevated them from those of us who tried to fit in, or at least pass.

And then, it was 2:45, and we sat like stone— shoulder to shoulder on our tawdry jade green velvet couch. I had begun sweating quite some time ago. A small fire burned to take the spring chill away, but the day was turning warmer than we'd expected.

"Those motherfuckers better show," El said. No one responded. Trinka and Matthew chose the moment I headed into the bathroom to arrive. I heard three sharp knocks as soon as my butt hit the bowl. Of course, in my imaginary scene, I was the one who answered the door. I leapt from the seat as though lava were spewing from the leach field. Just as I entered the living room Karl was motioning for them to have a seat across from us in the two equally fusty green chairs.

"We're both so sorry for your loss," Matthew said. He was florid, with a thinning fringe of pale hair that circled his greasy dome, and badly pock-marked bloated face. He reeked of onions. Trinka barely stood five feet, if that even, and had the same lifeless pale hair, but her eyes were a bright dark blue and her small pouty mouth belonged on the face of a child.

"Thank you," my mother said. "But it feels like a hollow and sentimental comment."

"We loved Serena, you know," Trinka said. "In any event, we just felt it was important to bring you her ashes in person." With this, she stood up, crossed to my mother, and thrust a Wal-mart bag at her. My mother actually closed her eyes and clasped her hands in her lap. Karl rose.

"I think you folks will need to leave," he said.

"Karl, right?" Matthew also rose. He was as tall as Karl. "What, exactly, have we done wrong? We've been friends with Serena for over 20 years. We were once all house-mates in our college days. Truth is, she couldn't tolerate life with you and Violet. She felt she had no choice. She felt that she had to escape an impossible situation. All we did was open the door."

It was me now springing up from the couch. "You let her kill herself."

"It's impossible to stop someone from killing themselves if they are intent on doing just that. She opened her veins in the tub— not us."

"That's bullshit," El said.

"Look, he said, "we came all the way to Maine to bring you her ashes, and we could have stuck them in a box and tossed them in the mail. Trinka and I didn't kill Serena. Serena killed Serena, and no, we didn't see any signs. Besides her being depressed, which she almost always was, she was her usual."

Matthew plunked down in his chair and reached for a large faded and frayed canvas tote with stenciled trees all over it. He pulled out a double-bagged bundle of Wal-Mart bags, gave them a shake and re-knotted them.

"Given that you all think we murdered Serena, we'll be on our way. I'll leave the bag here."

My mother sprung from the couch. "You put her in a Wal-Mart bag? Seriously?"

"You wanted a different bag? Like, what, maybe Tiffanys? What the fuck difference does it make?"

"You're a terrible person," El said.

"He's not a terrible person, actually," Trinka said. "He's actually a kind and caring man, and he cared deeply for Serena. I did too. We both very much loved her."

"And so you know," Matthew said, directly to Karl, "She very much loved you, but you couldn't keep your hands off her sister."

I never saw Karl move so fast. I truly didn't think he was capable of such vigor. But there he was, with his fist in Matthew's face. Trinka screamed. Matthew grabbed for Karl's collar, but Karl dodged his reach and pushed him into the chair. "I wouldn't, if I were you," was all Karl said before he walked out the back door.

Trinka moved to Matthew's side, took him by the elbow and pulled him up from the chair. "Let's get out of here," she said.

"They're all nuts." The two of them left.

Chapter 16

A few weeks after Serena's ashes were returned to us, my mother upgraded the Wal-Mart bag to a shoe box, refused to consider where the ashes should ultimately go, claimed it was her decision where to disperse them, if at all, and Karl withdrew from all of us for months. El was now never home, unless it was to take a shower and pick up clean clothes, having almost entirely moved in with the boyfriend, and I once again decided this was a shitty family and a shitty place to live.

Candace continued to promise a job at the 4-H camp in Wheeling. I knew nothing about West Virginia, but anyplace sounded good to me. I was heading into my senior year in the fall. I would do whatever it took to graduate early, or maybe get a GED, or anything in between to not have to endure another year at Back Kingdom.

"I'm thinking of trying to split," I said to El. We were sitting in the late May sun on the soggy bank of Fairy Shrimp Spa.

"Take me," she said.

"You won't leave your stud muffin."

"This is true," she said. "Very true. He keeps me sane, and I love him very very much."

I never knew what to say when El started talking about being in love. I was jealous, mostly, because I never got to finish loving Gemma. And I wanted someone to talk to about her. My unrequited love, and my truncated attempt to express that love. And if not El, who? So, I went for it. Another thing weighed heavily on my mind. What did The Lovejoys mean when they both spoke of their great love for Aunt Serena? I'd wanted to run this by El since their visit. Fairy Shrimp Spa had a way of inspiring courage and honesty.

"El," I said, "did you get the impression that maybe Aunt Serena was with both of them?"

"Both of who?"

"The freakazoids who delivered our beloved aunt to us in a Wal-Mart bag."

El stared me down with her purple snake eyes. "Like as in a romantic thing?"

I nodded, and tried to hold her gaze, but ended up looking at my feet.

"Where do you come up with this stuff? I mean, Jesus Liza. A menage et trois?"

"Some people do that sort of thing. I've read about it. Aunt Serena was a free spirit, so I could imagine that they might have all been together."

"Well, guess what? I'm not going to imagine it."

"Would it change your mind about her, I mean, if they were together?"

"I don't know," she said.

We sat. The damp was seeping through my jeans, and the sun was beginning its descent behind the Whites.

"Would you think differently of me if I told you that I fell in love with a girl when I was in Maryland?"

"No."

Five minutes later we were heading back to the house, and we never spoke of Aunt Serena's love life, nor mine, again. That August I headed out to West Virginia for my new job. Once again, I was on a bus. The sun rose in a purple splash as we rolled down I-95 South. I felt no dread, and only a little excitement. I wanted to feel more. But once I was gone again, I was gone.

And there was Molly.

Book Two
Chapter 1

Ann Arbor and Owls Head

My girlfriend Molly doesn't think we can leave Ann Arbor. "I want to grow old and grey with you in the city that I love," she says, as we prepare the same breakfast that we have every morning--whole wheat raisin toast and hard-boiled eggs.

"Good," I usually answer, "Since I already have my first greys."

"It's beautiful," Molly says and pulls me into her ample warm body, that smells slightly of onions, but I find it a comfort, that smell, like a kitchen.

"It's not beautiful, Mol, it's dingy. And I'm not ready for it. Twenty-eight's too young."

I gingerly withdraw from her embrace. She holds on a little too long, and I wonder if she notices the stiffness of my body. I return from the fridge with the soy milk for my gunpowder tea and resume my place across from her. At the last minute, I grab the cream instead. I pass the kitchen window from where I have a perfect view of the towering Balsam that's covered in blue lights and opalescent garland. Every year the neighborhood council decks this tree out in the middle of the small park where mothers collect with their babies. I think the tree is beautiful.

"I'm not convinced that Ann Arbor should be my home forever. There are other places I think I'd prefer to live and work."

"Like Maine, right? We keep having the same conversation,"

she says, but smiles at me. I miss the western foothills of Maine and pine for the company of my sister and mother—in that order.

"And I suspect we'll continue to as long as we never come to a natural resting place," I add. I pop an entire hardboiled egg into my mouth. It is exactly the right size.

"I thought you were terrified of going back there. To those people," she says, still smiling.

"Those people are my family, Mol." But it does terrify me to return to the dark dense North, the bleak mornings in the dead of February that leave me breathless from the cold. And the visits from Karl to my mother's bedroom, his heavy steel-toed boots clopping up the stairs. But mostly the low thrum of madness still resonates in my head. My mother's brittle smile lingers like a childhood image of an absurd Halloween mask. The one that scares you but you don't why it should.

In the years that our mother was a small, fragile wooden craft in a turbulent sea, and we her passengers, it was a strange life, full of unwelcome surprises, and I didn't want to add any more strangeness to it. So, when I met Molly at the 4-H camp where Candace found me a job, I, a 17-year-old ropes instructor was ripe for salvation. My vital juices were spilling over. And there was Molly. My 24-year-old boss, ready to lap them up with her tongue. And I followed her like a kitten.

"Aren't you happy here?" She fiddles with her heavy red glasses. Bites the end of the left ear piece.

"I'm happy Mol." And it is true that I am, just not most of the time. I adjust the chair so I can keep the tree in my view. I'm worried about the budworm.

"Well then there's no issue, right?" She bites the right ear piece. It's gross that she puts her glasses in her mouth. But I hold myself back from commenting.

"Well, I didn't say there was, baby. I just want to float out the possibility that there could be a life outside of Ann Arbor for us. That's all." I don't mention that there could be a life outside of Ann Arbor for me. How can I try to drag her away from her beloved park, her beloved dam, her beloved farmer's market? The daily rituals that hold her in her olive skin bejeweled with stunningly black freckles. Molly is a creature of pattern. These patterns create a design in which Molly and I are the center.

I carry our breakfast dishes to the little porcelain chipped sink as I have done for 3,000 mornings. I note the neat crusts of toast arranged on her plate that she leaves behind each and every one of those mornings, and that I feel I must eat because I can't condone the waste. Hence the size of my hips since I've been Molly's lover.

"But you float it out a few times a week," she says. And again, she smiles.

I do float it out a few times a week. And so, the conversation follows the script our stale union has penned over the past couple of years. And without the slightest variation, I turn from the sink, having eaten her crusts, smile, and say: "I know. It must be getting old for you. I'll stop."

At which point she says: "I love you so much, Liza. If I thought you'd be truly happy back there, I'd pack our stuff tomorrow. (I don't really believe that, and I run the water to drown her out for a moment.) But you're talking about the place you fled. The family you fled. I think you're just confused about your next move because you're finishing grad school. That's normal."

"You're right," I say. I shove Ms. Piggy, her favorite cat, off the table a little more brashly than Molly likes. She immediately scoops her up and kisses her. Molly has three fat lazy spayed cats, Miss Piggy, Kermit and Gonzo—her children, as she calls them. She's made it clear that she doesn't wish to "spawn." I never liked the Muppets. I thought they were stupid. And I'd rather have real children. My biological clock is now a grenade.

"Leave her alone. She's fine. She's a cat. She shits in a box."

She shoots me The Look. The one that says: This isn't about the cats. Don't take it out on them.

I know she's not right--I'm not confused at all. I know she'd be devastated if I contracted from her life. I know she loves me. And I know that she doesn't understand that I don't love her the way I used to. But I owe her so much; it's hard to fathom that I would ever disappoint her. It was Molly, doggedly persistent and supernaturally focused, who held my hand as I tentatively paved my way out of Back Kingdom. It was Molly that encouraged me to get my GED, go to community college, and onto bigger and better things. And mostly, away from "drama" as my Aunt Serena called it. She offered the sanctuary of sameness. The sameness of our bodies. The sameness of our meals. The sameness of our brazen declarations of love for the folds of one another's anguish.

"Well, I have to get rolling," she says. She places Ms. Piggy gently on the floor, sighs when she gets up from the orange wooden chair. Grunts when she bends to stroke Ms. Piggy one last time before leaving. She's too young to be making old sounds at 34.

"We have the entire junior high from Lansing coming to the museum today."

She places an uninspired kiss on my cheek and says: "We have to celebrate tonight! This is your very last day of grad school ever!" and goes off to her park ranger job. I linger at the window. It's a bright day and a ribbon of sunlight boomerangs off the garland hanging on my tree. I head to the phone. I call my mother, or Elspeth, when I'm weary of Molly. My mother is a particularly good listener. She attributes it to the years of her intense grief over my father, but she doesn't dispense advice. I don't believe that in such grief a person returns to "their old selves." I think they're transformed. My mother certainly was. She returned to us a good mother, but a different one that last time she was hospitalized, shortly after our visit from the Lovejoys. Subdued. Philosophical. Distant.

My sister, on the other hand, is quick to go directly to the advice she thinks I want. I call her. As the phone is ringing, I imagine her just waking up in the cavernous sun-drenched corn-flower blue Victorian on the coast that she and our mother live in now with Karl. I see her in a mustard colored T-shirt over black gym shorts. Her fine blue-black hair in the single braid she plaits every night to keep it from tangling.

I lean against the sink; we don't have a cordless phone, and the receiver doesn't reach the kitchen chairs. Ms. Piggy curls her long gray tail around my ankles and purrs. Elspeth cuts to the chase the second she understands why I'm calling. It's not a big leap. There have been calls like it before.

"Leave her, Liza. Molly is great in so many ways, but she's a colossal control freak."

"I know, but she's also really smart and loyal. And really dedicated to her job, and has been nothing but kind to me."

"You realize you just described a maiden aunt?"

"Okay, so maybe she's a maiden aunt, but what about Ted? Is he the right guy for you?"

"You called me to talk about whether or not Ted is the right guy for me? I don't think that's really why."

I hear the water running in the big cast iron sink.

"Well, he is married," I say. I don't add that he's 42 years old, and is a state trooper.

I wonder about Elspeth being in any position to give advice. She's 28 and has never attempted to leave home.

"I'm not going there, Liza. I'm not taking the bait. You called about you, not me."

"Elspeth," I say, "you're right. But I do still have some feelings for her. I'd miss her, El. I really would. Her skin is always warm. It's not so easy." And it's not.

"Okay, so we've established she's not a reptile. What else?"

"She rubs my feet."

"That's all you need? I think you're really reaching. And it is easy. You leave or you don't. You're happy or you're not."

"It's not a decision," I say. "It's a process."

"You're so full of shit. It's a decision. You commit and you figure out the details later."

"I don't know, El. I just don't know."

"And how's that going for you, all this not knowing? Of course, you know. You wake up every day and know. So leave already. Kiss her goodbye and go."

"I love you. You're crazy as a loon, but I love you."

"Fuck you," she laughs. "Come home."

Home. Come Home. And I repeat those words aloud. As though to roll them around in my mouth. As though to taste them. And they are salty.

"Yes, sister. Home."

But I'm not sure what that is. I've never lived in the big blue Victorian on the forlorn dead end street in Owls Head. I've only heard about it. Seen a photo or two. By the time my mother and Elspeth left the road house and moved to the coast I was already gone.

"Are you still there?" She clanks something in the sink. It's loud even over the phone.

"I'm still here," I answer. Ms. Piggy has jumped onto the counter and is rubbing against my hip. I reflexively dip my hand into her plush fur.

"Is the tree up yet?"

"This week-end," she says.

"How's mom?"

"Good. The nursery is getting busy again with Christmas coming. She and Karl make wreathes. The same old."

My mother seems at peace. I am mostly happy for her.

"Do you miss Aunt Serena?" I ask. This question surprises me.

"That's pretty random. Where did that come from?"

"I don't know. I guess I just sort of miss her lately. I keep thinking she'd have something to add to the Molly conversation."

"Does missing mom and Serena have something to do with why today is different?"

"What do you mean?" Elspeth is going in for the kill. The way she does.

"Well, today is different. Today you seem to have reached some critical pass, right? About you and Molly?"

"I'm not sure. Maybe it's school ending. Maybe it's the holidays," I say. And I think it is. I look at the tree again out my window. I want to smell it.

"For what it's worth, Aunt Serena would encourage you to do what's right for you, and I think you've made it clear that what's right is to leave Molly. But I gotta get to work. The psycho-kiddies are waiting to make papier mache Christmas angels. I'll leave you with one thought: come home."

"Okay. Okay. Maybe I will." And I half believe it. "I gotta go to class," I say. I hang up. Miss Piggy is now nestled into the curve of my thigh. I almost hate to disturb her.

I ride the bus, trying to get excited about my last day of classes and biological controls for the cherry fruit fly. As we glide down Cambridge, I marvel at what good lesbians we are. The historian and the organic farmer. With the dream we once shared of weaving her love of local history and my love of farming into a life together here in Michigan.

I ride the bus still, and I'm so pissed off I could spit. Or scream. Like the bumper sticker that says it's been lovely but now I have to scream. Our days are lovely. Filled with chick- singer folk music warbling through the apartment and little vegan dinner parties with other dykes. I dream of steak and cheese subs and soggy fries. And Molly and I never ever fight. Because Molly wants to keep me. She wants to keep me. To pat me and stroke me. And if she does it enough, I'll respond, like Miss Piggy, Gonzo and Kermit will never do.

I ride the bus still, and weep for the ending that I know is here, because spitting or screaming is not an option on the bus. And I despise the ending even though my life depends on it. And I weep more because weeping on busses is so tawdry, or is it ignoble?

I head directly to the student center for my daily sticky bun and espresso—my shadow breakfast—the counterpoint to my sepulchral conjugal repast. It's stuffy. The smell of dusty heat makes me dizzy. I try to drown out the shrill din of so many conversations because my head is starting to ache. I actually have 17 minutes before class and look forward to getting outside where I can sit in the brisk December morning on a solitary bench with my debacle of a breakfast.

"Come home," my raven-haired twin said.

Chapter 2

On my way back to the apartment the sky was getting purple and snowflakes were melting on the bus windows.

"Excuse me. I'm getting off."

I looked out my window. Had I missed my stop? "Of course," I said and moved my feet into the aisle so my neighbor could make her way to the exit. I wondered who this brusque middle-aged woman was in her dowdy brown hat and if she was happy with her mate waiting at home in a warm kitchen.

It was 4:50. I'd be home by 5. Molly would follow around six from work. Would I leave her tonight? What if she was making me a fancy celebration dinner to signify the end of grad school? Maybe I'd go along with it all. Keep it light and festive. Drop the bomb in the morning? Or maybe I'd just stay on here with my friends and get a research grant and climb into the messy sour smelling saggy double bed with Molly's dead grandmother's ugly-ass brown and orange quilt thrown over the top, all covered in cat hair.

I could see the beautiful tree lit up across from our place. I was almost home. When I got off, I looked up at our living room window. Lights were on. It was unusual for Molly to beat me home. I didn't want to go in yet. I crossed the street and stood at the base of the big sparkling tree in the park. I loved over-the-top trees. I shouldn't support tree farming, and cutting down trees to deco-

rate for three weeks and then toss to the curb. I shouldn't. But
I did. Every Christmas in Back Kingdom my Aunt Serena made a
huge deal about the winter solstice. We started in on preparations
for what she called the "big 3"—Solstice, Christmas, and Epiphany. We celebrated from the 21st through the 5th of January. "Solstice to Epiphany," Aunt Serena would day. Each 20th, we snow
shoed out past fairy shrimp spa into the deep woods that stretched
through the notch to Canada, and with Karl's help cut down and
dragged home an enormous tree. My mother didn't like to get
too cold, so she stayed behind and made glittery decorations, and
baked pecan sandies. When we arrived, the tree stand was filled
with water, positioned and waiting for us.

"Oh my God!" That would be Mom. "I think that's even grander than last year's tree!"

Molly wasn't a big fan. She'd conceded to a small tree to put on
our piano bench. "Not too ostentatious," she'd say. It went up on
December 23rd and came down on Boxing Day. I decided I would
have a stellar 9-foot tree this year. It would be exactly right for
the big Victorian in Owls Head, its silver star brushing against
the old tin ceilings El had mentioned a thousand times. As though
tin ceilings would bring me back. I planned to call El this evening
to tell her to expect me, and to wait for my arrival before anyone
even thought of decorating any trees.

I could hear voices as soon as I unlocked the vestibule door. It
seemed there was a party going on. No doubt a surprise for me. I
put my key in the door and silence descended on the other side. I
pushed it open to a dark and quiet kitchen. At first, I was relieved,
and then of course the explosion of sound and light.

"Surprise!" Eight of our friends stood with wine glasses in
hand. A banner strung across the double doors to our bedroom
read: Mazel Tov Liza in lime green letters. Ella Fitzgerald wafted
from the den and the center island was festooned with lime green
balloons and covered with various Mediterranean vegetarian dishes.

"Wow!" I said and smiled manically. "This is a total surprise,
guys! Thank you!"

"You really didn't know, right babe?" Molly encircled me in her arms.

"No idea!"

Our friend Cynthia passed me a glass of Chianti. "Here you go, darling. How does it feel to be finished grad school?"

"Fucking great." And it was true. That much was true.

Molly disentangled herself from me, plucked her wine glass from the island and raised it in the air. "Here's to my lovely, intelligent Liza, who I thank my lucky stars for each and every day. May she follow her dreams, and may I only hope to be a part of them."

"I'll drink to that!" Joanne raised her glass and clanked Molly's and mine, and the rest followed.

Molly whispered in my ear. "I hope this is okay? You look a bit dazed and confused."

"Moll," I said into her springy hair. "It's great. Really. I'm just pooped."

I drank too much wine. I just kept going back for more and more. It seemed never to run out. Every time I headed for the island to pour another glass, two more bottles were uncorked and waiting, all red and shimmery. Joanne and Cynthia were still there at 11:00. They were both shit-faced. I was well on my way.

"Lizzy Lou," Joanne said. I hated that name, but that's what she always called me. "Word on the street is you've been talking about leaving us?"

"Word on the street?" A little roiling in my belly juices signaled a hard time ahead. "Or word from Molly Schneider?"

"Jo," Cynthia said, and sunk back into the couch against her girlfriend, "it's really late. I'm drunk. Let's split."

"It seems you've been off all night, Liza," Joanne persisted. "What's up?"

Molly foisted herself from the bean bag with a grunt and began clearing off the coffee table. Miss Piggy trotted over and wrapped herself around Molly's leg.

"In what way?" I drained the last little silty puddle of booze from my glass. I registered the edge in my voice.

"Like you want to be anyplace but here."

Cynthia looked at me and shook her head as though to say here we go. She rarely stood up to Joanne, and Joanne loved to run all of our lives.

"Very astute of you Jo. Because that is exactly the case. But its between me and Molly." I stood up. My signal that the party was over.

"Indeed," said Jo, and stood up to her full 6 feet and stared me down. She had been Molly's best friend since college. "Let's go Cyn."

"Molly?" I called from the living room. I could hear the bathroom sink running, and Molly spitting.

"Can't hear you, babe. Water's running."

"Then turn it off."

I was fired up. Jo's abrasiveness always got me hot and bothered. I'd decided to have the Big Talk right now.

Molly emerged in her flannel shirt and sweats, toothbrush in hand. "What's up?"

"Sit," I said, and plunked myself down into the velvet chair next to Kermit. He crawled into my lap.

"Oh-oh. This is a sit-down conversation?"

"Molly, I've decided to go to Maine to see my family for the holidays."

"Am I invited?" She had not sat.

"No. Moll. I'm going alone to sort of think some things through."

"But you're coming back, though, right?"

"I'm not sure."

"Wow." She dropped onto the couch and buried her face in her hands. "I can't believe this is happening." She looked up at me, her face twisted into a knot. I didn't feel the slightest bit sad for her. I felt a little shocked at my callousness.

"I'll probably catch a bus tomorrow. I'll take as much as I can with me. Don't worry about the rest. If I don't end up coming back, just toss it."

We kept a futon couch in a tiny den off the back of the kitchen. It was always ice cold in there; it used to be a porch. I couldn't wait to just curl up alone under a bunch of scratchy army blankets and fall into a heavy sleep. But I wondered if my excitement about leaving would make it impossible to actually fall asleep, so I grabbed a Louise Erdrich novel I'd been waiting to read from the book case. I also snagged the receiver as I passed by the phone, dialed my sister and pulled it into the den with me. The cord bare-ly made it. I told her I was getting on a bus in the morning. She whooped and hollered. I felt fucking great.

Chapter 3

Molly was gone in the morning. I slept late, as cold as it was. It was well after nine. I wrapped the blankets around me and walked into the kitchen—found her note on the island under an empty wine bottle from last night.

My lovely Liza:

I am stunned at your cruelty. When Candy brought you to work at 4-H that first summer in Wheeling you were a gawky 17-year-old. Terrified of her own shadow. But I saw a light in your eyes that made me know you could escape your genetic burden and flourish. You once referred to me as your Svengali. I thought you were joking, but I can see now that you must have actually thought that. What makes me angry is not that you thought so, or not even really that you're leaving, but that you never had a meaningful and respectful dialogue with me about your real feelings, and now you just pack your shit and go? I do hope that you can stare yourself down someday and grow up. And forgive me for saying so, but I don't wish you the best, and I doubt you will ever have the best, because you're walking out on the best.

Molly

"Fuck you," I said to the letter. Tore it up in shreds and sprinkled them on the floor. The phone rang.

"Hello?" I was hoping it wasn't Moll.

"Liza! Why aren't you on a bus?!"

"I just woke up El," I said and scooched up on the island.

"I called Greyhound. You can still catch the 10:55. You can be in Augusta by eight tomorrow morning. I have to work, but mom and Karl can pick you up. Get on that bus!"

Gooseflesh sprang up all over my body. Suddenly, I couldn't wait. I glanced at the cat clock on the wall. 9:25. It was true I could make it to the bus station if I called a cab right now.

"I'm on my way!"

"Most excellent, sister." She hung up.

I was already dressed. I slipped on my boots, grabbed my coat, ransacked my closet and dresser for a few of my favorite things which I tossed in my back pack, threw a toothbrush in my pocket and grabbed my book. I called the cab and in nine minutes was climbing into the back seat.

"Bus station," I said. "I'm going home!"

"That's nice, honey."

I took a last look at the beautiful tree in my park, but I knew there'd be trees just as magnificent in Maine.

I woke up in New York. Drooling onto my back pack which I'd placed against the damp window to rest my head on, and I was starving. Not one morsel of food had I packed in my haste to flee Ann Arbor. A couple in front of me was arguing softly. But not softly enough.

"If you hadn't tried to bed down every guy from the office, we wouldn't be having this conversation at all."

"Oh right, Pete. From the man who slept with my sister."

"Yeah. Like four years ago after you'd said you wanted nothing to do with me."

Lucky for me I always had my Walkman in my back pack. I popped in my head phones and Tori Amos sang to me. My ass was aching, and my neck was stiff. Five big states ahead of us. So much like the trip from Maryland 14 years and 30 pounds ago. With my heart on fire like a flaming hoola hoop for Gemma, in canvas sneakers and Kyle's sweat shirt. Back then, I didn't love that quivering Back Kingdom girl. But now, a zing of love for that child nearly jolted me out of my seat. The bus hissed to a stop at an Arby's somewhere in the Hartford area. "Rest stop folks. Be back on the bus in 15 minutes."

I was relived to be up and stretching into the overhead for some money. And I was looking forward to a roast beef sandwich and a steaming cup of coffee. But mostly I was exhilarated by my crazy exodus, and so far, had not one pang of remorse or worry about my hasty departure from my life with Molly. And I was smiling. Really smiling. The Arby's food did not disappoint and the scalding sour coffee was restorative. When I boarded the bus again, I wanted to sleep, and I reclined in my warm seat in the pitchyness of night, but I was back at the Mistletoe waiting for Karl. Maybe because of the rhythm of the road, the snow everywhere, and smell of damp humans was so like that other time, or maybe because like that time I was going home from a place I hadn't loved.

The sun rose all pinks and deep oranges the further North we drove. The last time I saw any of my family was the day after I left for Wheeling. I'd thought I'd go back at least for a visit, but I was never able to bring their faces into focus. I pulled my backpack down from the overhead and rifled through it. Two things I made sure to pack remained with me always, as objects of constancy that seemed to contain atoms from different chunks of my life. One was Aunt Serena's purple lacquered chopstick that she used to make a bun from her long red hair; one was a small watercolor on a flattened-out toilet paper roll that my mother painted for me of a humming bird. I needed those in my hands as we closed the gap between my old life with Molly and the new one with my family of strangers. I had never actually worn Aunt Serena's chopstick in my hair, but I decided the time was right. I twisted my braid into a knot and slid the chopstick through. I wondered if I was beautiful.

The bus rolled to a stop in Augusta at exactly the time it said it would. I looked out the window and scanned the parking lot. I didn't know what my mother and Karl drove these days. But there she was. A plump olive-skinned woman with a pile of salt and pepper hair pushed up into a grey ragg wool hat, and an ample bosom pressed against a bright red parka. My eyes immediately went to the feet. I would know my mother by her thick soled work boots with a chunky heel so she could break five feet. She stood outside on the curb. She was scanning the windows, and I fell in love with her again.

I almost knocked folks off the bus as I hurdled over the steps into my mother's arms. Karl stood behind her camouflaged by the crowd, but his wide lop-sided smile was unmistakable. He had less hair, and what he had was now faded from the tow-head white-blonde to a dishwater grey. But my mom looked like a million bucks. Her violet eyes alarmed me under their dark plush lashes, and I couldn't detect any age minus the salt and pepper hair. She hugged me the way I always thought a real mom should. With a ferocity and strength that said: I will not let danger find you. Like the hugs I'd known before all the sadness.

Karl stepped forward. "I'm on time," he said. "You didn't have to spend the night at the police station."

This time I hugged him. What had this quiet saturnine man ever done but his best to take care of my mother? And El and I as well? What I hadn't been able to see, or perhaps accept, as a kid, I could now. That it's easier to hate. Hate requires no effort to understand or investigate otherness. It's for the simple and the lazy.

"Hey, I had all the donuts and instant cacao I could ever want."

"I'm donutless," my mom said. "But maybe these will do?"

From her coat pocket she pulled a baggie of pecan sandies. They were still warm. We walked toward the back of the lot where I tried to guess which car would be theirs. I chose a dark green Subaru wagon. But as we approached, they didn't stop. Instead, Karl stooped to unlock the door of a vintage Renault painted the color of yams.

"Cool car," I said.

"Your mother picked it out."

I got into the back seat. The car was immaculate. Not a speck of dirt on the floor.

"It smells like ginger," I said.

"Karl's addicted to ginger altoids. Is that Serena's chopstick in your braid?"

"It is."

"My God, I miss her."

"Yeah. Me too."

My mother put in a cassette. It was Joni. She sang about cutting down trees and skating away.

The car was warm. We were about an hour away from Owls

Head, a place I'd never been. When El wrote me that they were moving to the coast I really hadn't cared. I was finally starting college and was deeply entwined with Molly and her world, and reveling in my new family of friends.

"You don't want a last look at the old place, or a last walk out to Fairy Shrimp Spa?" El would ask each time I called home. "You don't even want to see the new place in Owl's Head?"

I hadn't. I was free, out and 21. Molly was helping me go to school, and there was no time or money for a trip up North. But here I was, going to that very place. I detected no rancor, nor sense of failure. I looked for it, but it wasn't there. I only felt relief and happiness, sitting in the back of the warm yam- on-wheels in the company of my mother, and even Karl. Sort of what I'd felt arriving home from Lewisville as Karl quietly navigated through the aftermath of a Nor'Easter.

"We're here," my mom said. I shook myself back into my body, wiped the drool off my cheek and sat up. The yam-mobile was parked in a narrow-crushed stone drive-way alongside a huge blue Victorian house. Two other smaller Victorians stood between ours and the Atlantic on a short dead-end road. A huge snow woman sat in a small gazebo in the middle of the front yard. She wore a rainbow knitted scarf and tam-o'-shanter and held a cardboard sign in her stick arms that read: It's about time.

"Courtesy of El?" I asked my mother and hauled out my bags from the trunk.

"Yes. She's teaching today, but she's trying to cut out before last period."

"I like the lights." The alders and yews were decked out in white twinkle lights and the big white barn door entrance sported a large evergreen and apple wreath. This I knew was the work of my mother.

"You made this?"

"I did. It's become quite the little cottage industry. I even teach workshops."

"I'm glad, mom. They're stunning."

"You should see the rest," Karl added. "Your mom has a work-shop in the carriage house out back."

My mother smiled up at Karl. "Well you help too!"

"You're the talented one, my dear," he said, and kissed her on the forehead.

I realized I was smiling. My mother must have noticed and smiled back at me. Some little current of recognition between us propelled me toward her, and she took my hand, and there were tears in both our eyes.

"Let's get you inside and feed you."

Karl held the door open for us. It was eerie how much the inside of this old house resembled Back Kingdom. The wide pumpkin pine floors and beadboard cabinets with heavy black hinges. The deep cast iron sink. The gentle sag of the ceilings. A squat little Ben Franklin wood stove was perched on a platform of charred bricks. My mother's familiar blue glass graced the window sills.

"It's a beautiful place, Mom."

"We like it."

"My room is upstairs?" I suddenly only wanted to be horizontal.

"Oh, for the love of Pete, you must be blitzed. I'll take you up."

The second floor smelled of wood smoke and the peach colored walls glowed in the morning light. Baby pictures of me and El covered the walls.

"Wow," I said, "I haven't seen these in forever."

"I know. I always regretted that I didn't hang them up in Back Kingdom."

"Mom, let's make a deal that regrets are like gall stones."

My mother laughed. She said, "I don't know what that means, but okay!"

She swung open the white door into a big corner room painted the color of an orchid. As a child it had been a color I loved. A high four poster cherry bed with a pile of purple and white quilts waited for me, and a framed print of my favorite Vermeer hung over a matching dresser.

"Go to sleep," my mother said. "We'll wake you for dinner."

"Perfect."

I awoke at twilight when El crawled into my bed. "Do you hear it?"

"What?"

"Listen! How can you not hear it?"

I wasn't sure what I was listening for. But I furrowed my brow and listened as hard as I could. But still, nothing. "I'm sorry El."

"Close your eyes, then."

And there it was. Unmistakable.

"It's the ocean. We can hear the ocean from this house?"

"Not this house. Our house."

I placed my arms around her neck. I said, "I love you."

"I know," she answered.

My mother called from below. "Dinner's ready."

"She's been cooking?"

"She's a different mom now, Liza. You missed a lot of good years. The wonders of modern psychopharmaceuticals. She's as steady as she goes."

I joined my family for salmon pie and lime Jell-O. More favorites of mine. We watched Heidi; a childhood classic that Aunt Serena adored. We made plans for a tree decorating party over the week-end. We discussed possible jobs for me and Karl said he had some connections at the University of Maine Extension program. El and I finished the evening with a brisk walk on Pebble Beach. I was sure that some catastrophe would befall us within the week.

The next morning, I was awake around 5:30. The sky was barely light. A soft violet glow rested on the ocean, glints of which I could detect from my window through the branches of an elm. I could not lay still in my bed in this room, dazzling as it was. Energy coursed through me. A long and arduous 2 and a half years of grad school, and a long and arduous 10-year relationship was over, and I felt like I might take flight.

I padded down the long hall to the big white bathroom at the top of the stairs. It was chilly and the anticipation of a hot shower excited me. I fiddled with the heavy antique hardware to coax the spray from the shower head and was delighted to find it was powerful and plenty hot. I stayed in for a long time, luxuriating in the steamy spray and fennel soap. It was Friday. My sister would likely be up soon to get ready for her school day. I didn't want to use up all the hot water my first day home.

After I was dried off and layered, I slipped out through the side door and down toward the beach. It would be easy to get used to starting my days like this—watching the sunrise on the slate grey Atlantic. Eventually I had to get a grip on real life. I was broke, like really broke. I had about $77.00 in the bank, and soon any student loans I had would be out of deferment.

Molly, much to my consternation, had picked up the tab for mostly everything. How long could I in good conscience, sponge off my family? But I wanted a break. I decided not to think about a job until after the New Year, and it didn't appear that they were struggling. Karl was now an adjunct history professor at U of Maine, my sister was a teacher, and my mom seemed to be doing okay with her green house. I was going to coast for a bit. Sleep in if I wanted; explore the peninsula which was gorgeous, and read all the novels I'd not had time to read in school. I sat on a rock for the light show over the ocean, and when the sun was done show-ing off, I strolled back to my family and wondered whether or not I would have pancakes, or an omelet.

On my way up the road, I noticed a light coming from my moth-er's studio. I knocked. "Come in," she called.

I pushed open the door. My mother stood in a circle of pine boughs. A small pot belly stove burned some well-seasoned oak. It was a hot and clean burn with a distinct aroma.

"My God, it smells good in here."

I sat in an old wooden grange chair painted an indigo blue.

"It does, doesn't it?"

My mother crossed the wooden floor to a tea pot on a rusty electric hot plate. "I have three kinds of tea," she said. "Lapsang Souchong, English breakfast, and fennel."

"Lapsang was Aunt Serena's favorite," I said.

"She'd be so proud of us all." She dropped the tea infuser into a purple mug I knew to be Serena's, poured in water from her old green kettle and passed it to me.

"I think so, too," I said. "Especially you."

I spotted an old blue velvet wingback chair that looked much more comfortable than the one I'd chosen and sunk into it. The fire was warm and I held the heady pungent tea against my chest.

"I make wreaths and grow plants, Liza."

"That's not what I'm talking about, Mom."

"Oh," she said, and worked her long fingers through a pile of boughs. "You're talking about how crazy I was?"

"I didn't call you crazy."

She kept at her wreath. "I don't mind, Liza. Don't be worried about that. It's a relief, actually. I was crazy."

"For what it's worth," I said, "when I got back from Maryland you didn't seem crazy to me. Those were good years, Mom."

"I was hospitalized."

"Once. For like five minutes."

She put down her wreath. "Then how come you beat feet and never came back?"

She didn't seem angry—no sharp edge at all in her voice.

"It was so hard to lose you again, Liza. Although I did understand that there was nothing for you in Westover and that being gay made it damn near impossible. But I thought you'd at least come back and see us all."

"I thought so, too. I wish I could tell you why. I don't even really know."

She walked over and kissed me on the head. "That's okay love. Maybe someday we'll all know more about those years. I'd venture to say you were still mad at me for abandoning you."

"Can you teach me how to do that?" I said, and motioned toward the pile of boughs at her feet. I didn't want any heavy conversations.

"I'd love to," she answered.

My wreaths sucked. I clearly had no fine motor skills or any artistic sensibility at all. But being close to my mother in that warm studio with my hands sticky with red pine resin was enough. More than enough. I was happy.

"What are your plans today?" My mother poured more hot water into my tea cup.

"Plans? I have no plans. I've had enough plans."

"Understood," she said. "But if you want to join me, I was

planning to head to the Camden State Park for some winterberry."

"I'm in," I said.

We came home three hours later with the entire back seat of the yam-mobile filled with the stunning red berried branches of winter.

Chapter 4

The morning we were all heading out to get a tree, some-place up the coast by Bucksport, it was grey and raining. The slush in our driveway was up to my ankles. I borrowed El's silly canary yellow rain boots. Karl and El were both on winter break, so tree day was a family affair.

"Why are we going all the way to Bucksport for a tree?" El was buttering her bagel. I suddenly remembered the laborious way in which she slathered it on every nook and cranny with great con-centration.

"They have blue spruces up there," I answered.

"So, what's the difference?"

"Good needle retention," I said.

"And they're beautiful," my mother said, entering the room. "That lovely shade of blue."

El plunked down on one of the church pews we used at the table instead of chairs. She stuffed half of the bagel into her mouth. "Good needle retention?" she asked while chewing. "Really?"

"Yuh," I answered.

"You are such a nerd," she said, and laughed.

"And you talk with your mouth full."

"That's true," she laughed again.

"Pancakes or French toast?" My mother pulled an old flowered apron over her head that I remembered from Vermont. And then I saw us all sitting at the base of a big lopsided tree covered in construction paper garland and papier-mâché angels. It was the last Christmas with both my mother and father. That apron had been a gift my father had chosen for my mother from us. El and I had been so excited when the three of us found it at a grange hall holiday bazaar and dad had said he'd wrap it up and put it under the tree from The Twins. "These are mom's favorite flowers," he said, and pointed to the little sprays of violets hand painted on a muslin background.

"French toast," I answered.

"No, pancakes," El said.

"I'll make both."

And so, I thought maybe this would be the day the wheels came off. In the week or so I'd been home, every day had been perfect. And every day I waited. Waited for someone to dredge up some ancient hurt, pick some family scab, or at least circle around, teeth bared, knives sharpened, but no. I didn't even miss Molly. And to my relief, she hadn't tried to get in touch with me.

I shuffled through the mail stacked on the table. And amongst the circulars was something from Aunt Kitty.

"I think you got a Christmas card from Maryland, Mom."

"Oh. Open it up, love."

I'd fallen out of touch with my cousins. After the New Year's Eve debacle Aunt Kitty had called Back Kingdom to apologize on Uncle Doug's behalf. She asked if I wanted to come back, but I really didn't and said as much. Bri got on the phone and said there'd been a big fight that morning when everyone finally realized I was actually gone, and that she hated her father. For a while we wrote, and she always planned to come to see us in Maine, but it never happened.

When I opened the Christmas card a photo fell out. It was Kitty, Frosty and Bri smiling from beach chairs. All three looked like movie stars.

"Weird, I said, no Uncle Doug?"

The card was signed Kitty, Courtney and Brianna. Aunt Kitty had scribbled a note as well: *Love to you all up there in the beautiful*

Maine winter. Please send my warmest wishes to Liza. You may have figured this out by now, but Doug and I are separated. Apologies for dropping such news in such an off-handed way. I owe you a phone call Violet. I'm loving my life these days. The girls are healthy and thriving. Courtney is getting married this spring. You all must plan to come! Bri is starting a new job at a pharmaceutical company in Chapel Hill. XXoo.

I read it out loud. "So Frosty's getting hitched?!"

My family had come to call Courtney Frosty as well. Once I had eased my way back into life at Back Kingdom, I often regaled them all with stories of life in the 'burbs. I had not, however, told them everything. I left out the part about Gemma. Uncle Doug had called my mother to tell her of the events leading up to my exodus. Not to apologize, but to paint the picture of me as vile and unnatural. My mother refused to speak to him after that.

"Good for Aunt Kitty."

"I agree," my mother said. "She's been through enough."

She flipped pancakes and French toast, in her well-loved apron. I watched her brow furrow as she slid a spatula under each, careful not to nick them.

El poured herself a cup of coffee. No adornment. Just black. She slid into the pew next to me. She smelled like Noxzema, soap from our childhood.

"It must have been so weird for you, Liza. The whole liver transplant thing; Uncle Doug being Uncle Doug. That morning Karl brought you home, you were like a lost baby deer. I never understood why you left us in the first place."

"Maple syrup or yogurt?" My mom appeared before her twins with pancakes and French toast. But I knew what she was doing.

"I feel like living dangerously today. Give me the hard stuff."

"Say when." My mother poured syrup for both of us.

"It was tough on me when you left, you know. It was especially tough on mom. It was quite cruel, actually."

"I thought we did this the first time I came home."

"Funny," my sister said. "I thought we didn't."

Karl's timing was superb. "Are we getting this show on the road?" he asked, with his usual lop-sided smile.

"We are indeed!" My mom sprang from her seat on the opposite pew, French toast half in and half out of her mouth. "Let's go! There's a blue spruce with our name on it in Bucksport."

"Guys!" My sister lurched out of the pew. "We have to have this conversation."

"Why?" I asked.

"So we can move on," she said. She leaned into the table and stared me down with her freaky indigo eyes.

"I have moved on," I answered. I was amazed at the softness and deliberateness of my voice. So well-regulated. So grown-up.

"Should we postpone this outing?" Karl asked.

"Fuck this outing!" El yelled. She bolted from the kitchen and thumped up the stairs where she slammed her bedroom door.

"No tree?" I said.

Karl laughed. My mother, however, pursed her lips in her beautiful love-worn apron.

"I'm sorry," I said. "I just didn't know what to say."

She ruffled my hair and sat down on the pew next to me. "It's okay," she said. "You know how she gets."

But I didn't really. Was she really the same moody kid of 17?

"Should I go talk to her?"

"You can try," Karl said.

I heaved myself up from the pew with a dramatic grunt.

"May the force be with you," Karl added. My mother cuffed him and smiled.

"You two need to get a room." But I think I loved that my mother was happy. I was never sure if that was true or not. But now it seemed so. Maybe it was my own break-up, or just pushing 30. But I wanted people to be happy.

"El, let me in," I said.

"It's open."

El's room always smelled like pine. Since we were little, she collected pine boughs and laid them all over the place. Mostly she piled them up on top of her armoire with twinkle lights.

"What's going on?"

El sat up on her bed, crossed the room and opened a window.

I could smell salt from the ocean, and her room immediately felt moist. She sat at her desk, which was strewn with lesson plans and the various debris of a middle school art teacher. She picked up a jar of India ink and tightened the lid.

"It's the same old stuff, Liza. I don't think you really get what it felt like to be left behind."

"You wouldn't have wanted to go to Maryland, El."

"It's odd how everyone assumes that. The fact is no one asked me if I wanted to go. It's just another part of this family story that was written by someone other than me."

"I don't think anyone wrote anything. We just did what we did."

"And that is precisely the issue. Everyone just did what they wanted. But I didn't."

"Sure you did, El. You moved in with your boyfriend."

"Funny. What makes you think I wanted to?"

"Then where do we go from here?" I didn't know what else to say.

"I don't know," she said, and crossed to close her window.

"So how about Bucksport?"

She turned to me. "It's not funny, you know."

"I'm not laughing. I just want to stick to the plan. I want to go get a tree. It's tree day, and I think it could be fun."

"I'm gonna pass."

"Mom will be sad."

"She's been sad before."

My mother, Karl and I had a quiet trip, devoid of excess emotion. Pleasant and well-modulated. Our blue spruce was nine feet tall and the three of us could barely wrap our arms around it. We tied it on top of the yam-mobile and drove home in the rain that turned to snow around Belfast. I was thrilled by the idea of trimming our tree as big soft flakes fell outside our grand picture window. My mother would gush and Karl, I knew, would put in his Johnny Cash Christmas CD and pour peach schnapps into the English Breakfast tea he so loved. And El would be over it and join us. And that is exactly what happened. Until around dinner time.

"I remember that angel," El said.

And I did too. Aunt Serena had found a carboard match box in a drawer someplace at Back Kingdom filled with rusty skeleton keys. She thought they looked like angels, and so we made pipe cleaner halos and wings to glue to the back of the keys.

El plopped herself down next to me on the couch and we stared in silence at our tree— the first one we'd decorated together since my return from Maryland so many Christmases ago.

"Didn't we have a ton more of those?"

Elspeth looked at me. The way Elspeth does with her creepy eyes, sometimes indigo, and other times violet, squinted to a slit and penetrating my brain. At these times usually what followed was not gentle.

"Ruh-roh," I said. "What's going on?"

"Please tell me your kidding?"

From El, this meant how can you be such a colossal and un-feeling boob. I did a quick drive-by through my memory bank and came up with bupkus. I did not know what I might be kidding about.

"El," I said, "I got nothing. I'm sorry. I just remember that we sat there in front of the fire with Aunt Serena and turned every single key into an angel. I don't know if there were nine or 30, but there was a pile of them on the coffee table when we were done. And she made lemonade for us out of real lemons and it was undrinkable."

"And that's where your memory of that night ends?"

I nodded and shrugged my shoulders, conceding that I was hopeless because I didn't have her steel-trap brain.

"Mom?" My violet-eyed twin called to our mother who was in the kitchen writing out Christmas cards. "Could you come here for a sec?"

Mom came in with a big smile and I felt suddenly protective of her and I didn't know why. My sister pointed to the skeleton key angel poised on the tip of a lower bough and asked my mother where the rest were. My mother sat on the edge of the arm chair closest to the kitchen archway and her smile vanished. She looked at her feet for a moment then rose her head and met El's glare.

"Why now, El? Are things going too smoothly?"

I instinctively placed my open palms across my abdomen. And once again, I didn't know why. But my scalp puckered, and the skin felt too tight for my hair. I couldn't finish this story about these angels. Whatever it was, and whatever its significance had been was lost to me.

"What's happening here?"

"Shall I tell you Liza, or would you prefer it be El whose role it is in this family to rattle all the old yellowed bones?"

"I would prefer if neither of you told me anything, because frankly, I don't give a fuck. Please don't make me sorry I came home."

"That's the night mom stole Christmas," El said.

And there it was. Like putting in the movie. You hear a slight click, whir, and the lion roars. Then the tree is in a pile on the floor, after having been ravaged by my mother who first pulled off the garland, then the ornaments and finally the lights—all of which was tossed in a snowdrift out the front door, and lay glistening in the full moon until Karl picked it all up days later.

"She was jealous of Aunt Serena and Karl that night. And there was vodka. And she was jealous of Aunt Serena's relationship with us, Liza. And there was more vodka, and a whole lot of manic bullshit. Is your memory refreshed now?"

"I'm not going to do this," I said, and heaved myself off the couch.

My mother stood partially in the archway, no longer perched on the arm of the big purple velvet wing-backed chair.

"You could stay, Liza," she said, and gently placed her chapped hand on my shoulder. I looked down at it, red and rough, nails worn down to a nub from hours spent wreath making. What else could this woman do, but ask me to stay? And I wouldn't walk away from her. Not again.

I returned to my seat. My folded hands instinctively nestled between my knees, and my eyes directed at the floor. I was positioned for a good dressing down from El—a sound and thorough dressing down.

My sister took the floor. Like a TV lawyer she gestured grandly at the tree.

"Do you like this tree, Liza?"

I had no idea where this was going. But I hoped it wasn't going to be a tirade. I don't know where El gets her energy. She can pontificate for hours.

"I do, El. You could say I love it."

"Yes," she said, and smiled at me. "I think you love us for our trees."

A deep and lustrous laugh welled up from my mother's belly. I looked at her and she'd put a cupped hand over her mouth as though to thwart another ripple of laughter.

"Are you guys smoking crack? I mean, really, what the fuck's going on? I love you for your trees?"

"It's an inside joke, Liza," my mother said.

"Is anyone going to let me in on it?"

I was so angry at these two ridiculous women who looked nothing like me, but so much like each other. Who'd made peace with whatever eccentric and debauched lives they'd led during my protracted absences. I would never be on the inside because I'd left. Not once, but twice. And I hadn't come back at all the second time. Till now. And I didn't know their secret language.

"Mom said it about you," El said, and dropped into the couch. "When you came back from the cousins."

"No one's going to forgive me in the end, right?"

"There's nothing to forgive you for, Liza," my mother said, and crossed to the couch where she sat next to me. "You did nothing wrong."

"That's bullshit!" El leapt to her feet and spun around to face me. "You sold your soul to the devil to get away from us."

"El," my mother said, "that's a bit over-the-top."

"Mom," El said, "she left us to live with your brother, who thought you and Aunt Serena were loser pieces of shit. She left us again and ran off with an older woman."

"It's pretty clear that I'm not really wanted here," I said, and stood to leave. But first I turned to El. "You begged me to come home, El. You convinced me to leave Molly and come home. But this isn't home. It wasn't home then, and it's less so now."

"Ouch," my mother said, and her hands seemed to instinctively sail up to her heart, where her long slender fingers rested. "Why do we have to do this?"

"I don't think we do have to do this. But apparently, El does,"

I said.

My mother walked further into the room. No longer was she one-foot-in, one-foot-out. The look on her face was one I'd never seen—resolute and fierce. Was she actually taking charge of a situation? I was intrigued to see where this was going, and returned to my seat on the couch.

"Both of you need to grow up," my mother said, and stood over us with her hands on her thick hips, and her lush salt and pepper hair sprung from her widow's peak like a geyser. "Live your lives. I was crazy. Crazed by grief, sadness, bi-polar and paralyzed by fear when your daddy died. Aunt Serena saved us. Fragile herself, as you know, and Karl loved us both. Big deal. We cared for you girls as well as any family would. And yes. Serena couldn't, in the end, share Karl. And she couldn't tolerate that Snoutly was killed. So, she left us. So what. We carried on. And just so you know, Liza, it hurt like hell when you left again after she killed herself. We needed you. So, forgive me if I side with El on that one."

"Oh, I see," I said. "I was running an entire 4-H Camp and taking college classes, but I should have dropped everything, as broke as I was, and come back to Crazy Town for visits? Because Auntie sliced her own throat? Really?"

El was sobbing beside me. My mother, all 4 foot 11 of her, towered over us like the pillar of strength she never was.

"Yes, Liza," she whispered. "You absolutely should have stayed, or at least visited. And I'm going to bed. I'm old, and I'm tired, and I have a lovely and beautiful man who adores me waiting upstairs in my bed who happens to think I'm the cat's meow. So, goodnight, girls, and by the way? I expect you'll be getting along tomorrow morning."

And with that, this tiny volcano of a woman who I'd only known as docile and easy to ignore stomped out of the living room with the ferocity of a Marine.

"Well then," I said to my twin.

"Indeed," she answered. And we climbed the stairs hand in hand.

Chapter 5

Sylvie appeared in a fuchsia velvet dress. Luscious and smelling of wedding cake. Our tree had been festooned with an assortment of Christmas balls that my mother and Karl amassed over their lives, and of course, the lone skeleton key angel. Many were familiar to me, and some I'd made as a child. But my favorites were decorations of Karl's that were from all over the globe. But it was Sylvie, standing in the glow of the soft blue and purple tree lights, dry and dirty martini dangling between two fingers, that slayed me.

My mother had planned this small gathering of neighbors. Cider was mulling and Jim Nabors was singing about shepherds herding their flock in his sonorous bass. El had warmed up to me in the past few days since the rainy Thursday we'd headed down east for our tree. We'd even found a way to talk about the pain I'd caused, which mostly consisted of my agreeing with everything she said and apologizing for things I'd never actually done. I was dreading a party. Even a small one. Not knowing anyone in their new lives on the coast made me feel like I was on parade.

Sylvie smiled at me as soon as I walked in with a platter of stuffed mushrooms.

"Ah, you're the difficult sister?"

I didn't know what to say. I have never been known as the one with a witty comeback. So, I just looked at her, and set the mushrooms down on the sideboard.

"I'm sorry. That was inappropriate," she said.

Up close, I could see all the colors in her hair. Brown like bark, but filled with copper. Short, curly, and close to the skull.

"I'm not too worried," I said.

"I'm Sylvie." She extended a very white hand with piano fingers. No rings.

"Liza." I clasped her hand in mine. I could feel the dreaded flush coming on. I knew I was red up to the tips of my ears.

"A blusher!"

"Yup. The difficult blusher."

"I'm sorry to hear about your break-up. Never easy, I know."

No one in my family actually took the time to ask me about The Break-up, but this woman I didn't know had heard all about it?

"I've got some pigs-in-a-blanket waiting in the oven."

"I did it again, right?"

Sylvie slurped at her drink, but it missed her mouth and dribbled down the front of her velvet dress. One drop glistened as it made its way to her cleavage. It dawned on me then that this woman was well on her way to being shit-faced at our tame little soiree. I passed her a napkin. She dabbed at the tops of her breasts. All I could think of was sweet rising yeast.

"Shit. You can't take me anywhere."

"No worries," I said, and exited to the haven of our brightly lit and friendly kitchen, where I traded out one platter full of finger food for another.

"You met Sylvie?" It was Karl, sliding a cookie sheet of spanakopita out of the oven.

"Yeah," I answered. I tried my best to sound as nonplussed as I could, although my heart rate belied my calm response.

"She'd be a good contact for you. She's an arborist."

It seemed unlikely. This woman who stirred me so, who appeared to be flirting with me, was an arborist?

"Cool," I said. I slid my mother's gourmet pigs-in-a-blanket off the top of the wood stove, transferred them onto a blue paisley platter and headed back into the living room. Over the archway between the two rooms hung a sprig of mistletoe. Sylvie had positioned herself directly under it. Was it on purpose?

"Oooh! Those smell amazing!" She dangled a fresh martini in her hand. "They can't be your basic hot dogs in Pillsbury dough."

"No. It's wild boar with fennel, and she makes the crust thingy from scratch, out of potatoes and onions I think."

"I so love your mom's parties. She puts so much love into everything."

I had a flash of anger. This plump woman stuffed into a silly fuchsia dress had no idea who my mother was.

"I wouldn't know," I said, and made my rounds with my platter full of pork. Sylvie avoided me from then on. The party filled up and by the time 15 or so people were milling around it was easy to avoid her as well. But I was aware of her trips back and forth to the drink station. I wondered how she was still standing. I counted four. I'd be having my stomach pumped. On one of my rounds into the kitchen to refresh a platter or two, she followed me.

"You're working too hard," she said. "Sit down and enjoy the party."

But I needed to stay busy. It's too hard to mingle and schmooze. A few of my mother's and Karl's friends had chatted me up. They were kind enough, but the conversations were stiff. And although back in Ann Arbor most of my friends were Molly's, at least I had a few. Sylvie's invitation relieved me some.

"I'll get you a drink. What would you like?" she asked.

In the overhead bright kitchen light, she seemed even prettier. All of her colors more vibrant and the contrast of hair to skin to eyes sharper.

"Sure, how about scotch?"

"On the rocks?"

"No, neat."

"Coming right up," she said, and left me with a huge smile on her face.

I circulated amongst the tipsy guests with a platter full of bacon wrapped scallops, collected some empties and headed back to the kitchen. Sylvie waited there with my drink.

"A nice generous pour," she said.

"Thanks, I think!"

We slid into the pews. I picked at the remains of a bowl of olives. Sylvie was quiet. I sipped at the scotch.

"Too too much to drink," she finally said, and slid her martini glass across the table. "Air would be good. Walk on the beach?"

"Sure." I surprised myself.

We gathered up our coats and headed out the back door. It was 22 degrees. But it felt great after the stuffiness of the wood stove. I was happy to be moving down this pebbled expanse of shoreline under the bright moon, but uncertain what it meant to be doing this with Sylvie.

"Oh God," she said. "I feel better already."

Up ahead a bonfire burned. We were heading toward it. Massive and bright. I realized it was the solstice. Aunt Serena's favorite day.

"Jesus. That's the biggest fire I've ever seen!"

"That would be our neighborhood wiccans and UUs. They do this every December 21st."

We were close enough to feel heat. A group of about 15 stood around the pit. Someone was playing the obligatory guitar.

"Do you want to keep walking, or should we sit and listen?"

"Let's listen," I answered. "But I'm not sure I want to sit on the ground!"

"I noticed you had a boney ass," she said. "And I took the liberty of pouring your Scotch into my flask. That should warm you up."

"Or we could just grab that log over there," I said.

Sylvie laughed. "Or that."

We hauled it over closer to the fire without crashing the party. I was glad she had my Scotch. The guitarist was playing a classical piece. I was happy we were right here right now and I said so.

"Me too," she answered.

"Even though my ass is boney?"

"Even though."

"Are we flirting?" I asked.

"A little. Is that okay?"

"I'm not sure. I left my girlfriend of 12 years a few weeks ago."

"I'm not trying to get in your pants," she said. "Just thought you could use a pal up here."

"The flirting is innocent then?"

"Completely."

We talked for an hour. I knew her back story, she knew mine. We were both from small towns, and were both a twin, although her twin brother had drowned when she was a teen-ager. She grew up not far from here in one of the mill-towns along the Androscoggin. She was close to her younger sister, Sidney. She had a prickly relationship with her narcissistic mother, and, of course, she drank way too much.

When we got back to the party it was thinning out and the few who remained were sitting in front of the fire killing the last bottle of red wine, my mother, sister and Karl included. Sylvie and I joined them. El raised her glass and invited us all to toast Aunt Serena. But everyone was a little drunk and sloppy. And it felt hollow and absurd. I joined the toast, with a bent head and limp arm. All I wanted to do was go to bed. The Scotch had hit me hard, and all the drunkenness irritated me.

"It's all so tawdry," I said under my breath. "I mean, she killed herself."

Sylvie reached over and placed her hand on mine, only for a second.

Chapter 6

A few weeks after Christmas I really needed a job. Neither mom nor Karl were applying any pressure, but I was losing my mind. They all got up in the morning and went to work. Even my mother, though only in her studio at the end of the driveway. She had a purpose-- getting all her spring seedlings prepared. Joining her was somewhat a fodder for my days, but I usually found myself getting anxious after a few hours of her relentless happiness. I marveled at how such a once sad woman had become pathologically happy.

I hadn't heard from Sylvie and although on the one hand was relieved, I did know she was the most likely person to steer me toward a job. She was an arborist for the state, and worked for the division of animal and plant health. Karl thought she diagnosed and evaluated trees. My thing was more about aquaculture, and I really wanted a Ph.D., but for now, I wanted a paycheck.

My sister suggested I speak to her long-time married state trooper boyfriend, Ted. She wasn't sure he would have any leads for anything "in my field" but explained that he knew everyone and that lots of people owed him a favor. Eventually I knew I'd need to acquaint myself with him. He and my sister had been an item for six years, and she reported on many occasions that he was the one and only true love of her life, "like mom and dad."

And so, my sister arranged for us to meet. Mom and Karl told me he was a great guy as well.

"I like his politics," my mother said. "He's really liberal."
They were selling him hard. I was curious why. A lunch was arranged at a local hang-out in Rockland. It was one of those days
when you're hopeful for spring. A genuine January thaw. Snow is
melting, and the sun is bright and it's in the 50's. You're imagining a crocus on your neighbor's lawn. You think that there will be
no more blizzards or subzero days, but you know that this is only
a bizarre blip on the screen, just to keep you focused on breathing
through the harsh Atlantic nights.

I ordered a big sprouty sandwich and some hot tea. I was just
easing into a booth in the back with El when in he walked. Oh
my. Matinee idol comes to mind. Tall, sandy tousled hair, a little long for a state trooper I thought. Root-beer eyes, with a dark
ring around the iris, and stupid dimples. It was a day off, so he
was dressed in regular clothes, which for him was a pair of baggy
faded jeans and a lumber jack shirt. He wore a small silver cross
around his neck.

"I'm Ted," he said, and extended a square hand.

After introductions and small talk about the weather and our
holidays, he asked what kind of work I was looking for.

"I'd take anything at this point that was reasonable."

"Do you like kids?"

"Not really," I said, and he laughed.

"Would you consider a job with disturbed teens at a residential
school?"

"Doing what?"

"Farming stuff?"

My sister was beaming. She knew I would, and I knew I would.

"Like a school for kids who live there and work on a farm?"

"Exactly. I know one of the social workers there, Daisy.
They're looking for someone who can help them design program-
ming that integrates work on the farm. It's a huge place up the
coast a ways, over by Stanfordshire."

My heart was beating faster. This sounded really perfect, and
like something that I could feel good about doing while I thought
about going back to school.

"But Liza," he said, and leaned into me across the booth. "I'd like you to understand a few things about your sister and me."

He was close enough that I could see the yellow flecks in his root-beer eyes. I could smell the cinnamon toothpaste he must have used that morning and could've reached out and pulled the errant grey strands from his widow's peak.

"You don't have to explain anything to me. Whatever arrangement you and El have is your business."

"Oh, I know I don't have to! If I thought I had to, I likely wouldn't. I want to."

El was looking down at her plate, and moving the black beans back and forth with her plastic fork.

"Okay," I said.

"Zelda is my wife. We met in Jr. High and knew right out of the gate that we'd spend the rest of our lives together. We went to the same college and got married the fall after we graduated. Four years later, she took a dive off a cliff and became a quadriplegic. We found out that she was seven weeks pregnant. She chose to carry our baby, a little boy, but in her last trimester she got very sick with respiratory stuff; not uncommon with spinal cord injuries, and our son was taken by C-section, but he died." He delivered this with no emotion. It seemed he'd had a lot of practice.

"Zelda is an amazing woman," El said, and placed her hand on Ted's knee. "You'd love her. She named her little boy Bonaventure after her great-grandfather in Canada."

"I'm so sorry," I said.

"Everyone in town gets our situation," my sister added. "Zelda is a devout Catholic, and even she accepts us."

Never one to think of myself as a prude, I still struggled with the idea of Zelda being stuck in a wheelchair while her husband basically waited for her to die so he could be free to marry my sister. But maybe that isn't the way it really was. Maybe he loved Zelda in one sort of way and my sister in another? I didn't know. But what I did know is that there are lots of ways of being in the world, and I didn't have dibs on what the right ways or wrong ways were. But I was pissed why my sister, who had six years to tell me this stuff, hadn't, and I said so.

"It wasn't mine to tell," she answered, with an air of superiority for knowing that she was right. But I had what I needed. The name and number of the clinical director of a farm school, who happened to be his wife's sister. And I liked Ted.

"I'll see you tonight?" Ted asked El. "I have to get back to the station."

"Maybe Liza could join us tonight?"

I had no idea what my sister wanted me to join, and I hated being in the position where I may rebuff a kindly invitation from a seemingly nice guy who just hooked me up with a possible job. But no.

"Sure," Ted said, and bent down to kiss my sister goodbye, and left us.

El danced in her seat, the way she did as a child. Just wiggled like a puppy, put both hands up to her mouth and actually squeaked.

"It will be so much fun to have you join us!"

"El, where is it that I'm going tonight?"

"A gallery opening. In St. George."

That wasn't so bad. I could handle that. A little wine and cheese, some grapes, maybe I'd even like the art, unless it was the usual coastal schlock.

"That's a relief. Good, I can wrap my head around that."

El leaned in to me, and like a teen-ager in a sotto-vocce whisper asked what I thought of "her man". Did I think he was cute, did I like him, didn't he seem nice, and had I noticed his eyes, and did I think topaz described them best?

"Yes, yes, yes, yes, and yes," I said, and she did her puppy wriggle again, and I was happy she was my sister.

Chapter 7

We pulled into a gravel parking area around 6:45. A tiny white clapboard Methodist church had been revamped into an art gallery. A brightly painted sign in yellows and organes hung above the transom and read: Zelda's. The Gallery by the Creek. I took this to be a tongue-in-cheek comment on all the galleries by the sea surrounding those of us on the rocky shores of mid-coast Maine. Oh, and wasn't Zelda Ted's wife's name? My sister had failed to mention this detail.

"El, is this The Zelda?"

"Yes," she said, and leaned over me to open the glove box and pop an Altoid into her mouth. "I didn't mention that?"

A classic El move is what this was, but I decided to let it go.

"Oh," I said, "I think you did." But I rolled my eyes just a tad, and El giggled.

Once inside, the gallery was bright and festive. A dozen or so people, all of whom appeared to share the same DNA, lingered by a long trestle table piled with platters of meats, cheeses, raw vegetables, and deviled eggs. A cooler filled with both beer and soft drinks sat on the floor, and a card table held several bottles of red and white wine.

"Didn't she do a great job?"

I assumed my sister was referring to Zelda. Her lover's wife—who was not easy to miss as she was the only one in a wheelchair parked in the center of the room. An older woman with the same long bones and oval face carrying a mountain of silver hair on her head stood behind Zelda, hands resting on the younger woman's shoulders.

"It's a cute place," I said, to appease my sister. It was cute though, and made a perfect gallery for a small touristy town on the way to Port Clyde where the ferries left for Monhegan. More importantly, the paintings were odd and striking. Small barrel shaped blue and green humanoid figures looked out of distorted boxes at their viewers. All eighteen paintings were hers.

"I'm going to introduce you," my sister said, and grabbed my hand.

She was calling out to Zelda as she pulled me across the pine planking. Zelda turned and smiled at us. The woman with the white mountain on her head left Zelda—stately and graceful draped in her sleek black wheelchair and clad in a kimono of a fiery plumage design. I was immediately intimidated and a little ashamed of my lycra jogging pants and clashing nylon T-shirt. Not to mention an ancient pair of my mother's after-ski boots from the 70's. And let's also not mention the one long coarse braid wrapped around the top of my head like a crazed milk-maid. In the presence of this glamorous painter I was a mere peasant.

My sister bent to place a kiss on Zelda's cheek. I thought I detected a flash of recognition between them. They could have been sisters. Goose flesh sprung up on the back of my neck.

"Zelda, my God, where did you get that kimono?"

"I'm not sure. Some uncle brought it back from World War 2, I think. It was in a cedar chest in the attic."

Her voice was low but resonant. She had a very black and very round beauty mark just above the left side of her upper lip.

"This is my sister Liza," El said.

"Oh," Zelda said, and smiled up at me. "You might work for Daisy?"

"I hope to."

"She's here tonight. Elspeth, introduce them?"

And I met Zelda's older social worker sister. Another blue-black- haired beauty only much less glamorous. We were both a bit awkward, standing at the food table piling our small paper plates with carrots and celery. I caught her eyeing the deviled eggs. I know I was, but I'd decided against the little cholesterol filled and mayonnaised torpedoes for fear of excessive farting.

"So, I understand you're looking for work at The Montello School?"

"I am," I answered.

"What has Elspeth and Ted told you about the job?"

I did my best to describe my understanding of what Daisy was looking for, and fluffed up my experience running 4-H programs for youth. By the 2nd glass of a sour red, I had an interview planned with Daisy. She excused herself to go on with her evening and make much of her artist sister, as she should. I stood my ground at the food table, on which someone had placed congo bars, and finding myself alone crammed at least three devilled eggs into my mouth.

I looked out at the lively and eclectic milling crowd—lobstermen in their galoshes, the twenty-something grunge and pierced group gathering in the corner and secreting ennui everywhere, the DAR matrons in pink sweaters and pearls, and the corduroy clad teachers and writers. I liked them swirling around in the brightly lit gallery warmed by the wood stove perched on bricks in the back of the room. I was sated. I felt calm. I enjoyed the feeling of my feet laced snugly into my mother's old boots. I hoped a demure snow would be falling upon taking my leave so that my foot prints would remain. Zelda startled me out of my reverie, just as I was pocketing a congo bar for later.

"Those are probably my favorite," she said.

"I'm so so embarrassed," I said. "Stealing your reception sweets for my own selfish desires."

Zelda let a peel of bright laughter rip. She was eerily reminiscent of my Aunt Serena. I wondered how I hadn't noticed this at first. It was my sister I thought she resembled, but now in the throes of laughter, I saw and heard Serena. Why hadn't my mother or El mentioned this? Did they not sense the same energy that I did?

"Some folks are coming by the house later. I'd love for you to join us if you'd like."

"Will there be congo bars?"

"As far as the eye can see. I don't have to worry about looking good in a bikini anymore."

"I'm in," I said, and she let out another great bellow and wheeled back into the center of the room where the elegant woman with the snow-capped mountain on her head once again rested her boney hands on the younger woman's shoulders.

I sauntered through the small gallery and examined up close the quirky oil paintings. All of them, large and small, contained a circus artifact. The spookiness of her work was much more apparent when you were upon them. I had once seen a show in Anne Arbor with Molly, a modern art lover, of Philip Guston. I recognized something of his macabre treatment of humanity in Zelda's paintings. In my limited knowledge in almost everything, I thought she must be considered very good. I wondered who up here might understand that about her, and if she ever sold any work. I wondered if she was good enough to show in New York City, my only litmus for what is important work and what is not. Silly, but I'd lived with an art snob for ten years.

"I heard that you were joining us?"

My sister and Ted approached me with armfuls of yellow and orange roses that had been placed around the gallery. They must have cost a fortune.

"That's the word on the street," I said, hoping to sound blasé, but I was actually dancing inside. It felt like I might have a life here, albeit a weird one.

Chapter 8

The three of us drove in silence to Ted and Zelda's house. My usually chatty sister was still. I didn't really know Ted well enough to decide whether this was odd for him as well, or if he was just generally reticent to blabber. Mostly, I was curious if there might be a sense of foreboding for them to be attending an after-party with Zelda, or me. Or both. The ride was short, and we pulled into the crushed stone driveway of an A-frame house on the river, surrounded by conifers.

Several other cars were parked in the driveway already. The moon was bright and small ice flows bobbed on the surface of the slow-moving river. Everything, including the towering firs, was a silvery-blue, and the sharp scent of pine floated light in the air. I didn't want to go straight in. It was too beautiful a night to abandon for warmth.

"I'm going to walk for a bit," I said, and headed toward the river.

Ted looked a bit perplexed, but El squeezed his arm and said, "My sister has a thing about pine trees."

She then turned to me. "Don't stay out too long. It's cold and you'll miss all the fun."

I watched them, arm- in –arm, first only in the bright moon, and then enveloped by the circle of warm yellow light from the outside flood. My sister's profile as she looked up at Ted, just as they were to head inside to the home he shared with his wife, so lovely; beatific and serene, made me cry for her. As long as there was a Zelda, she would never have a nest in the woods where she could wake each morning to his heartbeat.

I stood on the bank of the river. All the different shades of blue and silver transfixed me. Something about the light here was different than anywhere else I'd been. Certainly, different than West Virginia, and even Michigan. I would have to look into what that was all about, but for now, I just let it make its lapis shadows in the snow. And of course, there was the crack of ice on ice from the river—and the chatter of nocturnal winter animals scrambling for branches. I stayed until my lungs hurt from the frigid air. The gentle thaw that had started this day was gone.

I headed back and I saw her coming toward me. The bobbing curls, no hat, was a give-a-way. Sylvie. I'd not known she'd be here, but it was a small town and everyone seemed to be in the same circle.

"Hey," I called. "I didn't see you at the reception."

"Cuz I didn't make it. Had other stuff to do, but your sister nabbed me as soon as she walked in to come and save you from the river Gods. Communing with nature or trying to avoid the weird-ness?"

I was relieved that someone else seemed to be curious about the unconventional nature of my sister and Zelda's arrangement with Ted. Of course, my mother and Aunt Serena had had a similar arrangement with Karl.

"You're somewhat troubled by it too?"

By this time, we had fallen in to the same stride up the em-bankment to the front of the house, and had entered the circle of the flood light.

Sylvie stopped, turned to me, and kissed me on the forehead. "'Hello,' she said. "I'm troubled about everything. Let's just join the party."

I felt like she'd been heaven sent. And this, coming from a rabid atheist. I wondered if that was the definition of love. Did we feel that people we loved were sent by God, despite our faith-lessness? I was cold, alone and confused by everything that had happened in my few weeks in Maine. I was cut off from Molly, my choice, I knew this, but still the taste of being away from her was alien and acerbic on my tongue. And here was this woman with the same black curls who seemed to appear when I felt the most alone.

"I'll follow you," I said. When we walked into the door the A-frame engulfed us. Zelda's tree was still up, towering over us all with majesty and grace, donning twinkling lights and glittery baubles with dignity, as though for us, at its own shame, and I loved that tree.

A game of charades was unfolding. Most of the party-goers appeared lightly inebriated and spirits were high. It was too warm and too small and too many people were stuffed together on couches, in bean bags, and leaning in corners. Zelda, once again, was holding court. She'd shed her kimono and was now clad in a black tank top, her long be-jangled arms were held aloft and swirling around.

"What are we walking into," I asked Sylvia.

"One of Zelda's epic Charades. She likes to do song titles. She's quite a diva."

"I see that."

I wanted to leave, but getting my sister to go would be an ordeal. She was sitting on the floor at Zelda's feet, smiling up at her, and Ted looked on from the couch— hard to read, but if I'd had to guess I would have said he looked sad.

"What do you make of this triangle," Sylvie said.

"You know too?"

"Everyone does."

"Sylvie, could you give me a ride home?"

Someone in the group shouted, "Tangled up in blue!"

"Ding, ding, ding! We have a winner!" Zelda let out another one of her raucous hoots, and the room erupted in applause for their hostess' brilliant pantomime of *Tangled Up in Blue*.

"You want to split, yes?"

"If you don't mind, that would be great," I said.

"Roger that," she said, placed her hand on the small of my back and ushered me out of the house.

Once we'd climbed up into her vintage Rover I was immediately at ease. Sylvie glanced over at me and smiled. "Jesus," she said.

"I felt that over here."

"What?"

"Your relief, Liza. What's going on?"

"At the expense of sounding nuts, that Zelda has an energy about her that absolutely freaks me out."
Sylvie started up her car, which she called Esmerelda, and backed out, expertly I may add.

"Why?"

"She reminds me so much of my Aunt Serena."

"The one who killed herself?"

"The very one."

"How are they alike?"

Molly had already sucked me dry about my aunt. It was like an immersion into really bad therapy. Molly had not relented, with her constant barrage of questions about my Aunt Serena. She'd been sure that some strain of DNA gone rogue ran in my veins, and that I too, may one day decide to flee the planet by my own hand.

"I'm going to pass on that," I said, and smiled at her so she'd know I wasn't upset.

"Of course," she said, and smiled back.

The drive to my mother's big blue house was silent. I was heavy-limbed and craved sleep, but I suddenly wanted to tell this woman everything. The whole story of my Aunt Serena. How she lived and how she died. So much for passing.

"Do you want to come in?"

"Very much so," she said.

I felt like a school girl— a little light-headed and a mild tremor in my hands, a smidge breathless. The house was dark. My mother's car was absent. I was pleased we'd have an empty house, at least for a while. Talking about Aunt Serena is not anything I'd ever think of doing with my family. I'd tried once, shortly after it happened, but we'd all had such vastly different takes on her suicide it was as though we were whirling around in different galaxies.

I pushed open the heavy blue door. All the lights were off, but

the tree was lit. Her needles were dropping, and branches arthrit-
ic—she needed to be burned at our next bonfire. Tonight, though,
she sparkled and glistened, and the soft blue and green lights cast
a mystical sheen over the living room.

"Sylvie, can I make you a drink?"

"I'm off the sauce," she said. "I do that once in a blue moon—
give my bod a rest."

We settled into the couch. Neither spoke. I stared into the
light of the tree, transfixed and content. Sylvie's head was tilted
back on the wall behind the couch and her eyes were closed. I
worried that she was tired, and would fall asleep if I didn't dive in
soon.

"So, my Aunt Serena," I said.

She turned her head to the side, opened one eye, and said, "
We're talking about her after all?"

"Yeah. Is that okay?"

"Make me some coffee?"

I laughed. Sylvie laughed. It was good. And I made a pot of
the strong stuff, from Karl's special beans from Ethiopia. One of
his few extravagances.

"Cream? Sugar?"

"Don't be shy with the cream, but no sugar, please."

And I made the most bad- ass cup of Joe that I could. Threw
in an extra-large splash of straight-up cream, and watched the
swirl complete itself in the most astounding shade of early spring
wheat. And I delivered it in the heaviest stoneware mug we had.
Purple. Aunt Serena had bought this for my mother many Christmases ago. She'd bragged that the mug weighed 15 ounces. It
must have weighed as much as a human heart.

"Here you go," I said, and placed the mug on the wooden coffee
table in front of us.

"Awesome. Shit, this smells amazing. Thank you, Liza," Sylvie
said.

And so, we settled in for a night of story-telling. I began at
the beginning. My father's death, our exodus from Vermont to
the suburban wasteland of College Park, Maryland, Uncle Doug's
wrath, and our cousins' snobbery, and finally our salvation in the
form of our Wiccan exotic Aunt Serena, and my mother's descent

into a temporary madness, and the bizarre love triangle of mom, Aunt Serena and Karl.

I spent an hour bringing her up to speed about my lengthy time away, Molly, West Virginia, and Ann Arbor, and how I eventually arrived back home. But I circled around my Aunt's suicide.

"Liza, there isn't enough coffee to keep me awake much longer. Are we getting to the part that matters tonight?"

This woman's bull-shit detector was most impressive. She appeared to have no fear of offending, and only focused on getting me to the crux of things. I had some mixed feelings about her brashness, at once applauding her chutzpah, and deriding it.

"I'm not getting to the point fast enough?"

"No. You're pussy-footing around."

"Well, excuse the fuck out of me," I said. I was pissed. Who did she think she was?

"Liza. I am here. I'm drinking your coffee. I love your coffee. I'm tired, and would, frankly, like to be sleeping. But I'm here. My eyes, heart and ears are open, and your job is to get to the point."

I couldn't come back to this. I pressed on. "It started when Snoutly was killed by the game warden," I said. "He was a bear that Aunt Serena insisted on feeding. My sister thought he was our dead father. And finally, he was just too enmeshed in the community and folks were scared, but my crazy fucking aunt wouldn't fucking stop feeding this fucking bear, and so he got killed, and she got all sad."

Sylvie turned to me. "Your aunt offed herself over a bear?"

"No. there was more, I think. This is where the family all goes sort of nuts and stops being able to talk about it. My mom and Aunt Serena were both in love with Karl. He looked just like my dead dad, apparently. My memory about my dad is filled with holes, but I think he actually did look like him. A lot. So my mother fell for him when we first got to Back Kingdom, but he fell for Aunt Serena, and then he sort of fell for my mom, so he was servicing both of them. But not at the same time. I mean it wasn't like that. But he visited both at different times. Anyway, it was weird, and I don't think my Aunt Serena could take it, and she was a little crazy to begin with, so she ran away from home to

Colorado, and killed herself."

"She just left us notes and got the hell out of Dodge. She slit her throat in the tub. Classic, right? These fuckers in Colorado cremated her and dropped her off in a Wal-Mart bag at our house."

"So that's the story?"

"Yes," I said. "Sort of."

"Okay, then. I've got to go. You're fine."

She stood, kissed me on the forehead, thanked me for the coffee and left. I thought she might be just what I needed.

Chapter 9

By April, Daisy had hired me to head up the farming component of her program. We had 36 beds and a waiting list. On top of that, I had applied for a Ph.D. program at the University of Maine in Orono. Sylvie and I had been hanging out a few times a week since she'd saved me from the party at Zelda's. We weren't lovers, although it seemed like we'd cross that line, and I was looking forward to it, because I had fallen in love. Maybe. Just a tad.

The week before I was to start my new job Sylvie suggested we go to the "Big City" to celebrate. We were grabbing a drink at The Sea Captain's Saloon one rainy evening in Port Clyde, and I was pondering some heavy flirtation—thinking of what rakish things I could muster up the courage to say. But Sylvie, per usual, cut to the chase.

"I think we should head to the Old Port to celebrate starting your job--do it up right!"

In all the time I'd lived in Westover we'd only made it to Portland once. Aunt Serena had taken us to the mall Christmas shopping the December before she left us. The Old Port was another story. I'd never been, and it seemed ridiculous that a city 70 miles away seemed so unattainable.

"Don't let me stop you," I said.

"So, it's a date?"

"It's a date," I answered. I felt a little lightheaded and leaned forward against the graffitied wooden bar.

"You mean like a date date?" She tilted her head slightly to the left and squinted at me. A glossy curl bounced against her cheekbone.

"Sure, why not. It can be a date date, maybe I can even wear some pretty underwear." I was proud of myself for being so bold.

"You'd give up your granny panties for me?"

"If you'll give up your ugly long underwear shirts."

Sylvie placed her slender white hand on her chest and gasped, feigning shock. We both looked away then, and sipped our Old Fashion's with great deliberation. Oh shit, I thought. Are we regretting this already? But Sylvie broke the ice.

"Can I keep the green one?"

"The green what?" I asked.

"Shirt."

"If you must," I answered, and she reached over very slowly and planted a silent kiss on my forehead.

We were together every day after that for three months, and not one argument. About anything. Ever. To top it all off, I loved my job. I bided my time as a hot summer on the coast gifted us with uninterrupted sunshine. And I ended almost every day in the surf of the harsh Atlantic from where I emerged salty, tumescent and stupid with lust for Sylvie. It was the week after Labor Day when the letter arrived. Just before I was to start my PhD program.

It was from Zelda. I thought it quite odd that she'd write me a letter, when I was living in the next town over and had socialized with her on several occasions since meeting her the night of the gallery opening. I'd come from the beach that particular Saturday. It was a hot fall, and I continued to swim for ten minutes a day in the Atlantic for as long as I could tolerate the frigid water. Usually, a warm autumn meant that I'd swim at least through Halloween.

A little zing of dread pulsed through me as I sat on the rocker on the side porch and turned the letter over in my hands. I was afraid to open it. It wasn't an invitation sized note. What was it she felt she had to write, and not just call up and say, or wait to run into me somewhere in the village?

So, I tore into it. So sloppy I was, that a corner of the first page of the two-page letter tore off.

Dearest Liza:

I hope this letter finds you well, and loving our Indian summer, and life. Our creator really does allot us all such bounty. It's easy to forget that when bad things happen. But for me, it is an absolute truth and a constant reminder that although our "human condition" is a fickle one, it is a brilliant dalliance in time that we must not denigrate, ever.

You've likely learned some of my past from your lovely and kind twin. I was pregnant once, and young and fearless. I jumped from a cliff at the canyon that I'd jumped from hundreds of times, since I was 7, in fact. But the winter had been reticent to come, and the river was low that spring. And so. Here we are. We've tried to conceive since then. In my state love-making becomes a creative, often pain-staking and courageous act. I'm 36. I believe my womb will bear no fruit. What I long for more than all the stars in the heavens is a child.

Adoption is a lengthy and expensive process fraught with many obstacles. Ted and I have discussed this option a zillion times, but we are both certain it is not for us. So, we've decided to proceed with finding a surrogate. Someone willing to be inseminated with Ted's sperm, the old-fashioned way or the modern way!   I will not endure egg harvesting, I am sure, so whoever might gift us with a baby will need to be comfortable with passing on her genetic material, and live life knowing she has a biological child that she won't raise. That being said, neither Ted nor I would ever wish to keep a surrogate mother from being engaged with our child.

I'm sure this is all quite crazy sounding. You're likely confused, possibly angry, maybe laughing at the insanity and presumptuousness of such a request. We are desperate people. If you're wondering, your sister supports this completely, and was, in fact, the one who mentioned you. Someday she'd like a child of her own with my husband. I would never ask that they forego this dream. Just not now. It would rip me in two should another woman give him a child first.

Before you completely dash this idea to the ground, please sleep on it, search your soul, discuss with loved ones, consult with clergy, whatever

you need to do to give our request the respect we think it deserves.
  Sincerely,
  Zelda and Ted Duncan

I read it over at least three times. The sun was going down, and I began to feel cold from my afternoon swim. The side porch was now entirely in the shade. I folded up the letter. It smelled like asparagus. I'm not sure why I smelled it, but I did. It was all that Zelda said: presumptuous, insane and then some. It was arrogant, outrageous, and inconsiderate. Not to mention manipulative. I decided then and there that Zelda was more than a diva; she was deviant. And I was angry—she was right about that as well. I was not, however, confused. I'd certainly not entertain such a narcissistic request under any circumstances. For anyone, least not a woman I barely knew. And my sister gave her this idea? That I, the least maternal person I know, would have any desire to carry and birth an infant?

I let the porch screen door slam behind me, and hurtled up the stairs to El's room, where she'd likely be preparing a lesson plan— her Saturday afternoon ritual. I didn't knock.

"El, what the fuck are you thinking to offer my uterus up to Zelda?"

"Woe, there, tiger," she said.

I closed her door behind me and leaned up against it. I stared her down.

"You got a letter," my sister said.

"Did you actually suggest to Zelda that I might agree to be a surrogate?"

"You know how it is when folks are just brainstorming. Everything is up for grabs, no matter how ludicrous," she said.

"El, this is obscenely ludicrous. I will never, ever, carry a child for anyone. And especially not Zelda. My genetic material ends here."

"Okay, okay," my sister said. "Forget I ever put your name in the hat. I'm sorry, really."

I was turning to leave when she landed the zinger. "Why are you so disgusted by your genetic material?"

My hand was resting on the corner of her dresser. With a life of its own I swiped everything within reach onto the floor. "Fuck you, Elspeth. Who do you think you are?"

"Have you not hated yourself for most of your life?" She sat back in her chair and folded her arms across her chest.

"What do you want from me?"

"I want us to be sisters. Like I feel that I know you, and that you know me. It will have a really settling effect on us both, I think."

I felt suddenly exhausted. By this heavily therapized woman. My sister, whom I loved and still did. But she had to drill down into the gristle and fat.

"So, Liza, what do you say?

"I already feel like your sister. If you don't feel like mine that's on you. I think it's completely inappropriate and impossible, what you're asking."

But I already knew she had me. All I wanted to do was fall back into her high four posted bed, into her pile of jasmine smelling quilts and yellow pillows. I was working at the school sometimes seven days a week, and farming with severely emotionally disturbed adolescent girls was not for the faint of heart.

El leapt onto the bed and giggled like a 9-year-old about to play Barbies. But we'd never actually played Barbies. Aunt Serena hadn't approved.

"So," she said, "wanting us to get reacquainted is inappropriate and impossible?"

She feigned incredulity. One full black eyebrow was cocked, and her index finger rested on her pursed upper lip.

"I feel like your priming me for confession, El. Like we're about to disect our lives. That's sort of heavy for a Saturday night."

She smiled and play-swatted me across my left thigh. "Silly Liza," she said. "It doesn't have to be heavy at all. It can be fun."

I laughed out loud. I knew no one who'd ever said that toiling over the uninterrupted series of tedious and often terrifying acts that is life, can be fun.

"Fun? How so," I asked.

"Universal longing to marry our soul and spirit. We all have this as humans. It's fun to reach for that by observing our experiences," El said.

"You sound like Aunt Serena, but way nuttier, and more Catholic. Is Ted rubbing off on you?"

"More like Zelda," El said.

"Is she a little wonky?"

"Don't think you can divert me. No fuckery will keep me from my work here tonight, Liza."

"Well, I'm going to need some fortification."

"The red kind?"

"And you think we need to get reacquainted? Seems you know me quite well," I said.

"Yes. You can be bought with a cheap Chianti," she said, "and I love you for that. Be right back."

"I appreciate your understanding and cooperation," I said, and El, in return, graced me with her white and glistening teeth.

"Do I still crack you up?" I knew what her answer would be. But I liked hearing it. My most beloved compliment was that I was funny.

"No worries about that. You're a regular Phyllis Diller."

She returned with a full mug.

"Here's your wine, love," El said.

She'd poured it into my favorite childhood mug—the one with Snoopy's pal Woodstock on it—my most loved Peanuts' character. She was populating our stage with the correct artifact to invoke the mood—preparing me for confession. Woodstock felt small and inconsequential, bogged down by the world, as I often did.

"In a coffee mug?"

El plunked down next to me and a little wine sloshed out of the mug onto her bedspread. She giggled and swiped at it with the palm of her hand.

"All the wine glasses are broken," she said, and laughed. "Karl keeps throwing them at the squirrels." I knew that wasn't true. It was funny, though—a reference to the one time we saw Karl respond strongly to anything— he threw a can of tomato soup at Snoutly. "This goddamned bear is coming to the back door now," he'd said.

"It strikes me as odd that our only friend was a bear. I'm sure there's some meaning in that, but I've no idea what."

"I think we needed the spirit of a wild thing," El said.

"Why do I never know what you're talking about?"

"Perfect segue. Let's talk about the winter mom lost her mind," El said.

"Don't we already understand that? In retrospect it makes perfect sense. It's crystalline."

"Our father died when we were seven, though. Did we understand it then?"

"I don't know, El. But we're almost 30 now. When I think back on those years with both of them, I just remember the love."

"It was sort of story-book idyllic, wasn't it? Almost unreal--like looking at life through a lens soaked in hair-spray," my sister said. And I think she's not far off. Our parents, to hear my mother describe it, loved each other beyond reason. My mother said it was as though they alone were in love, and that the rest of the world who coupled up really didn't have a clue--that they couldn't have possibly felt toward each other the way my parents did, because that much love on the planet would simply lift it off its axis and send it hurtling into outer space.

El snuggled up to me and nudged my wine again, only this time it spilled on me. She gasped, lurched herself to a sitting position, and began rubbing the wine off my jeans, but only managed to rub it in. I didn't care. I'd already drained the bird and was sort of lit.

"I'm so sorry, Liza," she said.

"Stop being sorry and just refill the Bird," I said, referring to Woodstock. I passed the mug her way and she laughed. I followed suit and at least a minute went by when we both found my inane comment uproariously funny. This hilarity ended in an abrupt and simultaneous sobriety. Neither spoke for several minutes and I thought I might nod off.

It was El who picked up the thread and kept us moving forward. "They met in college?"

"So I've heard. Tomas and Violet. The Pennsylvania Dutch boy from Lancaster, and our French-Canadian mom from the streets of

Baltimore."

"And they ended up in Vermont." El said. "Life is so weird."

El placed her head on my chest.

"Dad got a job there. They packed up their crap and drove to Vermont a few weeks after they got married."

"Tell me more," El said. "It's romantic."

The second mug of wine was hitting me hard. I wanted to sleep. But El's head was somewhere in my armpit, and her breath was warm on my neck and smelled of licorice tea. This intimacy scared me, but I'd be hard pressed to name any other time in the past decade when I felt so solid.

"What's to tell? Dad died. The end."

"It's all so sad," El said. "We could have had such a much better life, all but for a freakish snow storm."

"How would you have liked it to be better?"

El pushed herself up on her elbow and stared me down. "You're kidding, right?"

"I don't think it was so heinous. It was okay. Just okay. And sometimes okay is the best we can hope for."

"I so disagree," she said, and plopped her head back into my armpit.

"Of course, as I knew you would."

"Well, then I'm at least predictable."

I didn't bite. I closed my eyes and searched for the sound of the waves. A faint lapping, and from Owl's Head Light the onerous belch of a fog horn. El snored. A soft sound like the flutter of tiny wings.

Chapter 10

The next day at Montello School was particularly strenuous. One of our more challenging students, a young woman named Michelle, but who insisted on going by Lytta (in Greek mythology the spirit of mad rage) performed fellatio on the therapy dog, a large Shepard named Bongo. Naturally the lovely silver-haired matron of the community who volunteered Bongo for the program was appalled and a bit rageful herself. I'm sure that Bongo had a great time. The staff who was supervising the therapy dog visit quit, and the other four girls in the session could not stop laughing.

Nothing in our policy and procedure manual addressed this type of aberration, and all the staff had to emergently convene to figure out the correct consequences for Michelle. Many of our students (who were also residents) were hyper-sexual, having been sexualized at a young age by friends of the family, babysitter's husbands, friend's big brothers, uncles and/or fathers.

Since the animal therapy programs were my domain, I was chosen to meet with Michelle as well as be the liaison between the program and the state of Maine under whose care she was; all interested parties had a say in whatever would befall her next. I felt for this child, and adored her veracity and integrity. I regretted her unfortunate attraction to Bongo and struggled with how best to address this with her. It seemed to me this was the job of her therapist, who would apparently follow-up, but the first conversation was mine and I was unprepared.

At two that afternoon in a small stuffy conference room that smelled of curry, Michelle and I faced off.

"So, Michelle," I said, fiddling with the end of my braid and wondering where to go from there.

"You know I want to be called Lytta." Michelle folded her arms across her thin chest and slunk down in her chair.

"Yes, but you know it's against the rules to use other names."

"It's a stupid rule," she said, and stuck a fingertip in her mouth and began to macerate what was left of her nail.

"What was going on with Bongo today?" It was the best I had.

"Bongo," she said, and leaned forward in her chair, "is hung like a horse. It's been a really long time since I've had sex" and here she paused, "of any kind."

"Oh, well that's a relief. For a minute I thought it was just one of the Michelle stunts for some shock value, like the time you ate the pollywog."

"The time I ate the pollywog I was hungry. Today it was a different kind of hunger."

This child was hard to like, but I did. I wanted her to suc-ceed. I wanted her to stop eating pollywogs and sucking on doggie dicks. I wanted to slap her. Hard, and across the face.

"Next time eat a cheeseburger, and as far as the sex is con-cerned take care of yourself. Just so you know, the powers that be are thinking about how to address this. Do you want to get booted out of here?"

"I thought you'd never guess," Michelle said, and slunk fur-ther down in her chair, refolded her arms across her boney chest, tossed her purple hair back and laughed.

I wanted to come back with something pithy and sharp, but had to remind myself that I was the grown-up, and that pissing contests with children, even bright old souls like Michelle, were like running up a down escalator. Instead, I opened the door to the conference room and gestured for her to leave. Our little chat had concluded, and in 45 minutes so would my day. I was looking forward to an evening at Sylvie's. She had promised something with eggplant, and there'd be plenty of tequila, her favorite—not so much mine. I could already hear her rich belly laugh when I'd tell her about the letter from Zelda over shots. I would not tell her about Michelle. I didn't talk about work on dates.

The house was quiet when I returned home. No cars in the driveway and I savored those moments, unusual and sensuous. Sitting in a well-ordered quiet and cool kitchen that smelled of grapefruit and ginger, at the round table in the floor to ceiling window where a sturdy aged maple whose leaves were indolently turning gold, filled me with a sense of possibility. My days of ocean dips were falling away—it was getting colder, but I would not squander the gift of a daily salty dunk.

In less than ten minutes I was at Pebble Beach. My sensible one piece navy blue speedo was slightly damp from yesterday's swim—just uncomfortable enough to motivate a merciless headlong dive into the next wave—better to be soaked than damp, and the wave that rolled toward me was frothy and bellicose and I wanted it. Sylvie liked my skin to taste like the sea. "It's delightful," she always said, so I'd stopped showering after my early evening forays into the biting Atlantic.

The thing about being in love with Sylvie is that I never worried about preparing for our dates. Stripping off the stiff frigid suit my skin felt silky to my touch. I let my fingers slip between the lips of my vagina, wet and briny, and I could barely wait to be with her. A warm flannel shirt and some lose jeans with my one indulgence—almond body oil, and out the door. I had taken to borrowing Karl's bike for the two-mile ride to the South end of Rockland. Sylvie owned a run-down Victorian that had at one time been chopped up into a six-family apartment building. Slowly she was letting tenants go and reclaiming the units. Our favorite weekend activity was tearing out walls with her Sawzall and sledge hammer. I loved the opal painted bathroom, cast-iron sinks, and walnut wainscoting.

 I knocked on her screen door just before seven. She answered in a royal blue sweatshirt and her black curls were haphazardly piled up on her head, tilting slightly to the left.

"Oh," she said, "it's my very own mermaid arriving on time straight from the deep," and she pulled me into her chest and kissed me.

"Tongue," I said. "what's the special occasion?"

She laughed and pulled out one of her lime green chairs for me. "Ready for baba ghanoush?"

Sylvie knew it was my favorite. Dipped in warm pita bread.

"Always," I said, and she ran her hand over the back of my head on her way to the counter. The 1940's feel of her place set me back in time. It was easy to imagine a young mother with bright red lipstick, two-toned pumps and a calico apron heating up tomato soup for Susan and Billy, waiting for her lobsterman husband to return, big band music wafting from the RCA Victor in the Parlor.

Sylvie carried our dinner over and sat across from me, filled my wine glass with a fizzy fruity home-made sangria, and began ripping up her pita. Not one for small talk, this woman. I don't think she'd ever once asked about my day, and I loved her all the more for that kindness.

"Are you ready for the wackiest story maybe ever?" I'd planned to wait to spill the Zelda letter but I couldn't. I knew Sylvie would find it as bizarre and hilarious as I did and I anticipated the two of us laughing throughout dinner. I adored making her laugh; she was often blunt and serious.

"Sure. Hit me with it," she said.

I launched into the letter, which I'd read so often I knew it pretty much word for word. I saved the zinger (that the whole idea had been Elspeth's) for the end. But the laughter I waited for didn't happen. Sylvie was twirling her wine glass around, looking down at her bare feet, and the vertical crease between her eyes intensified.

"You're not laughing," I said. "What's wrong?"

She slid her chair across the orange linoleum until we were knee to knee. She pulled my hands from my lap, took them in hers, and looked me directly in the eyes.

"I would love nothing more than to have a child with you."

I pulled my hands from hers as though they were covered in acid. True North seemed a dream someone had. I tried to string together some sort of viable sentence, but no words came forward. Sylvie took my hands again and resumed.

"I'll be the surrogate, love. You don't have to do anything. Just be by my side. Rub my feet, buy me pickles, coach me through labor—all that corny stuff. Let's do this."

She leaned into me and tugged on my braid. "You look just like an Andrew Wyeth in this light. My very own Helga. Let's have a baby and be the crazy aunties."

I stood with such force that the chair fell backward. I would not be manipulated by this woman, or any woman, and certainly not by any man. I would not have any part of this modern morality play.

"You're not making any sense. You've lost your mind, Sylvie. Is it the water up here? Everyone's insane. I feel like I'm living on the wrong side of the rabbit hole."

"Or maybe it's the right side?" She stood, and approached, but I bolted before she could put her hands on me. I was on Karl's ancient Western Flyer 10 speed and heading out of Rockland before she made it to the porch. I could hear her calling my name as I pedaled up 73 to Owl's Head. Soon, the sound of blood pumping in my ears was louder than my name on the twilight breeze.

Chapter 11

A few days after our dinner date Sylvie was still calling and "popping" over. I wasn't ready to handle her well-modulated and meticulously organized rhetoric regarding all the excellent reasons we should proceed with plan Zelda. The love of my life wanted to screw my sister's married penal husband and carry his child so we could be the fun aunties? This, I could not tolerate.

I'd rehearsed rebuttals in my head: my favorite was to calmly and maturely explain that Sylvie was of course free to make any choices she saw fit with her own body, but that should she proceed with a pregnancy I would not be by her side. That was my position on this absurd matter. I would not budge.

I headed into work-- a classic Northern New England late September day. The sky was cornflower blue with only a smattering of curvaceous cumulus clouds. At 8:30 in the morning, on my commute to work, it was a dry 60 degrees with the promise of sunlight all day and a high of 66. The cows looked happy. Lots of tail wagging and soft mooing. Each dairy farm I passed found me more in love with the small farming towns on the Mid-Coast, as if the sea wasn't enough.

Today I would find out the state's decision about Michelle's future. I had bigger things on my mind than Sylvie and I. Almost as big, anyway. Ever since Sylvie's aunty comment Serena's ghost just wouldn't leave me be. I felt her everywhere, and I wasn't even a believer. I derived no comfort from thinking that our dead are hanging around.

Daisy was waiting for me in the staff lounge. She clutched her delft blue coffee mug in both hands and was not smiling.

"Michelle ran last night," she motioned for me to sit at our old battered yellow Formica table.

Nothing good ever came from girls who ran. They either returned to abusive families, addicted boyfriends, or ended up trafficked up and down I- 95.

"Any info?"

"Not yet. If she truly wants to be gone then she'll be gone, but I think she doesn't."

Daisey always called it right. If she thought we'd see Michelle again, then we would. As far as I was concerned, she would be back within 48 hours, and hopefully not pregnant. We couldn't keep pregnant girls.

"Keep me posted," I said, poured my coffee and headed to the stables. Nothing feels quite like a warm, moist, furry nuzzle of a horse's nose. They are so quick to tell you how deeply they love and appreciate all that you do. The time I spent in the stables before mixing it up with the girls was on par with my evening dip. I chose to begin and end my days with moments of joy. It made the whole middle-weary passage of time so much lighter.

Tevah, one of our stage four girls who'd been granted more privilege as a result of her wisdom and tenacity, asked to check in with me after lunch chores. We found the old bench in the pumpkin patch empty. Tevah's long russet colored hair, thick and curly, was pulled onto the top of her skull and fastened with a number two pencil. The pores across the bridge of her wide nose were blackened by dirt and I wanted to hug her.

"What's up, Tev?"

"I might know where Michelle went."

"Did you know last night when she left?"

"No. Yes, actually, but not really."

"Oh, Tev. You gave her a head start."

"She's trying to get on the ferry." Tevah twirled her hair a few times and worried a small scab on her knee.

"To Canada?"

"Digby. In Nova Scotia."

"Any more details? Names, times? Do any of the other girls know?"

"That's all I got. Truly, and please don't make me a stage three."

"You withheld serious information from us. Consider yourself a stage three."

"Right," was all she said. I walked her back to her class and filled Daisey in. Michelle would be likely getting off the ferry in Yarmouth any minute now. And hopefully she had a plan. It was out of my hands at this point. On the drive home that night I could already feel the ocean on my skin. I grabbed a few things from the co-op in Belfast, hit a snarl of unexpected traffic in Camden, un-usual for this time of year, between Labor Day and Columbus Day we usually had a bit of a reprieve.

When I got home, I tossed the groceries on the kitchen table and headed upstairs for my swim suit. I was worried about Mi-chelle, and a good swim seemed to be in order. My routines often saved me from despair. I sat on the bed--unmade and rumpled, and dotted with gold fish crumbs. A long heavy sigh rolled out of me. I wasn't quite thirty and I sighed like an old woman. El came in and plopped down on the foot of my bed. She stared at me for a few seconds.

"Hey, deep-six the swim, let's go to the movies."

"What's showing?"

"Does it matter?"

"You know what El? It doesn't, and your brilliant."

She looped her arm through mine, and we nearly skipped down the hall.

Chapter 12

After the movie El and I stopped for a drink at Jo-Jo's. I loved this dive. Jo-Jo left an artificial Christmas tree up year-round from which customers hung random items, including a few tampons, some bottle caps, and perhaps the most macabre, lobster carcasses. Jo-Jo also poured a generous Scotch, and a tiny black and white TV always blabbered at the bend in the lacquered bar top. The late-night news was on. I wasn't paying any attention. El and I were playfully bantering about the gratuitous violence in the grizzly movie we'd just seen. But Jo-Jo exclaimed, "Oh shit. What a shame," and cranked up the volume.

I turned to the TV and there was a photo of Michelle. She'd jumped from the ferry between Bar Harbor and Yarmouth. The skinny blonde newscaster with the hard eyes was referring to her as another statistic—a "troubled" teen-aged girl from a "reform school" who leapt to her death from the ferry. The blonde then described the futile rescue attempts and reported that the "victim," 17-year-old Michelle Dubuc from Lamoine, was sucked into the propeller.

"She's from your school, isn't she?"

"I have to get out of here."

"Of course," El said. Jo-Jo peered over her pink plastic readers. "You okay?"

"She'll be fine, Joe. I think the Scotch just hit her hard. I'll get her home."

El led me across the parking lot, opened my door and lowered me into my seat. I was light-headed, sick to my stomach. This young woman, this brilliant child—a tender 17 years, what madness was this that she couldn't figure out how to live. Was she so angry—so fucking terrifyingly enraged that being mangled by a propeller seemed like a good idea? I couldn't catch my breath.

"I'm taking you home. It's okay."

No. Nope. It was not okay. I kicked the dash board, reduced to a tantrum like a three-year-old. I kicked it and kicked it and the glove compartment sprung open. McDonald bags rolled to the floor. There must have been a dozen balled up McDonald bags. And now I was nine, and I was furious that my sister was clearly making clandestine trips to Mikey D's for illicit poisonous food. My sister, my twin, was hoarding greasy food bags in her glove compartment. Why were we all bat-shit? What was wrong with us? I swooped in on those bags in a sudden swift attack, like a kookaburra. I scooped up fistfulls and pelted them at El.

"What the fuck are these? Why are you doing this? Why do you eat this shit and save the bags? You're grotesque, El. You are a savage, a monstrous thing."

El pulled off to the side of the road. The car was so cold. She never turned on the heat. She hated the heat.

"Liza," she said, over and over, reaching for me, encircling me in her long dainty arms. "Liza, stop. Just stop. It doesn't matter. Those bags don't matter."

I pushed her away. She smelled of patchouli, so much like Serena. I had to get out of her car.

"I'm walking from here," I said.

"It's cold, hon."

"I've been cold," I said, and slammed the door. She drove in the shoulder, behind me for the last mile—this crazy secret McDonald's eater, with a glove compartment full of bags that reeked of fish fillets.

By the time I was home, the house was lit from within. Everyone was up. My toes were numb. November was coming in angry.

El cut her engine behind me, as I pushed open the door. They were all there. My mother, Karl, and Sylvie. So, they knew about Michelle.

The first was Sylvie. "Sit down, love," she said, and pressed gently on my shoulders till I was solidly on the bench. Karl paced, wringing his hands, one and then the other, big-knuckled, red and calloused. My mother slid a glass of wine in my direction—an arm's reach away, in case it had been the wrong thing to do. And then they retreated, all lined up against the kitchen counter, as though planned, from tallest to shortest, staring at me. Waiting for what I couldn't tell. They just stared at me. This random gaggle of folk; this ersatz family.

"I'm fine," I said. "Really. Obviously, there was way too much pain there to live. You know. Well, some of you know."

Sylvie, once again, was the first to move. She crossed the kitchen in two long strides, pressed her body against mine on the bench, and pulled me into her. She reeked of garlic, and an underlying unclean smell. I needed to get away.

"It's hotter than balls in here," I said, and headed for the living room where I cracked a window. The three women followed me.

"What's the best way we can help?" My sister sat directly across from me on the hassock, placing both of her dainty hands on my knees.

"Guys," I said, "this is all a bit over-the-top. I'm tired and I just want to go to bed." But I didn't really. I didn't want to hang out in the living room with all the hens, either, but I definitely didn't want to go to bed. No way could I have slept. I'd already begun playing Michelle's suicide over in my head. And although I wasn't silly enough to blame myself in any way, because I certainly knew there was no blame on me, I did wonder where in Michelle's trajectory to suicide I may have been able to change her course. A different word in a sentence, or different sentence all together? Or silence, or a lingering touch, or a feigned disinterest? I'd once been convinced that the Lovejoys should have known that Serena was going to off herself. I didn't believe in an after-life, and had mostly disdain for those who did, but yet I found myself musing about Serena taking care of Michelle somewhere in the place of the dead.

The dead. Today was November 1st. All Souls Day. In Aunt Serena's world, it was Samhain, in Old Irish, summer's end. Aunt Serena loved pagan celebrations. We'd spent many a Halloween making offerings of our candy booty to ensure a mild winter, and hopes for an easy time of waiting for the light to return on the solstice. Aunt Serena would tell us that the membrane between the living and the dead was like paper on Samhain, and that it was the perfect time to think of our father, as he'd likely be listening then. We'd go to Fairy Shrimp Spa, dance around in a circle, and then burn all but a few pieces of the most favorite candy.

"You want to know what would be helpful?"

All three of my women bobbed their heads and smiled like dashboard dogs.

"Go get Aunt Serena's ashes. It's time. It's Samhain."

El took off running toward the staircase. My mother threw her hands over her mouth and squealed like a baby pig at the trough.

"What did I miss," Sylvie said. "Samwhat?"

"I'll explain later," I said, "Go grab your coat. We need to do this before midnight!"

"I am mixed up with some crazy bitches! But whatever," Sylvie said. "I'm in."

 My mother was at the bottom of the stairs calling up to El to hurry.

"Where's the fucking box?" I could hear El opening and closing things, and then the squeak of our mother's cedar chest lid being lifted. "Never mind," she yelled. "Found it."

"What did she find," Sylvie asked me. "Do I want to know?"

"Ashes," I said. "She found Aunt Serena's ashes."

"I can't come back to that," she said, and laughed a little.

Karl walked in. "Where are you taking them?"

"Where do you think we should?"

"I think she'd love to float with the seals. Maybe Port Clyde?"

"Great idea," my mother said, and squeezed his hand.

"It's 11:20. We got to go right now," El said. She grabbed a book of Emily Dickinson poems off the shelf-- Aunt Serena's favorite poet.

"I'll drive," Sylvie said.

We climbed over one another to our seats, me shotgun with

Sylvie, and mom and El in the back. Sylvie fired up Esmerelda, and screeched out of the drive way, sending the crushed stone into a wild spray. We made if from Owl's Head to Port Clyde in 18 minutes. The harbor was dark, and we held onto each other as we walked down along the wharf to the end.

"Look at those stars," Sylvie said.

"How should we do this?" my mother asked.

"Let's each of the three of us scatter a handful," El said. "We can read one of Emily's poems."

"It's too dark," I said, but Sylvie rescued us with a flashlight she kept in her glove box.

"Here Mom," El said. "You start. Pick a poem."

"Find *I Felt a Funeral In My Brain*, please."

El turned to the correct page, and my mother read the poem, softly, almost to herself, and flung her handful of Serena onto the placid sea. Then she passed the box to me. I turned the pages to a poem about madness, caught by a line about being "straight-away dangerous," and read only that one line. I let her ashes sift through my fingers. It was harder than I thought to let her go. And finally, El. "I heard a fly buzz," she started, but couldn't finish. She shook out the remaining bits of Aunt Serena, let out a monstrous roar, and we were done. She hurled the box into a garbage barrel in the parking lot.

"Last call at JoJo's?" Sylvie was on her game. I, at least, thought it was a brilliant idea to raise a glass to Aunt Serena.

"Fuckin'A," my sister said.

"Ditto," answered my mom.

The next morning the sun shone in my bedroom like 100 spotlights. Or so it seemed. I was clammy and tangled in a twist of blankets. Sylvie was clutching a pillow and drooling, her black curls stuck to her cheek. It took a second or two to bring the previous night into focus. We'd released Aunt Serena, gotten shit-faced, and I vaguely recalled a sloppy pillow conversation about Zelda's insane request.

"Jesus, could you close the blinds?" Sylvie sat up, yawned, and unstuck her heavy breasts from her ribcage.

"No. You," I said, and Sylvie laughed, crossed the floor and let them down.

"Coffee," I said, and she stroked my hair, slid her T-shirt over her lovely Rubenesque body and padded barefoot out of my room. Maybe I would. Maybe. Maybe I'd stand by her side while she grew a baby.

"Hey you!" El danced into my room and flopped down on the foot of the bed. "One too many rusty nails?!"

"At least."

"Well, I'm off to work. Last night was stellar. I love you." She kissed me on the forehead and left, trailing her piney scent behind her, into the brisk autumn morning.

The End

About the Author

Shellie Leger is the author of the novels Lonely Specks and The Treadwell Place. She holds an MFA from Stonecoast and teaches fiction writing. She lives in the western foothills of Maine under towering pines, and is surrounded by water.